DETECTIVE IN THE CROSSHAIRS

MURDER IN THE DESERT

A Meredith Ogden Hollywood Legwoman Mystery

PENNY PENCE SMITH

150 Hamakua Dr. #357
Kailua, HI 96734

ISBN: 978-17-372084-4-0 (Ingram print)
ISBN: 979-88-650036-7-0 (KDP print)
ISBN: 978-17-372084-5-7 (EPUB)

Cover design: Cynthia Gunn
Author photograph: Malia Leinau Myers
Cover photo © Raul Hernandez Balbuena | Dreamstime.com
Interior design and book production: Elizabeth Beeton

What our readers say about Meredith Ogden,
Hollywood Legwoman Mysteries

Shadow of the Wave—Stranded and Stalked

"Terrific Read…third in the series…excellent."

"…fascinating story, and the author's descriptive writing is a pleasure to read."

"Brava for another enthralling Meredith Ogden adventure."

Sunset West—Guns, Grit and Gossip

"If you're a mystery fan like I am, you'll enjoy *Sunset West— Guns, Grit and Gossip*…."

"…second in a series and…so much fun to read, once again, about the Hollywood/entertainment scene…."

"…fascinating story…a pleasure to read."

Nicole Monton
Midweek Magazine
Honolulu Star Advertiser

The Last Legwoman— A Novel of Hollywood, Murder and Gossip

"…really good story…writing was beautiful…"

Don Wallace
author *The French House*
editor, *Hawaii Book Review*

"…an engaging storyteller…"

Honolulu Star Advertiser

"…a joy to read…"

Meredith Ogden
Hollywood Legwoman Mysteries
by Penny Pence Smith

The Last Legwoman—
A Novel of Hollywood, Murder and Gossip

Sunset West—Guns, Grit and Gossip

Shadow of the Wave—Stranded and Stalked

Also by Penny Pence Smith

Under a Maui Sun
Reflections of Kauai

To Dixon, always Dixon—who brings ideas,
accuracy, the male perspective, and love.

It takes a family.

CHAPTER 1

A slight rustle of fabric brought her awake with a start and a fearful shudder. She cautiously opened her eyes and glanced around without movement. The solid sleeping human usually in the bed next to her was missing, but a glow from the bathroom solved the puzzle as a gentle nudge to her cheek brought her to her elbow, sleepily glancing over her shoulder.

"Got a call, gotta go," whispered the tall man bending toward her. Wife, confidant, and hard-core Hollywood journalist who shared his life, Meredith Ogden shook her sleep tousled copper-blond hair and asked, "Why? What time is it?"

"Three-thirty." He answered, "Go back to sleep."

"Why you?" she groaned, pulling herself to full sitting. "Isn't this why you have a staff of super-detectives to handle these emergencies?"

"Yeah," he sighed, "but Ted Belin, Sheriff out near Desert Hot Springs, called and said they had a 'situation'—translated—a dead body. He said, 'it had my name all over it.' I'd understand when I got there. I kind of owe him, anyhow. So…." Meredith nodded half-heartedly.

"Any idea what that really means?" she asked sleepily.

"Nope, but I need to get on the road before commute traffic. I'll call." He reached down and kissed her quickly on the lips, grabbed his jacket and headed for the steps to the lower level. He quickly stopped, turned and whispered, "Take Riley to school?" He normally dropped off their three-year-old at preschool on his way to work. Meredith nodded, murmured, "Of course," then glanced toward the adjacent room, listening for any sounds of an awake little girl, heard none. When she looked back, T.K. Raymond was gone.

The tumultuous murmur of the surf, the audio wallpaper for the home on the bluff above the Malibu Beach in Southern California, grew louder as T.K. Raymond walked into the garage. The tall, solidly built, slightly silvering fifty-something-year-old was Captain of a "Special Profile" unit of police detectives overseeing criminal cases involving VIP personalities in high visibility industries—sports, real estate, finance, and the nascent technology sector. His own expertise, for years, had been cases around the entertainment industry—movie/TV/music celebrities and executives. Elevated into management, he rarely, individually, managed single cases. But his presence on certain movie-TV-land crime scenes was always insightful and this one as the sheriff had said, had his name "all over it."

Climbing into the clumsy department-provided sedan he pondered the route to the remote high desert location. "Drive south and pick up the I-10, or take the scenic longer drive though Topanga Canyon, connect with the Ventura Freeway and then the I-10 East? At three-thirty in the morning, he knew he should take the fastest route to Desert Hot Springs in the high desert above Palm Springs. But the curiosity of it all had him hungering for a meditative route.

Two hours later he pulled off the highway into the lonely glow of a large casino in Cabazon—an off-road oasis for gambling midway to Palm Springs—not far from the turn-off to the upper desert towns, ultimately Desert Hot Springs. At the adjacent truck stop he bought a coffee and some trail mix, returned to the car and began the climb into the sparse highland communities. Many were characterized by legendary L.A. hideaways— "Jack Rabbit estates" —tiny scrappy cabins on land granted by the U.S. government decades earlier to anyone who agreed to build a livable structure. Some of these rough-hewn domiciles had been constructed years before by would-be collaborators with space aliens that would surely one day visit. Some small oases developed originally in anticipation of those celestial visitations. The remote and ethereal desert inspired such imagination.

The community of Desert Hot Springs had always been an enigma. Off and on it was a trendy and discreet get-a-way for L.A. celebrities avoiding the attention surrounding the more public and celebrated centers like Palm Springs. A hotel or two sprouted up and for a while would become the "it" place for the enlightened celebrities. Such resorts would fade and then resurrect as a new generation "discovered" the town. Some built large Spanish-style homes in order to live just a short distance from the metropolis where they made their livings. Others built small, artsy cabins to entertain friends away from the eyes and ears of anyone who might know them. Unobtrusive and remote was always the character for the area. Permanent residents were often artists and folks who didn't need—or want—the public eye on their lifestyle. But now in 1993, as Palm Springs and some of the nearby cities and towns were growing and overgrowing, the venerable high desert oasis with its natural hot springs was becoming a suburb.

The sun emerged eastward toward the mountains bordering the daisy chain of dusty off-ramps to tiny rag-tag communities and shopping centers along the I-10. Raymond checked his notes and followed the directions sheriff Ted Belin had dictated on the phone. Good thing he had them, he reflected. The small town had grown since he last visited, long before, and where he was headed was well out of the mainstream. The journey took him further and further out of the small town itself until streets became mostly unmarked—and uninhabited. He hesitantly pulled off the main road on to a rutted, badly eroded drive that took him up a hill to a plateau where a decaying once-grand mansion was under massive renovation. Apparently, again, someone had been bitten by the get-a-way bug, found the bones of a promising-retreat and was working to enliven it. Law enforcement personnel swarmed around, clustered in various locations. Raymond showed his ID to a young officer at the driveway entrance and was directed to park on the street and then join the Sheriff at the back of the property.

He walked around the side of the imposing stucco building and stopped to take in the view from the back area. Looking across a large, debris-strewn, waterless swimming pool, he saw a desert ravine painted with vegetation and brush subtly alive in earth hues, and cacti of various shapes and heights, climbing the slopes of the camel-colored hump-backed mountains. As he took it in, his reverie was interrupted by "Hey, T.K. Raymond"—the voice of Sheriff Ted Belin calling from down the hillside. "Down here!" Raymond carefully navigated the craggy rock hill.

"Quite a place," he huffed.

"Yeah," Belin barked. "But we have a woman's body that's gonna keep us all busy for a while. Rolled out of the ground under the house while the contractors and carpenters were starting work." The two looked at the half-dozen technicians working around a lump which Raymond assumed was the body, invisible under the number of humans at work over it.

"Who is she?" asked Raymond.

"As far as we can tell, her name was Lindy Fuller— apparently an actress. We hope you can help us with more. Being a Hollywood guy and all. She's been here a long time," said Belin. "Not very recognizable…but the gunshot in the front of the skull pretty much tells us how she died."

"How do you think I can help?" asked Raymond, frowning, confused.

"Well," began Belin. "She must have been buried with her purse. It's here with the body and managed to survive. Probably because it's such thick plastic, kind of impervious. Survived better than she did. We have a badly deteriorated driver's license issued in 1963, about thirty years ago and a Screen Actor's Guild membership card from 1962. But also a piece of torn-up notebook paper with your name written on it—along with someone named Tad Oakley-something-or-other. The last word—probably another name—was either torn off or deteriorated over time. Whatever, it's not going to help us. But you know Oakley? Know her?"

The scowl deepened on Raymond's face as he repeated the names over and over in his mind, trying to place them. He shook his head and murmured, "Not that I can recall…."

"Well," the old sheriff coughed, years of smoking, desert sand and wind rattled in his voice, "we figured since you're the celebrity expert for the entertainment world—and your name was one of the last ones on her mind—or at least in her purse—you should be here."

☆☆☆

In Malibu, snapping on the reading lamp next to the bed, Meredith Ogden slid from the covers and quietly padded to the door to the adjacent room, peering carefully into the darkness. The fluffy pink and lavender bundle of three-and-a-half-year-old Riley Elinor Raymond chuffed slightly in deep slumber. Meredith watched silently—somewhat awed, as always—that she was responsible for this small, fragile package of life. Raymond, of course, had something to do with it too. But Meredith still considered the child some kind of surprise from God or the universe or…well, whoever. Riley certainly had not been on the somewhat haphazard life-planning charts. A subtle movement at the bottom of the miniature bed caught Meredith's eye and she saw the wily head of her own twelve-year old cat Paco. "Traitor," she mouthed. The feline had quickly realized when the tiny human arrived in the Malibu house and challenged his special position, his best defense against an alien was a good offense. And made short work finding a pleasurable home in the blankets around the tiny person. He turned his head back into the soft fabric.

Meredith retreated to her own bed. Three-forty-five a.m. She pulled the covers up to her chin as her normal cache of concerns about Raymond's crime-solving activities—now, in the desert—ebbed into sleep.

CHAPTER 2

Raymond and Sheriff Belin climbed the stairs to the second floor of the house, construction debris and grit under their feet. The once-sparkling-now-faded red tiled main floor became wooden slats in the upper story. They felt the "give" that came from time and neglect as they explored. "Lot of work to be done," mused the old lawmaker. "But, well, folks these days have more money than sense. A/C here in the summer is out of the park. Temps get up to one-hundred-twenty-five on bad years. One-fifteen on good." Raymond winced. Today, mid-February, it was a mild eighty. Picking through the rubble in the big estate, the two worked their way back down to the front entrance.

"Who lives in these houses?" asked Raymond noting three neighboring older ranch style houses, one kept up well with manicured lawn and shrubs with an older SUV in the drive, the other two less maintained but seemingly lived in. A rusted truck sat in front of one of the garages. The two law men walked down the street, observing the three nearby domiciles.

"One's a vacation rental…" Belin's voice carried off as if to say, "But why here?" He gestured at the other two. "The nice one is owned by the daughter of the original owner. Teaches at one of the high schools in the Valley. Husband runs a garage close by. The other," he pointed at the most rundown of the three, "not sure anyone's been there in a long time. This is just second hand. I'll have to get the actual details when I get back to the office. Ready to get dirty?" he segued.

"Dressed for whatever comes along," Raymond answered as they headed toward the backside of the big house. "Seemed like the body rolled out from here," said Belin as the two dropped to the ground, planting their elbows on the slightly slanted slope, and peered under the building. "They blasted out a concrete wall to be remodeled and there was like a small basement—too small for any real use—maybe a wine or food surplus storage. Maybe stocking up for the apocalypse—or the alien visitation. But totally enclosed in concrete except for a small trap door. When they knocked out the side, well, the woman we assume is Lindy Fuller rolled out. With the decomposed body of her little dog— shih tzu, I think—and her little purse. At least we assume it is Lindy Fuller. M.E. and tech folks will have to confirm that."

"But she's pretty well preserved," Raymond observed. "Hair long, facial features kind of frozen like leather. Mummified."

"Isolation and weather," the gruff voice of the sheriff answered back. "Let's grab some breakfast and talk about this stuff." Raymond enthusiastically agreed since he'd left home so early and now would be the time he'd be heading for work. He'd had a cup of bitter truck stop coffee and a small pack of trail mix. "Lots of new eating spots along the road," Belin offered, "but I like Tiny's—a diner that's been on Palm Drive for a long time. Serves a pretty good plate of eggs and sausage."

Raymond followed the old gent, but his mind was on the mummified starlet and why his name would be associated with it.

CHAPTER 3

Riley's preschool was located in Santa Monica, about 15 minutes from home. Meredith pulled into a temporary parking slot, opened her door and walked around to the back of the car, unhooked the car seat holding the child, who babbled with enthusiasm, anxious for the day to begin. Her mother lifted her from the auto and set her on the ground as the school's teacher/steward of the day came up and held her hand out to Riley. Laughing and waving goodbye as Meredith hugged her, the child took the teacher's hand and off they went toward the school building. Thank goodness she likes learning, thought Meredith, and is a happy child! Mostly.

It was a blustery day on the beach around the house where Meredith lived with Raymond and Riley, and worked. She toasted a bagel in the kitchen, poured a cup of coffee and brought a jar of apple butter and a knife into the alcove office. Then, settled at her desk, munching on the chewy bun, she looked through the waiting stack of possible stories or leads to others. As a highly respected columnist covering major Hollywood issues and events, and feature stories about major celebrities and entertainment industry happenings, her work was never dull, the subject matter always available. Since her days, some ten years prior, as the Legwoman, or assistant, to the then-most widely read Hollywood columnist Bettina Grant, Meredith's professional aura had blossomed and escalated. She was sought-after as a guest on news and talk shows, speaker at major journalism gatherings, and was revered and somewhat feared by celebrities and movie/TV moguls as well.

Snapping on four small TV monitors atop a small bookcase, she checked the happenings on the major morning shows: Joan Lunden and Charles Gibson on *Good Morning America*, Bryant Gumbel and Jane Pauley on the *Today Show*, and Paula Zahn on *CBS*, Amanda Borkin and Millie Nesbit filled out the ranks on *NBS's It's a New Day*. Meredith mused that her office was reminiscent of her late boss's in the 1970s. Then remembered the day she arrived at work in 1983 to find her famous gossip column boss murdered. Meredith shook off the memory.

Checking her voice mail, she heard a low, near-whisper, almost conspiratorial, a voice speaking so rapidly Meredith had to strain to catch the words. "It's Sarah, um…Sam's in trouble…big time…."

Meredith quickly dialed her long-time colleague and friend Sarah Freeman. "What kind of trouble is Sam in?" Meredith drove forth, anxious about Sarah's long-time boyfriend, also a close work friend of Meredith.

"Oh jeez. He's been arrested…well, taken into custody whatever that means…for…um…Benjamin Salisbury apparently seems to have been killed…" she fumbled for words, then blurted out, "It's ridiculous but…I knew you would want to know…I don't think it's been released anywhere yet but…I better go. I'm not supposed to even know. Can you find out anything…?" The line clicked off. Sarah Freeman was a freelance publicist, or publicity representative, for major movies and a good friend to Meredith and the girlfriend of Sam Bethel— another publicist. Sam was the normal press representative for the films of super star Tanya Meile, a chart-busting singer/performer and also an Oscar winning actress. Benjamin

Salisbury was the artist's agent, manager and husband who governed her appearances and other work with an iron hand. Why Sam would kill Ben made no sense to Meredith. She'd never heard of discord in the relationship, and the agent generally determined Sam's appointments to Tanya's movies, and managed the process.

Meredith sat down in her seat with a thump and stared out the adjacent window. Sam was one of the most logical and grounded problem-solvers she knew, a characteristic required by most publicists—turmoil was generic to movie publicity—but Sam was one of the best. Meredith rose and refreshed her coffee in the kitchen, then sat back down at her desk to figure out what her next steps should be about the information she'd just received. She shuffled through the pending paperwork, but her mind was elsewhere. She finally picked up the receiver and called Raymond's car phone. "Call me," she implored.

CHAPTER 4

Sheriff Belin scraped at the last of the yellow yoke on his plate, sucked it from the fork, then wiped his mouth with his paper napkin. Raymond finished his own scrambled eggs and tomatoes and had taken a small notebook and pen from his shirt pocket. "Ted, how can I help you on this? It's a long way from my jurisdiction, but I understand that my name being associated with the deceased pulls me in. Still, thank God it's in your backyard not mine."

The old sheriff picked up his cup, holding it with both hands. "Yeah. I know. But T.K. you've got the movie beat so you can help me by doing some research for us…who's this Lindy Fuller? Your guys probably got more info on her than we have. We'll be finding out why she's here in our county—if that's who the dead girl is. And then how she's involved with the house up on the hill. And, 'course anything else about her here in our area. But she must have some history in L.A. and with you and this Tad Oakley guy."

Nodding his head in thought, Raymond agreed, jotting down notes. "Did anyone talk with the neighbor who's the daughter of an original owner—maybe was there when Fuller lived there? Might remember something about her?"

"One of my officers went across the street but the wife—daughter of the former owner—had left for work, husband hadn't lived there long enough. Have to check back."

"Who owns the house?" Raymond persisted. "Who owned it—what—thirty years ago when her driver's license was valid? Owned it then and who's the one remodeling it now?"

Belin shrugged. "Current owner lives in Chicago and is not around right now. Waiting to connect with the real estate agent who sold it to them and gonna talk to the contractor as well. Real estate gal is Rita Lazlo, hot shot who they tell me has lots of contact with the celebrity world. But she's playing golf today. I'm thinking of taking a ride out to Palm Hills and interrupt Ms. Lazlo's morning walk in the sun. Come along and see the 'other side' of the Coachella Valley— the snazzy side." The reference amused the detective, but the more he thought about it, Raymond realized his name was associated with the situation and that every hint of "why" was worth knowing.

"Yep. Let's get going. I'll follow because I have to get back to town as soon as I can." Belin dropped some bills on the table and the two left the diner for their cars. Bright sun overtook a cloudless sky as the two-vehicle caravan dropped down to the I-10 and made its way east about five miles then north again a short distance to a sprawling verdant golf resort. Raymond mused about the Sheriff's descript—"the snazzy side" and had to agree. And, the resort did give some context to the situation. They wended their way toward the sport center and parked. Rita Lazlo's group was projected to be teeing up on the tenth hole. The game starter called an assistant to take the two lawmen to the location in a cart.

The three interlopers to Rita's foursome sat silently as one of the women lined up a shot from the tee. As quickly as she smacked the ball into space, both Raymond and Belin stepped from the cart and approached the ensemble. A short, squarely-built blonde in a golf skirt and matching polo shirt imprinted with bright blue and green golf flags—turned and walked quickly up to them. "What'cha need?" she asked, eyeing them defensively. Her sun-baked complexion was shadowed under a chartreuse visor that tamed a head of unruly hair.

"Rita Lazlo?" said the sheriff. She thrust her manicured hand forward to shake. "Yep, and you are?"

"Sheriff Ted Belin and this is Detective T.K. Raymond." Both men perfunctorily shook hands, then automatically pulled ID from their pockets and flipped open the wallets.

She glanced at them. With a raised eyebrow asked, "Am I in trouble?"

Both shook their heads. "No ma'am. It's about the house up on Elderwood Ridge," Belin answered. Rita signaled for the other players in her group to play on.

"What about it?" she asked. "It's been sold. Guy took ownership more than three months ago."

Raymond stepped into the fray. "We were hoping you could give us the ownership history of the place—so we don't have to go digging through the county files." Rita looked at him suspiciously.

"Why?"

"Ma'am there's been an 'incident' at the house during construction." Belin filled in the story and cautioned against talking about it yet. Rita sucked in a deep breath, gritted her teeth, then looked around to make sure her golf companions, now clustered in their carts, did not hear.

"Damnation," she spat. "That house has been nothing but a problem—one escrow fell apart because the buyer didn't have the money. Another fizzled when the buyer found something 'more modern' she liked better. God, I hope this one isn't a deal buster. What can I do to make this all go away?"

Both men smiled at the idea. "I think if we can get some history on the place—have the crime techs give it a good look, which they're doing now by the way, it may not impact the current place at all."

Rita looked worried. "I can have my assistant pull the records from the Title Insurance search. And any other files we have. You still may have to go back to the county records. These old places have a troubled history—most of them. But I can send what I have. I'll call when I get back to the club house. Also contact information on the owners. They're in Evanston, Illinois. Wanted a place to come when the weather is—well, kind of like it is there now." She glanced furtively at her friends waiting nearby. "Wish they'd played on," she murmured. "Guys behind us are gonna start hitting into us." Belin and Raymond quickly pulled cards from their wallets and handed them to her, as she did the same. They thanked her and were in their cart and headed back to the club house as the foursome gunned their vehicles forward to play on.

Raymond agreed to investigate the names on the SAG card, and also the other name scribbled next to his own in the L.A. and entertainment industry records he could find. The rumpled sheriff returned to the clubhouse, used the phone to check in on the investigation, and planned to return to the scene after stopping by his office. Raymond pulled back onto the interstate headed toward Los Angeles. It was just about the time Meredith would be leaving to pick up Riley. From his car phone, he returned her call. She picked up with traffic noise in the background.

"The guy with his name written all over a dead body!" she joked, hearing his voice. "Tattoos?"

"You'll be interested to know the dead body was a woman about 26 years old, pretty actress. I was apparently on her mind just before…well…need I say more?"

"Mmm. And?"

He told her the story, adding, "She died probably twenty-thirty years ago, and I need a little simple help."

"Of course. What kind of help?" Raymond asked her to peruse her extensive celebrity files to see if there was anything included about Lindy Fuller, the actress who succumbed so long ago. And if her colleague—former assistant—Sonia could use her data base and library contacts to look for both Fuller and Tad Oakley, whose name was jotted down along with his own. "It'll cost you," she snickered. He sighed.

"Raymond," she began and he immediately sensed the change in mood and a gravity in her voice. "Why I called is that Sam Bethel has been 'taken into custody,' apparently, for…" her voice caught as she tried to explain. "For I guess…maybe killing Ben Salisbury—the Vegas star Tanya Meile's husband. It cannot have happened, Raymond. Sam's a gentle soul from the hills of Tennessee—an amazing publicist—but not a nasty bone in his body which is why Tanya's always insisted on him as the pub guy on her films, and Ben's been solid with it. But, besides, that, Raymond," her voice pitch rose and the pace of her words doubled. "Ben was the golden goose for Sam. He wrote the checks and signed the contracts, makes no sense and…." Her dialogue trailed off. She was pulling into the drive to the preschool and took a deep breath. "I'm picking up Riley right now but…."

"I'll go by the office on my way home," Raymond interjected. "See what I can find. But then I'm headed back to the barn. I've already put in a ten-hour day. I'm beat after four hours on the road. But calm down—I'll find out what I can. Kiss Riley for me." He hung up and Meredith hurried out of the car to open the door for the smiling child with the deep brown eyes and blonde curls.

CHAPTER 5

The drive from the Coachella Valley desert into the extended boundaries of Los Angeles frequently included entry into a large cloud of haze and smog, a grey and yellow portal welcoming drivers into the inner-galactic breath of the giant metropolis. Sorry he had ever mentioned his own tiredness after a shortened night's sleep. The suggestion of weariness only deepened the reality through the monotonous hours on the interstate. Now it pulled at him. He took the off ramp at West Covina, gassed the car and bought another cup of bad coffee. Behind the wheel again, he mused at the barter with Meredith, reflecting on how they started the relationship when they met ten years before, bartering about finding the killer of her boss—he the special profile detective on movie cases, she the intrepid assistant ("legwoman") to the famous columnist—with a target on her back. And a giant juggling act to keep her own professional life together. Oh yes, and her dauntless focus on Raymond, himself. By the end of the investigation, she had him by the short hairs in most every way. And ever since.

He smiled thinking that in those days, never would either of them have imagined a settled life in a comfortable home on the water—and adjusting life to the giggles, tantrums and early morning hugs and kisses of a happy little girl. He shook his head musing that she was the product of their own souls. Or maybe just one night of glorious, inebriated sex. He thought back to the six years pre-Riley of living with Meredith—first as an occasional overnight guest, then as a household member in her former condo. Even when she became the cohabiter in his Malibu house both were free agents bound together by passion, interest and well—desire to be there, he supposed. He was twelve years her senior, a widower with a grown son. But then one night at a friend's annual Christmas party, Meredith handed him a surprising gift. The pregnancy she quietly announced to him was a development she had professed she would never undertake. When he reminded her, she explained, "we must have crossed the gods, Raymond. There was no mistake or forgetfulness. But nothing is one-hundred percent. Not even birth control, apparently." They muddled their way through the Christmas season that year with new film screenings, studio and other entertainment industry cocktail parties, holiday crimes among the rich and famous. Added to the mix were Meredith's disdain for the physical changes she was encountering—and, simply fending off the astonishment of the few friends aware of the situation.

The previous year, they'd put on weddings for Raymond's son Will and his then-girlfriend, for Meredith's coworker Sonia, and toasted a few other newlyweds. But even as the holidays morphed into New Year's Eve and then into actual next year, no mention of a wedding of their own was brought up, hinted, or suggested. Weary of holiday and other volleys coming his way, Raymond booked a short break, a several-day trip to Hawaii. Unobserved, he checked out Meredith's column and article schedule and saw it was written well ahead. He'd readjusted his own case load to allow the vacation time he already had coming and was set to talk with Meredith.

Home from work, he pulled off his jacket as he came into the kitchen from the garage, and put it on the small entry room hook. Meredith heard him from her office, quickly closed the calendar she was updating and walked into the kitchen. Both noticed a tension in the room.

"We need to talk about a couple of things, Raymond," she blurted out with a big near-gulp, pulling her hair into a messy ponytail, a nervous habit. His spirits plummeted. The "we need to talk" subject was never good. Especially considering the gravity of the possible current subjects.

"Okay," he agreed meekly and gestured toward the small table in the corner of the kitchen. They sat down facing one another.

"This past six months has been pure chaos between the New York morning show adventures, getting stranded on the rusty ship, the holidays and…well…um…this," she pointed at her belly. "We need to talk about the forbidden subject, don't you think?"

He found himself without words, hoping he understood hers, wondering what "forbidden" choices she was about to make. "…which subject…love…baby…." He couldn't quite continue, finally stammered out, "wedding?"

She laughed. "Yeah, wedding." Raymond breathed a silent sigh of relief. She went on, "And I thought I was terrified…the hold-out." He shook his head. "So, this is going forward," she said, again pointing toward her midsection—still taut and unsullied to outside eyes. "But we should, too. Don't you think? For the sake of this?" pointing again at downward. "I'm usually the one who just doesn't want to rumple the covers. No need. But, well, now it's different."

"What does that look like to you? Wedding," he probed gingerly, making certain not to call attention to her over-observance of her barely changed stomach.

"Nothing big or elaborate. Just getting the job done. We're kind of there already and just need to dot the i's and cross the t's." Raymond stood up, went to his briefcase, opened it and extracted a large envelope.

"How about this?" He laid the tickets to Hawaii on the table. "You've outrun me, as always," he sighed. "But I already planned out—at least—an escape from the circus we're going through right now."

She grinned slyly, "And you thought you'd just kind of woo me to 'I do' on vacation in the tropical sun?" He shrugged and sheepishly nodded. She stared at him for a moment then grinned. "Works for me."

"Hold on!" he directed. Grabbed his brief case and brought out a small envelope. "I had planned something a little more romantic for this…and well, never thought of the kitchen that way…." He stood up quickly and reached for her hand. "Come on," he gestured with his head toward the terrace. He led her through the living room onto the open expanse overlooking the surf. Sunset was just wrapping up its glossy canvas with only the promise of a starry horizon. Raymond fumbled with the envelope and brought out a small ring. "Not getting down on my knees or anything. Too showy and we're so far past it…but, was going do this in Hawaii…but, now's good. It's my grandmother's ring. For now or forever—depending on what bling you had in mind to decorate your fourth finger." She thrust out her finger and he wiggled onto it the sparkling diamond set quietly in gold.

She smiled softly, blinked, then burst out with, "Oh, yes, yes," dramatically pantomimed, hand against her heart. Then they both laughed. "Seriously, though," her voice took a quick turn. "This is serious, Raymond. Kind of seals the deal. Maybe immortalizes the past few years? Something like that."

He smiled almost nostalgically. "However you want to say it…Does this mean we have to get a station wagon?"

"No," she winked at him. "But we do need to go to Hawaii. Even though a beach wedding is one of the most cliched icon in books and movies, it's perfect for us, I think." She reached up and held his face, with its strong angular features and the day's slight almost-silver stubble, smiled softly then added, "…but right now, while the mind—and the body—are able, there's more…." She pulled him by the arm into the house and up the stairs to the bedroom….

CHAPTER 6

Kailua-Kona, Hawaii
January 1990

"The license took less than an hour. Finding the dress, most of the day," Raymond joked with George Masner on the phone from L.A. Masner was the detective's former roommate and still best friend now serendipitously conveniently married to Meredith's college roommate and still best pal, Gloria. "There's some perception that 'baby fat' has emerged—which by the way she's the only one who sees it right now—so…well, the attire cost three times as much as the license, photographer and minister combined," he chuckled. "The hotel found us a minister. I'm not sure what his religion is but he is certified, so I guess it's legal."

Raymond's tall, tight, athletic body seemed incongruous wrapped in a bright palm tree-imprinted Hawaiian shirt and Bermuda shorts as he slouched, barefoot, against the wall next to the hanging phone. The hotel, referred to him by George some weeks earlier, was one built in a remote beach area which, originally in the '60s, only boats and planes could access. The policy still allowed no phones, radios, TVs in the fashionable "hales" or thatched huts—complete with air conditioners and refrigerators. The only available phones resided in the lobby building.

"We needed a break—and some privacy," he reminded Meredith the day they arrived. All she could say, looking at the view of the Bay and adjacent ancient fishponds and welcoming squat hales, was "oh…!" After a day of errands—license, arrangements for the location, appointment with the minister, and dinner reservations—Meredith had set out to find the perfect attire for the ceremony itself. Now framed as a simple ceremony with only the couple, the hotel manager—a portly German gentleman, jovial and accommodating as witness—and the minister.

At the end of her shopping day, Meredith reported back that she'd visited four local clothing shops, found the perfect traditional muu muu in the last. "It's called a Bette. Lovely heart shaped neck trimmed in velvet and kind of mutton chop three-quarter-length sleeves. Apparently one of the most desired classics. This one was a vintage." The fabric was a soft lavender shade with deeper violet and white orchids. Raymond wondered what she was talking about but nodded and reached out to feel the gentle fabric.

"Oh, and I ran into a fascinating woman," Meredith continued. "She recognized my name—was also shopping—is the head of the film commission here and talked to me about the annual film festival coming up. She asked if we could get together and talk about it, hoping, of course, for coverage…." Raymond sighed, rolled his eyes and winced. They'd agreed to doing no business during the trip.

"I said 'no,' that this is strictly R&R and gave her my card."

"That's my girl," sighed Raymond with relief.

"Girl…S," corrected Meredith, glancing at her torso.

"Sure about that?"

The look she gave him said, "Are you serious?"

☆☆☆

"This whole thing feels like costuming for a play," she said to Raymond, as she pondered the old Hawaiian story handed down for generations: flower behind the right ear—available. Behind the left—taken. She wondered where it should be worn facing the next life phase. Maybe on the bosom?

"Like an episode of Gilligan's Island," he replied. And so true to culturally popular idea of the personal, private wedding—most often held on a beach, and frequently in Hawaii.

They met with the minister, as was his custom, at his lovely church on a side street in the small but bustling town. Once past introductions, he invited them to join him to talk in the small, lush garden behind the building. Tropical blooms, red, yellow, fuchsia, flourished, and their fragrance was a tonic. Thick, tall shrubs and trees, some with deep green leaves and some fern-like enclosed the serene outdoor cloister. Sitting on teak benches, they lost track of the busy tourist activity outside and the oddly intense pressure around their whole trip and its reason.

"This is my idea of an intimate and personal space," Meredith commented as the conversation had moved well beyond the prescribed minister-bridal couple conversation and into genial new-friend discussions. Pastor Juan Medieros was born and raised on the Island of Hawaii, but journeyed to California to study for what he'd hoped would be a career as a veterinarian, got side-lined by chemistry and the Vietnam War, came home a different person and went into the ministry. Not unlike Raymond's own story— with a different pathway. Knowing the couple's work and usual lifestyle, the minister recounted comedic and sometimes bizarre stories of celebrities whose nuptials he'd overseen over many years. Two hours had passed during what was usually a half-hour of pre-wedding counseling.

"Do you perform weddings here? It seems almost like your own personal place with God," said Raymond to Juan. The swarthy minister laughed and shook his head. "It's a place with God for anyone who wants to enjoy it. We do some weddings here. Most folks want to go to the beach. Better photography." He snickered.

Meredith looked at Raymond. He smiled and nodded. "Could we?" Meredith asked.

"Now?" asked Raymond in surprise as he and Meredith glanced quickly at each other for affirmation.

"Sure," said Juan. "But let me call my wife Celi to come over and witness. Are you sure this is what you want?" Both bride and groom blurted out, "Yes."

"We have the licenses you just signed, the rings are in my pocket. What else will we need?" posed Raymond.

"Just your desire to be here—oh yeah, and your love," the minister chuckled. Twenty minutes later a solidly built Hawaiian woman arrived, wrapped in a flowered frock, a long dark braid reaching to her waist, and carrying two delicate plumeria leis over her arm. "Hi, I'm Celi," she announced as she entered the church office. "I brought you each a lei. No one should get married here without some flowers." She placed a floral ring over the head and around the neck of both the bride and groom, who were a little taken back by the gesture and the flowers, and even themselves. They stammered out their "hellos" and appreciation for the thoughtfulness.

So here we are, thought Meredith. We're doing that thing I never have embraced—marriage, kids, Hawaiian Wedding Song. She couldn't help remembering her former boyfriend/fiancé's comment, "Your wedding is one of the only times you get to write, design, produce, direct and star in your own production." She smiled at the recollection and thought sardonically of TV's treacly *Love Boat* episodes.

Juan introduced the brief ceremony, his wife standing as a

witness, Raymond in Bermuda shorts and a blue golf shirt and Meredith in white shorts and a Northwestern University T-shirt. Vows were short and to the point. And mostly impromptu since the drafted copies remained behind in the hotel suite.

"Meredith," said Raymond, "I walked a solitary road for a long time, thinking I was happy—satisfied. Then I met you. You fill up my world. And every day you thrill, amaze and often even frighten me. But you have brought me to the point where, after the years of avoiding the word, I'm surrounded by love and that's all about you."

"T.K. Raymond," she began, "I know the word love and feel it every day with you, even though, as you say, we haven't actually said it often. From the moment you rescued my cat Paco from the intruders to my home, to right now with this unexpected wedding moment, I've never had a question in my heart or mind that we were wrapped in love from the start and will be so forever."

Juan smiled, said, "The rings." They exchanged gold bands subtly adorned with minute, simple native Hawaiian etchings. "Hope the ratings are great and the critics are kind in the next phase of this union. I now pronounce you…well, you know, husband and wife." He winked at the couple.

Juan's wife Celi took out a camera she had carried in her bag and photographed the couple as they stood with the minister, then placed them in a couple of other strategic view locations. The last "click" of the shutter finalized the ceremony. The bride and groom seemed to heave a sigh of relief.

"I guess we can wear our wedding costumes for dinner tonight," mused Meredith. Raymond invited Juan and Celi to join them, but the minister declined and suggested a raincheck until the following evening.

"But make sure to take some photos in your wedding finery tonight," Celi reminded. Plans were set and Meredith and Raymond walked out of the church holding hands—slightly stunned.

CHAPTER 7

Merging from the I-10 to the 405 in the West L.A. area, Raymond was comparing the wedding to Meredith to his first nuptials, years-earlier, to his late wife Lily and chuckled. So youthful, reverent, anxiety-ridden, important simply in the fact that a wedding took place. Two adults in the beginning of their lives—all ahead: fantasy, hopes and expectation. Family and friends urging them on. And no concept of what "ahead" would be—or as it turned out, not be. The jubilant birth of son Will, the gut-wrenching departure of Raymond-the-soldier to Vietnam. Lily had succumbed to cancer very young, leaving a husband with a four-year-old son and a life to arrange and manage. Even her parents, hopeful to partner in the rearing of the child, were struck down too early, further forging the slim family life of the father Raymond and son Will.

The impromptu ceremony that took place in Hawaii, helped by the connection to the spiritual but jovial emcee, Juan Medieros, was more a metaphysical transformation, a journey into a new and unknown galaxy. Raymond and Lily were earth with nascent seedlings waiting for the promise of the season; Raymond with Meredith, the springtime of the mature orchard preening in its prime. He felt the emotional charge remembering the moment when he realized being together with the copper-blond love partner was real and sure.

He turned east on Olympic and through the maze of West L.A. streets to his office. Parking quickly, he jogged into the building and initiated the search for the name Tad Oakley. Then made the phone calls about Meredith's friend Sam Bethel's situation. A few comments and exchange with Marty, his long-time colleague, and Roberta, his office administrator, and he was back in the car headed north to Malibu and home. It had been a long day. And a complicated one.

★★☆

"Shh…" warned the mischievous face of three-and-a-half-year-old Riley, greeting her father as he came into the kitchen from the garage. A small finger at her mouth, another wagging at Raymond. "Paco is having his nap on the fridge. He doesn't like to be disturbed."

"Paco is always having his nap on the fridge and he'll be yowling for his dinner in about five minutes." He reached down, hefted the tot into his arms and kissed her on the nose. "Where's your mom?"

"In her office. Working. But Lola and I are baking cookies." Raymond was suddenly overtaken by the swirling fragrance of hot brown sugar and chocolate. And noticed the culinary chaos a kitchen took on with an almost-four-year-old engaged in baking. He realized that he was hungry. As well as tired. And glad he was home to remedy both. He walked into the small alcove they'd built out enclosing the farthest end of the terrace to house Meredith's office space including Sonia's desk. Meredith leaned back in her chair and smiled at him. "Home is the traveler." He reached down and tousled her hair then quickly pulled back.

"It has been a long day. I kissed my child on the nose and tousled my wife's hair. Backwards. I'm confused." They both laughed as she rose and hugged him.

"A drink and a cookie before dinner?" she teased.

"Shower first," he groaned, turning into the living room and heading up the stairs to the master suite. Serious conversation was most often held after Riley was tucked away in her upstairs bed and Lola, the twenty-year-old college student who worked as an "everything" helper in the household and lived in the small, built-out studio apartment under the wide terrace, had retreated to her own quarters for the night.

The three-story house sat on a bluff overlooking a quiet section of Malibu Beach north of Los Angeles. Raymond had purchased it from an aging and long-time friend four years before, after living in a small cottage he owned further up the sand. Meredith moved into the comfortable home with her cat Paco and until the room, transfer of her workplace into the house from external offices, and arrival of Riley, the original 2500 square feet was a comfortably adequate for the couple. To accommodate the newest family member, the weekly arrival of Meredith's news assistant, and now a household helper, the house was slightly enlarged. A small section of the veranda was closed in for additional workspace and a ten-by-ten-foot room and bath added underneath the veranda with an external entrance for Lola, the household helper.

"Tell me," urged Meredith when the household was silent except for the dishwasher churning softly and the outside surf's rhythm providing a subtle never-ending backdrop. Raymond grabbed a small glass from a kitchen cabinet and poured scotch into it. He rubbed his hand across his face and sat down at the table. Meredith, joined him, bringing her leftover wine from dinner. She leaned forward, elbows on the table. "First things first: about the body with your name all over it?" she prodded intently. He offered a more complete story than she'd heard by phone earlier in the day. He finished with a shrug.

"Well, our side found Lindy Fuller." Meredith spoke up hesitantly. "But not much of her, unfortunately. Sonia went to work on her library of resources. Lots of calls to sources and found one brief mention of Lindy Fuller as a supporting cast member in a 1963 movie from the old Starsystem Studios. A party film with a lot of 'B' actors. Nothing else. But, Sonia has a call into the acting union to see if they have a contact for an agent or manager. Could have been contracted directly through the studio, but…."

"Think we can find an old photo…or a poster? Even a biography?"

Meredith shrugged. "We'll dig more tomorrow. But Raymond, does her name ring a bell with you at all?"

He shook his head and tinkered with his drink. "Not anything. And the notation was made so long ago. If it was even only twenty years ago, I was really young. At the earliest, '64 – '67, I was in Vietnam. Later, well, not associated with anyone in the movie industry— mostly law enforcement and long before the special profile assignments. My dad, of course, was involved, but at some point, he and mom moved from L.A. to Orange County so he could begin to semi-retire, step away from the business and disconnect. And my mom never was much involved—why they moved." They pondered the timing, Meredith with pen and paper drawing out a simple year-by-year chronology.

"What about Tad Oakley?" Raymond asked. She shook her head.

"Nothing anywhere. But look, we only spent a little time on it this afternoon. Let us dig more tomorrow. Find some old files somewhere, someone with a long memory. Sonia will make some calls from home. It's her day out of the office. And I can work on it. How about your team?" she looked at him with some expectation in her eyes.

"Not very helpful. In the office, Marty's on it and I have the office admin slugging through the data bases we have available now. It's Sheriff Belin's jurisdiction and the fact that Lindy Fuller's body was found there and probably lived around there, well, he's bound to uncover something locally. My name and the other guy's may have nothing to do with anything."

"On the other hand," Meredith murmured, looking at Raymond, eyes intense.

"I know. These are the stones that can't be left unturned..." He mimicked something she had said years before.

"...if you want to get to the truth,' she finished her own statement. "And your turn...did you find anything out about Sam being arrest for Ben Salisbury's murder?"

Raymond grimaced. "Not much either. All took place in Las Vegas. That's where Tanya and Ben live. Again, not my jurisdiction. But Marty talked to someone at the Vegas police department. They're faxing over the report. That's the start. I'll put in a call to the lead detective on the case tomorrow. Marty said it sounded pretty solid—but then, the circus is only just starting on that one. I'm not sure I want it in my ballpark, to be honest. Tomorrow..." he started but fell silent.

CHAPTER 8

"Just a name? That's all you got—from a couple of decades ago?" Fred Barton's energetic voice caused Meredith to flinch. Barton, editor of one of Hollywood's most important daily trade publications, was one of Meredith long-time friends, responsible for her initial job with gossip columnist Bettina Grant so many years before. Barton's lofty position made him a major resource of entertainment trivia, data and gossip. Meredith often repaid the favor with news and insights from her work. If anyone knows starlets, even from the 60s and 70s, it'll be Fred, she reasoned.

"That's all, Fred. We also have the name of one movie she was in. No starring role, but in the poster credits. Lindy Fuller. *The Beach Moon Caper.* Starsystem Studios," she half-snickered as she mentioned the name of the long-defunct studio. Fred echoed her snicker.

"Must have been a stinker. Starsystem wasn't known for its 'cinematic' quality. I'll look in our archives and see if anything shows up. And I have an old publicist buddy—out at the Old Age Farm now but he did a lot of the publicity work for the studio back when. But you'll owe me!"

"I know," Meredith exaggerated a sigh. "Lunch at Musso and Frank! You'll have it! But wait, there's more…." Fred sighed dramatically. "You know how busy I am, Merri!" he said using her long-ago nickname.

"Yes, and how much you love Musso and Frank! So, does the name Tad Oakley ring a bell?

Fred thought for a moment then murmured, "Nah."

"Here's the last question: what have you heard about Sam Bethel's arrest in Vegas for the death of Ben Salisbury?" She heard a deep sigh of frustration. Then the sound of Fred 's chair squeaking as he got up, walked to his door and closed it.

"It's a shit show," he groaned. "You probably have as much info as I do, but I know there was a lot of drama and fighting in Vegas during the past six months."

"Over what?"

"What do you want? Salisbury, as you well know, ruled Tanya with an iron hand—why she stayed in Vegas instead of touring, recording, all that. But he also had a new and different show in mind, one with all the chorus girls and big production techniques, bells and whistles. Tanya never wanted it. Her song style was always mellow, jazzy, with subtle graphics around her, real harmony surrounding. Kind of cabaret. Apparently, Ben had planned to eliminate the back-up group and crew who'd been with Tanya for years. Great identifiable sounds, solid support and good friends. And, on the personal front, Tanya wanted to live in L.A., record and spend time with her daughter. Friends in Vegas said the argument became a battle. I'm guessing their publicist, your friend Sam, got caught in the middle of it. He and Tanya have always been close. But…." Meredith could hear his elfin face crunching up.

"Wow," she breathed. "I've always been fond of Tanya and Sam—never knew Ben other than in a couple of social situations. Trade info as we get it?" she proposed. He responded with his usual "Yup." They rang off without much ado—as old friends can do—also understanding how fruitful the Musso and Frank conversation might be.

CHAPTER 9

One week later

Slogging his way through morning traffic—even late morning traffic—on L.A. freeways was an exercise in patience, good radio, and mental puzzles to allay the boredom. Raymond was familiar with them all and currently playing with mental puzzles. He was again on the road to Desert Hot Springs, or at least the adjacent area. Sheriff Belin had contacted him the day before to invite him to join a meeting with the former neighbor of the Elderwood Ridge house, the mother of the high school teacher currently living across the street.

"She's been visiting a sister in Wisconsin," the sheriff had explained. "Just returned home yesterday. Lives in one of the nice gated senior living communities in Palm Desert. I said we'd come to her. Think it would be good for you to be there." Raymond couldn't fault the logic. As he hit the road the next morning, he idly thought about the process of leaving the house most mornings. Twice a week Meredith was up and by seven, at the TV studio for the *Morning Coffee Show* studios. Most of the time, like today, he took Riley to preschool. Meredith usually picked her up but if she was involved in an interview or meeting or movie set visit, Lola would do the honors, bring her home and keep her occupied until one or another parent arrived. But this morning seemed unusually chaotic. "The ocean castle," as Riley called the Raymond household, was a study in comparative opposition from the early days of Meredith and Raymond's relationship. Quiet then, private, their own.

Now, at eight a.m. on a Wednesday morning, the bustle of the day was palpable. Meredith adjusting Riley's shirt. Riley tapping her foot and reaching for her lunch box. Lola the student helper cleaning up the kitchen and readying herself for classes at nearby Pepperdine. Sonia on the phone probing information for her question/answer column.

The 50-something-year old detective captain was glad to have the time alone on the freeway. When he pulled off the I-10 onto Cook Street and followed it into the center of the resort-laden desert valley, he geared up for the all-too-usual police work. Pulling into the coffee shop where he'd agreed to meet Belin, he saw the sheriff already seated at a booth, scraping onto his fork the last remnants of a large breakfast plate.

"You eat?" he asked, wiping his mouth. Raymond nodded and called over the waitress for a cup of coffee as he sat down. "She's a spry one," said Belin referring to the senior citizen subject they were about to visit. "No old folks drabble for her. She may be helpful."

Fifteen minutes later the two drove through the gates of a handsome townhouse community. They stopped at a guard stand where a uniformed attendant checked their names on a visitors' list and directed them to a nearby street. They made their way up the walkway of a well-kept up earthen-colored townhouse, manicured desert plants and other xeriscape pleasantries coloring the pristine front yard. A poised, straight-standing woman, easily in her 90s, opened the door and smiled at them. "Come on in," she instructed. They did. "I'm Victoria." She wore white capri pants, open sandals and a turquoise sweater. Silver bracelets and jewelry lightly clattered at her wrists.

Raymond had expected a wizened elder, stooped and accompanied by a helper. Clearly not the case.

"Come on out to the back veranda," she beckoned them through the comfortable, eclectically furnished house to a covered patio surrounded by lemon, orange and grapefruit trees. The perfect desert retreat, Raymond thought. A plate of cookies and pitcher of frosty iced tea sat on the glass table. "Tell me more about what you need to know," she said, sitting primly, pouring tea into three ice-filled glasses.

"Well," Belin began, "we have a puzzle up on a house on Elderwood Ridge, across the street from your daughter's place. We understand that you once lived up there—a long time back—and might be able to give us some information on the residents who lived there at that time."

"This is about that body found on that property, isn't it? My daughter told me about it."

"Yes, ma'am," said Belin. "We believe the victim was a young woman— probably in her thirties, named Lindy Fuller. We have some identification that suggests she lived at the house maybe twenty or thirty years ago. An actress. Does any of that ring a bell?"

Victoria sat back in her wicker chair and puckered her lips. After a few seconds she began. "I do remember a young woman and the name is familiar but maybe not totally. She didn't live there long. Or rather, she wasn't there long. I don't really know how long she owned or occupied the place but seems like she was there for a while and then just like that, gone. Eventually someone came and moved everything out.

"She arrived with her husband. A swarthy fellow, kind of short and bulldog like. Several inches shorter than she was. Never said much. When we first saw them moving in, she was pregnant. Then we didn't see them for a couple of weeks but when they returned, there was a new baby."

"Do you recall the husband's name?" asked Raymond. She shook her head in thought.

"No, I think it was something like Novato—Donato—maybe Italian. He was short—seemed curt and arrogant. But I'm not certain. He was seldom around. She told one of the neighbors he was in the movie industry and stayed in town—L.A. I would guess—a lot. Truly I only saw him about a half dozen times in the…oh maybe a year and a half or so…that she was there. Mostly I remember her because she was a movie actress. Sweet though—kind of airy."

Raymond showed Victoria a photo Meredith and Sonia had managed to locate. In it, the actress was overly made up, as was the style of the day. The older woman looked for a few seconds, fingered it as if trying to feel the character in it, then nodded. "Pretty sure it was her. She had shorter hair and I hardly ever saw her with makeup on, but the eyes give her away. She had amazing sparkly eyes. This black and white shot doesn't do them justice—they were a deep, violet color you couldn't avoid."

"Do you, by any chance, remember the name of the baby?" asked Raymond. The gracious silver head shook from side to side.

The two lawmen probed and conversed further with Victoria, allowing her to reminisce about the early days in the remote location hope to pique her memory more. "Is there anyone else who might have known her or more about her. Another neighbor?"

Victoria's eyes went vague. "No." she shrugged. "They're all gone," sadness slipped into her tone. "Mostly no one ever stayed very long out there. It was hot and dry and quite ugly in those days. It's changing and I'm still surprised my daughter and her family want to be there, but I'm pleased I could offer them a place to live."

It seemed obvious to the two lawmen they had gleaned all there was from the gracious and regal Victoria. They thanked her profusely leaving their business cards, and headed out of the gates. "I think I might like senior citizenship in a place like that," murmured Raymond, thinking that with the amount of noise and activity currently in the Malibu house, the quiet, gated community seemed tonic-like.

"Any news from around here about Fuller—or Tad Oakley?" he asked Belin. The grizzled officer seemed to chew on the inside of his cheek then sniffed and responded. "Well, nothing on either of the people. Our real estate friend, Rita, is digging for a clear flag on the house from that long ago. Should be simple but it was never in the name of the woman or anyone sounding like 'Novato.' In those days the place was owned by some corporation but passed on to one and then another as each one seemed to go out of business. Finally sold to the last previous owner about four years ago. Rita's trying to unravel the actual owners of the corporations."

"Fax me those names—the corporations. I've got a specialist works with us who can probably unravel that faster. It's her area."

The sheriff nodded, turned toward his car and said, "'Kay. You be careful on them L.A. freeways. Thanks for comin'." Raymond realized he'd been dismissed.

CHAPTER 10

"Teeth are brushed, we're bathed, and in bed—after some stalwart negotiation and a couple of tears—hers, not mine," sighed Meredith, entering the living room from the upstairs bedrooms, including Elinor Riley's bright lavender one. Named for Meredith's mother's maiden name—Riley, Raymond's mother's name—Elinor, the child had a legacy of strong, willful women to live up to, or, fall back on. At the moment, she had finally fallen asleep. Meredith flopped down on the sofa next to Raymond.

"Another year and she'll be in school most of the day, not just through lunch," Meredith recounted without thinking about it. "A little less complicated."

"You happy with life these days?" Raymond asked quietly. Meredith nodded her head of coppery hair. "Yeah. Bigger footprint, more family than I ever expected in my life. But…well…yeah. It's constant learning and I'm happily into it, Raymond."

He looked at her with raised eyebrows. "That's academic. But how does it feel down here," he laughed pointing at his heart.

"A new depth every day—of wonder, pleasure and…love. New words because of new feelings," she simpered. "And you?"

"Also surprising. I've been through the kid rearing once before. Figured it was all I needed then—all I'd ever need of it.

Will turned out great and it's totally satisfying and pleasing watching his life with and without me-us. But you know how shaken I was about fatherhood this time around—especially at my age—a kid in the works and the whole family thing starting again. We already had a pretty good and deep thing going. But a little girl— my oh my! Terrifying! No one told me how special—and yes, challenging— it would be. Little girls argue more often—and stridently— than little boys." His grin said it all. Meredith snuggled against him and he put his arm around her. They allowed the evening quiet to fill the house and sat unmoving for a while, knowing that the next day would have its fill of activity, chaos and stress.

CHAPTER 11

"Here we are again," announced Meredith's old mentor and friend Fred Barton as he approached the pristine table at Musso and Frank where Meredith was already seated. With the elfin demeanor of a Billy Crystal or Jack Lemon and short, bulldogish in stature, Fred led the way in front of a much older, worn man, dressed in slightly wrinkled slacks and polo shirt, shoulders curved, his face a road map of years and experiences, and a thin scattering of reddish-grey hair.

"Hi, I'm Morton" he beamed, extending his hand. Meredith shook it, murmuring greetings.

As the two made themselves comfortable in the thick leather booth, Fred explained. "I asked Morton to join us today. He was the primary publicist on the old Starsystem movies. He said he may have some stories about their stars."

"And it was good to get out of the old folks' home," Morton added. Meredith had to laugh.

"I kind of feel the same when I leave the chaos of my home first thing in the morning," she agreed as Fred waved over the waiter, greeted him like an old friend—which he probably was—and ordered drinks.

"I asked Morton to come along because I think he may have something that helps on your story."

"It's a little more than a story," Meredith explained. She unraveled a small slice of the antiquated homicide and her husband's involvement. As soon as they'd ordered and settled in with their cocktails—Fred with bourbon, Morton, scotch, and Meredith, iced tea—she turned to the older visitor. "We're trying to dig out anything we can about an actress from a long time ago—Lindy Fuller."

"She was one of the starlets in that dog of a movie, *Beach Moon Caper*," Fred interjected. Morton winced.

"She was one of the kids—well, young contract players—as I remember. But let me think about it," Morton muttered. Food arrived while he continued to scowl and contemplate. "Yeah. Now I remember her," he suddenly blurted just before he took a bite of his sandwich. "Pretty thing. Like all the kids in those day, liked to party—slurp up Hollywood, if you know what I mean. Not too talented but very sincere and serious. Let's see. I think she landed a couple more below-the-headline roles but Starsystem was only limping along by then. I think I recall she was dating some producer, or manager or agent. Maybe married him? Don't remember exactly."

"Remember who it was?" asked Meredith.

The withered old head shook subtly. "Donahue? Hm. Maybe, well, he was an agent then, but not sure he was the guy we're talking about. Can't recall exactly, but Lindy Fuller—not sure he was her squeeze. But could have been. Was supposed to have been some big muckety-muck manager or agent. Name on the door kind of guy. Sorry, haven't kept up with the lower level thespians, I'm afraid," he said as he bit into his sandwich.

"Ever heard of Tad Oakley?" Meredith persisted.

"Nope. I'd remember a name like 'Tad'"

The information was a beginning that both Meredith and Fred silently acknowledged. Later as they finished up their meal and Meredith called for the check, she looked at Fred and asked about her friend in Las Vegas, "How about Sam and Tanya?"

The venerable powerhouse, wiping his mouth with his napkin, shook his head vehemently. "Above my pay grade. Get the police report. All I get is gossip and trivia. But, you know Tanya's three back-up singers are in town from Vegas right now recording an album…maybe you could…well, you know." She thanked him.

"Are we even now?" she tossed a jest his way.

"'Till next time," he looked at her wickedly.

CHAPTER 12

"What's happening?" asked the tall muscular woman wrapped in a well-tailored dark blue wool sheath dress and spike heels. LAPD's Corporate Crime Specialist Margo Flaherty lowered herself into the chair in front of Raymond's desk, crossed her legs slowly and flipped her long tawny hair back. Raymond thought she was flirting—a behavior she'd directed at him for too many years—but instead she looked directly at him and commented, "You look good, Raymond. Your life seems to be going well for you." He nearly blushed, chastising himself for thinking about the less professional relationship they'd shared a long time ago.

"Now, what can I do for you?" she asked.

"Thanks for dealing with the Friday afternoon traffic from downtown," he said, then told her the story of the house on Elderwood Ridge. "I need your expertise to sort through the various owners of a house in the desert over about a five to ten-year period of time."

"Can't you just go to the property records in Riverside County and find that out?" He handed her the materials Ted had faxed to him with the names of three corporations listed, one selling off to the other and then to the third.

"We can't find information of any real kind on these entities. Each has been dissolved eventually and each seems to have been a front for something else. You're our corporate unravel-er. Think you can parse this one?"

"Pshaw!" she spat out. "Of course, but it'll take some time." She chewed on her lower lip and gazed at the pages intently. "I'll have to shoehorn it into the current projects, but let me take a crack at it. Pretty sure we can get somewhere—whatever that is—on it."

"Thanks," Raymond muttered. "Tough one—nothing evident anywhere—the homicide is so old."

"And that's all you need?" she asked. Then smiled mischievously. Raymond wagged a scolding finger at her and they both laughed at the old joke. She stood up, stretched languidly and left.

CHAPTER 13

"Where are we going, mama? It's Saturday."

"Yep, and we're gonna visit our old friends Alan and Potty. You remember them. They live out at the pretty farm." Meredith hadn't seen her former colleague/mentor/agent Alan and his partner Potty Parker, for several weeks.

"Aren't I going to Sally's to play today?"

"Yes, but it's not until three and we have lots of time to visit with our friends at the farm."

Riley scowled and snatched up one of the small stuffed ducks lined up on the sofa. "All you do is talk. Why do I have to go?" A storm was brewing, Meredith could tell, within the tiny girl.

"Because they like to see you—they're your honorary grandpas. They love you and I'll bet they have a surprise for you—maybe something yummy."

The small expressive face screwed itself into a wrinkled portrait. "Will they have cones again?"

"Cones?"

"You know. The little soft cookies with the tiny red dots in them."

"Ah—Scones!" The child clapped her hands and jumped up and down, her face lifting into a broad smile.

"Where? Where are the scones?" Raymond's voice broke in as he puffed into the living room, fresh off the beach from his daily run.

"You have to go with us to see Grandpa Alan if you want scones," crowed the emphatic almost-four-year-old. "And then I'm going to Sally's for a play date. There'll be cake."

"Sorry gup," he said, calling her the nickname she'd given herself—guppy—during an aquarium visit. "Dad's going to play golf with Uncle George today."

"A boy's day off," snickered Meredith.

Riley looked at Raymond, puzzled. "Trey says when you golf you just drink beer and smoke cigars." Trey was the adopted eleven-year-old son of Meredith and Raymond's long-time friends. Riley had long before bonded with the young boy as she would with a dear cousin.

"Well," stammered Raymond. "We try to golf good, too."

"Com'on," Meredith hustled the little girl into her jacket, then turned with a placating smile to Raymond. "Alan says he's going to gift Potty with a Seine River Cruise this summer. Kind of the last bucket list for Potty. Slipping fairly quickly now, and is already stressing because he can't find his passport—or his mother's wedding ring. He is afraid they were lost in the move a couple of years ago. So, we're going to have scones and calm the waters. Maybe I can help look for stuff."

Knowing how important Alan Jaymar was to Meredith— once a neighbor, a close and supportive friend through the death of her boss Bettina Grant, adviser and mentor in much of her professional career, Raymond smiled appreciatively at her. He walked over, kissed her on the lips, bent down and brush-kissed Riley's forehead. Meredith waved 'bye, Riley called it out. And they were out the door for an adventure no one anticipated.

CHAPTER 14

Spring tarted up the west San Fernando Valley with bright sun and pleasant weather. The undulating hills around the Calabasas area, resplendent this year with green hills, golden foothills and even fulsome scrub brush and trees. Meredith pulled into the ranch-style gate of the Movie-TV-Music Farm, the retirement enclave for members of the entertainment industry. She navigated her Mustang around the winding streets through the various style of residences—small cottages with bright gardens, duplex and four-plexes. In the distance, larger stucco buildings, several stories high, happily adorned with red tile roofs and shutters. Some units with gracious patios overlooking the bucolic countryside. Those larger buildings housed the more seriously infirm residents, mostly older and more in need of the health support. Alan and Potty enjoyed one unit of a fourplex tucked in the shadow of a thicket of trees.

Meredith pulled into the guest parking space as Alan opened the front door to watch her and Riley make their way up the path. Potty, Alan's long-time partner, former TV star actor, joined the group hug at the door. Once inside, Riley glanced around. "Are we having scones?" she asked. Alan and Potty looked at each other.

"How about banana bread instead?"

"Are there little red dots in it?"

"No," smiled Potty. "But we can put some strawberries over it. You can help me finish baking it. We're going to lunch first so we'll save it for dessert."

Riley thought for a minute. "Okay." She followed the slightly potato-shaped man, thinning ring of hair around his head and a small mustache, into the kitchen.

Alan took Meredith by the elbow and guided her toward the patio where a pot of coffee and two used cups sat on the table. "How's it going for him?" she asked.

Alan shook his head. "Downward spiral. But that's why I want to book this cruise soon. He's talked nonstop about it since we moved. I'd like him to experience it and remember it." Both stood silent and watched a graceful hawk meander across the horizon. In the distance three horses grazed.

"He's totally unnerved about this passport thing. Before I file a lost document claim, I need to go through this place again. A lost passport means going through the awful hassle to obtain a new one—it takes time. We have it, but it just adds more stress. Right now, we need a smooth transition. Bad thing is he also realized that his grandmother's engagement ring isn't with the belongings he packed up— specially—to move. He dithers about that constantly. Getting old isn't for sissies, Merri. Soon we'll have to move into a memory care building. I don't have the expertise to deal with the behaviors that are popping up."

"It makes me sad, Alan. Can I help?" The wise old gentleman only shook his head. The two sat there while nonstop voices and laughter came from the kitchen. The horses on the hillside glided slowly to new feeding grass. Soon chatter and clatter arrived from inside as Potty and Riley arrived.

"We're going to lunch!" announced the youngster. Meredith ushered the three into the car, squeezing Potty next to Riley's car chair in the rear seat. They found their way to a lovely outside table at the Plantation Café in the Farm community. Styled as a casual open dining area, windows and planters lightened the fact that it was an institutional venue. Idle conversation, mostly designed to address Riley and her typical childish questions and inquiries, filled most of an hour. Lunches ordered and served, the party finished their meals and Meredith ordered coffee, cocoa for Riley. Coffee for Alan and Potty as well. But soon Riley spied a nearby fountain with fish in the pool around it, squealed in delight as Potty suggested they walk over and explore.

Meredith carefully focused on the idea that Alan may have some insight into the mystery hanging between Desert Hot Springs and L.A. She turned her chair subtly and said to him. "Every hear of an agent or manager—maybe twenty-thirty years ago—named Novato or Donato or maybe even Donnelly. Supposedly well known, principal in a firm?"

Alan thought for a moment, shook his head then thought again. "There was a Max Donaldson but…well, he worked alone in his own business. And let me think…how about…Odenato? Malcolm Odenato…I think. Probably not right. He was a partner in RNS Agency. Raymond, Odenato, Schmidt. T.K.'s father's firm. But before you get too engaged in it, check it out. I could be remembering it wrong and I seriously doubt it's the same person."

Meredith felt a dark grasp on her entire body and mind. Couldn't be…not that close to home, to T.K. Too much of a coincidence. For years the agency arranged the work and careers of well-known actors and other movieland personnel and became a major influence in the entertainment industry. But could it be the connection to T.K. Raymond's name in the book? "Alan, what about the name Tad Oakley?" The old gentleman pondered with a deep frown, then shook his head.

"Describe Odenato, if you remember him," she probed.

Alan's brow knit tightly. He closed his eyes and stammered out, "I just have vague pictures of him in memory. Kind of shortish. Dark, Italian, hair curly—a little long and a little slick. Swarthy. Maybe small moustache. Recall he kind of swaggered. But he had the reputation of being a tiger of an agent. So...?"

"Any idea what happened to him?"

"Well, I remember the agency was sold soon after T.K.'s father died. Both Ken Raymond and Odenato had stepped way back, semi-retired, and the younger team pretty much ran the place. They ultimately bought it. Seems like Mal Odenato kind of disappeared. I haven't heard of him but then...well, I've been out of the fast lane for a long time."

"What about Donaldson?"

Alan stroked his chin and scowled, finally answered, "Also short. Also dark hair but as well as I remember, very natty. Very professional and buttoned-up. Still..."

"Well, he did own his own agency, you say. Name on the door..." Meredith added. Alan nodded.

As she dropped off the two old friends at their pleasant townhouse, Riley clutching a colorful banana bread-laden bag, Meredith wished them a great trip, "If I don't see you before you navigate the Seine." Potty immediately started fussing about his passport. "Potty, when was the last time you used it?" asked Meredith.

"I just don't remember. Maybe that trip to Puerto Vallarta. When was that, Alan?"

"Three years ago."

Do you remember packing or moving it?" she pressed.

"Merri, I can't hardly remember moving. It seemed so chaotic." Alan looked away and Meredith knew it was wasted conversation.

"Love you both," she called out, then focused on delivering Riley to her friend's house for the promised play date. Ninety minutes to kill, she thought with a sigh. Maybe some shopping, or even a quick workout at the fitness center while the little folks passed the time doing what little folks do. Then she thought of something more useful.

CHAPTER 15

Raymond stood off to the side of the fifteenth hole tee box, watching his friend George line up a shot, adjusting his body and swinging the golf club effortlessly. The tight white ball zinged off the ground and into the distance—straight at warp speed.

"Damn," said Raymond, kicking his foot into the grass. "My drives aren't worth all the work they require today."

"Yeah, but your short game looks great. You just need to spend more time…oops. We've got company." Both men watched a course attendant's cart rushing toward their location, the driver waving his arm.

"There's an emergency call for you, Captain Raymond. There's a phone on the 16th. I've got the number. I can give you a ride." Raymond glanced at George, wincing.

"I'm not supposed to be called out on my day off but somehow, whenever I get on a golf course, it's never to play golf!"

George waved him forward. "I'll catch up." Raymond slipped the club into his bag strapped to the rear of the cart, stepped into the attendant's vehicle and they drove off with a whoosh. By the time George had played up to the next tee, Raymond was grimacing as he spoke into the phone hanging on the wall under the small waiting area.

"It's my partner Marty," he mouthed to ward his golf partner. "Where are they and will they be there for another thirty minutes?"

"I'm heading over now, about fifteen minutes out, told everyone to stay put," Marty reported with a tone of patient assurance. Raymond hung up, ran a hand through his hair and shook his head.

"Apparently Meredith is being held by the cops for something she did at an address I think is her friend Alan's old house up in Bel Air."

"What the fu--?" snapped George. "Please tell me Gloria wasn't with her," he whimpered.

"Don't really know, but gotta go. Damn. I guess I need to take up racquet ball. The game's shorter." George urged him on, offering to pack up the clubs and paraphernalia from the aborted game. As Raymond and the attendant sped off to the clubhouse, his friend picked up the phone and called his own wife Gloria. He was relieved when she answered and reported she was working on paperwork at home. Gloria, Meredith's closest friend, was also an attorney. She didn't pack up her expertise and head to Bel Air, but she instructed George to keep her informed…just in case.

CHAPTER 16

The muted noise of a walkie talkie laced through the heated conversation of the two police officers, a wrinkled shirt and shorts-clad man, his face flushed with anger, hair uncombed and rabid, machine-gun-insinuations spewing from him at Meredith, matched almost by the spittle flying from his mouth. "…broke into my home…don't care who she says she is or her husband…no right…" and on it went. The young patrol office tried valiantly to calm the situation down, encouraging everyone to wait until reinforcements arrived to sort out the problem.

Meredith thought quickly about Riley at Sally's house about ten minutes away—the reason she had decided to make the detour. She looked at her watch furtively, worrying about the time. Controlled, logical, self-sufficient—normally—Meredith, the journalist, was ready to pounce the moment any questionable indication called for it. But, she knew, shakily inside, the spit-tossing guy had a point.

As she had left the filmland farm, she heard Potty's blatant cry about his lost passport. And his grandmother's ring. It sparked a memory for her from years before when she spent a Saturday at their house working with Alan on contract issues. Alan excused himself to prepare some tea. Potty was busily puttering around the small pool cabana. "What're you doing?" she asked. "Well," he answered, "I worry about certain valuables and so I have a secret hiding place. Never tell anyone—but if there's ever a question, you and I alone know where it is."

"And where is it?" she inquired in a whisper. He beckoned to her, and they walked to the very back unseen wall of the pool cabana. He tussled with a small brick, one of many in the surface, and wrestled it out.

"See? Perfect spot. Almost a tiny cavern." He then recited all the valuable things he could store there without anyone finding them. At the time, Meredith acknowledged the smartness of the idea and directed her attention elsewhere. She hadn't brought it to mind in years. Driving on the freeway from the west valley, she suddenly thought, why not stop by the old house? It's only a few blocks from Riley's play date, and if I can help the guys by locating Potty's possessions, everyone will be happier. She took the circuitous route over Topanga Canyon across the mountains, winding through neighborhoods into Bel Air. Riley chattered in the back seat until they pulled up in front of Sally's welcoming two-story brick house. Meredith walked Riley in and offered help but was assured the girls were great pals and Sally's mom and grandma could oversee the fun.

Pulling into the portico drive at the elegant one-time home of her friends, Meredith exited the car quietly and rang the doorbell. The familiar tones brought back years of memories from her long life working across the street in Bettina Grant's former home, visiting and relying on the two wise seers who lived where she now stood. But when no one answered the door, she knocked, then moved to a side window and knocked, calling out, "hello!" No answer. "Damn," she thought. She felt so sure she'd solve Potty's trauma easily and now.

An idea crept into her mind and she slipped around the white wood slab fence on the side of the property to a spot that only a few knew had a hidden latch. She reached to the top of a particular slat and pushed it. A slim gate opened just a crack. She leaned into it and was suddenly in the pool yard, behind the small cabana. Once more she called out, "Hello"—to no response. She quickly took a few steps forward to look for Potty's secret vault. She fingered the rough edges of the wall until she felt a brick she suspected could be the magic hatch, working it back and forth, feeling some give, then pounding on it. The block loosened and she wiggled it out, seeing an open space behind it. Reaching a hesitant hand into the dark maw and hoping no spiders, scorpions or snakes were residing here, she felt a couple of small boxes and a flat oblong object as well as several pieces of thin and deteriorating paper. Gently she extracted them, replacing the brick and turning to hurry back to the car.

Reaching for the hidden opening in the fence, her hurried focus was rudely stunted by "Hey, what are you doing on my property! I've called the police so don't try anything! Breaking and entering!" She turned to see a bulbous man, wearing flowing Bermuda shorts, a faded Hawaiian shirt stretched too tightly over a protruding belly. He spat out threats from a beefy florid face surrounded by scrambled red-grey hair. His fists were clenched at his side.

"I rang your doorbell and called out a number of times..." Meredith began.

The man spat on the ground and snarled, "So what? I was in the can and didn't hear you and you still don't get to break into my house and take things!"

"If I could explain...." Meredith tried to bluster her way but there was no interrupting as the man continued his tirade, pushed her through the gate and toward the car in the front.

As advertised, a black and white patrol car careened up the lane and stopped abruptly in front of the house, blocking the Mustang parked in the portico roundabout. Meredith took a silent deep breath. She knew how this would eventually work out, at least she hoped, as she dug into her purse for Raymond's card. "Took you long enough," blared the messy man, holding tightly to one of Meredith's arms.

A young male officer started to diffuse the situation but was close to restraining the big resident who couldn't stop shouting about "breaking and entering." Meredith explained how and why she was there and why she had entered the property through the unknown fence gate. Harold insisting that breaking and entering was still breaking and entering. Meredith slipped Raymond's card to the young officers who seemed a little taken aback. One stepped away and pulled out his radio.

Oh God, Meredith whined silently. Raymond's on his way and it won't be pretty.

And true to expectations, Raymond's car soon slammed into park behind the Mercedes and both he and his partner Marty, rumbled out. More conversation, with Harold the homeowner continuing to insist, "She broke into my property and stole something." Meredith had long before showed that the items taken from the hidden cabana vault bore the names of Porter Osborn—Potty—previous owner of the house. For Harold, it meant nothing. "Don't care if you're the mayor of California," he bellowed. "Arrest her."

Another car pulled around to the side garage, and as the door rolled up, it drove in. Everyone glanced at the sound. Harold wilted a bit. Then, stomping through the patio door came an ample-bosomed woman, hair in tight red curls, dressed in a caftan and gem-laden sandals. "What the hell?" she demanded. Raymond stepped up, offered his badge and card, and tried to explain. "She broke and entered," simpered Harold. The woman introduced herself as Madge Meecham, Harold's wife. Meredith quickly offered her hand and introduced herself, offering apologies and an explanation.

Madge looked at her squinted, and said, 'I know you. You're the woman on TV in the mornings. I see you the days you're on *Morning Coffee*. You report on Hollywood." Meredith nodded humbly. "What are you doing here?" Madge asked with a certain amount of reverence. Meredith explained about Potty—Porter—Osborn and his lost belongings. "Porter Osborn? The round guy who was on the detective show from Florida?" Meredith nodded. "Shit," said Madge.

She turned toward Harold. "What's the matter with you? You knew who used to live here. All you had to do was listen to the story. These nice people…" She gestured toward Meredith—the TV celebrity, Raymond—the police captain, and the rest of the entourage. "They're just trying to solve one poor man's memory problem and you…well, never mind. Go in the house." He did.

A few minutes of conversation ensued, and the temperature of the encounter simmered to a low bubble. Meredith signed an autograph for Madge, allowed her to take a photo with a camera she'd retrieved from the house. As the group flowed toward their cars, Raymond apologized to the two officers. Marty called his wife to say he'd be back home shortly. Raymond shook his head at Meredith with a slight grin but serious glare in his eyes. Oh God, thought Meredith, I've done it again. Another kerfuffle.

"I have to pick up Riley at Sally's house," she quickly spoke up. "I think we need to get the little one home and all of us calmed down." She knew there would be conversation later—a lot of it.

CHAPTER 17

Indeed, there were words in the Malibu house. General discussion topic wasn't new, but more adamant than usual. Raymond had always worried about Meredith's unwavering focus on complex and developing stories, and her ability to trip out of the third-party description and into the first-person involvement. Usually inadvertently.

"Remember our mutual vow not to do anything knowingly that would threaten our family safety or balance. And you just took it upon yourself to…well, overstep. Actually, commit a crime."

"Raymond, I thought it was an innocent, understandable, entry into the pool area. Literally five steps from the fence to the brick hiding Potty's passport. And it was Potty's—so it wasn't like a theft of something valuable to the people who lived there. It wasn't their property. I never thought it would be something that would involve the police, accusations…the whole clusterfuck."

Raymond just looked at her. "Breaking and entering. What it was—however it is rationalized." His stern gaze had softened to the point where there was almost a smile on his lips.

"Okay. I was stupid and I didn't think it through. I did try to get legal entry first. And the guy was pretty much of a blow hard."

"Yes, you were. And yes, he was a classic blow-hard." A grin etched into his face as he shook his head rapidly. "But it was a little embarrassing to me."

"For THAT, I'm sorry. I admit to not thinking straight. But my intention was good. And I'll try not to be that stupid again."

Later, a breeze wafted through the open windows, anointing the household with its soft fresh breath. In the glow of the lamp, Raymond mothered the files open on the teak table he used as a home desk, and breathed in the ocean's whisper. It had been a strange day fraught with anxiety, play acting and yes, concern for the two females in his life. Meredith had certainly flirted with danger and drama often but had never before put herself on the wrong side of the law—that he knew of. And it was a stupid situation that didn't really require the attention of so much law enforcement and angst. Meredith was right—Harold was an idiot. Even his wife got that.

Riley's wily recognition of family stress and obvious dissention made him smile. Just attention, apparent assessment, and patience. So much for so young. Not like the rest of the household.

At the moment, after a simple dinner of hamburgers and salad, the tot was curled in her bed snoozing softly. Her mom curled around her. And Paco the cat perched atop their blanketed mound in the bed.

And Raymond attended to the documents and ledgers from the box of files he'd retrieved from the garage storage cabinets— files from his parents' home before his mother moved into the retirement community. Very little existed now from the business. A copy of the sales agreement including lists of assets, client transfers and the rest to the new owners of Raymond, Odenato and Schmidt, the theatrical/creative management agency his father and two partners had owned. Nothing from or about the partners. No subsequent correspondence from them or reference to their follow-on plans.

Taking a large piece of drafting paper, the detective did what he often did when he needed clarity. He created a timeline to figure out where he was in the chronology of the business, surprised how little he'd ever thought about a time/life event continuum.

1960—Raymond graduated college, married Lily, worked for his father

1962—Will born, still employed at dad's, buys beach house

1964—Vietnam, drafted, deployed, Lily working as nurse

1965—Parents move to Laguna Beach from L.A., spends half-year in London, father semi-retired

1969—Home, Law School, part-time intern law office

1970—Father dies, business sold

1972—Lily dies, Raymond joins Police Academy

So, 1965-70 was the pivotal time in this investigation, especially if Malcom Odenato was connected to Lindy Fuller—the body in the desert. Finding him would be the next step. But, Raymond also needed to research Max Donaldson. Both names Alan had given to Meredith. And, Raymond reminded himself, there could be more that Alan didn't remember or know. Those names would surface. He made a note to pass on the two he did know and their backgrounds to the irreverent sheriff in Desert Hot Springs.

Stacking the paperwork neatly and turning off the lamp, he couldn't stop mentally calculating the timelines. As he brushed his teeth, he realized the one person who had definitely been there and who might have some intel—at least on Odenato. His mother.

When Raymond finally climbed into bed, Meredith had returned from Riley's room and was softly breathing. He turned off the light and she whispered, "I'm so sorry."

"It's okay," he responded. "It's over."

"Wait," she snuggled against him. "There's more…" and began to trace a light finger down his chest.

"You think this will make up for everything?" he murmured, turning toward her. "You're a vixen."

"I know."

CHAPTER 18

"What's on the agenda for next week-end?" Raymond inquired at the breakfast table the next morning. It was Sunday. The family finished up scrambled eggs, bacon, a bowl of fresh melon and a stack of toast—and had thoroughly debriefed from the tumultuous day before. Raymond's golf clubs still leaned against the wall next to the garage door.

Meredith looked at him, half smiling and half in puzzlement. "Why? You have an agenda to propose?" Riley ignored the conversation in lieu of a picture book in front of her, and a glass of orange juice.

"I'd like to ride down to Laguna to see my mother. I'll tell you more later, but I thought we could make a week-end of it. Get out of Dodge for a little break." Meredith thought about it for a moment.

"A family break might be a good thing. And I can probably make that work. Shift some of the household stuff to earlier in the week with Lola's help. Friday night there's a screening of a new movie, but we could leave early on Saturday morning. Would that work? I do have to be back Sunday night. Monday, I have an interview on the set of director Sid Belamy's film down in central Hollywood. It's the set that's the star of the show."

"Huh?" puzzled Raymond.

"I'll be interviewing set and production designers for an article on how—and why— they choose various locations and backgrounds. There's a lot of drama about movie locations. I've got some great stuff about what went on for the first Godfather movie. Sid's upcoming film is set in one of Hollywood's old, legacy apartment buildings. Apparently, some of the original rooms, built-ins, paneling, and a lot of interesting history. It's an old Hollywood-time legend. Anyhow, it'll be a good start and hook for the article. So, as long as I'm back and on deck Monday morning first thing."

"Great." Raymond agreed, silent relief in his bones. He didn't want to make a big deal of the conversation he planned to have with his mother. It would artificially alert everyone— especially his mother— to something that right now was only one small tentacle of a many-faceted mystery. And probably had nothing to do with the puzzle he was working.

A sudden urge prompted him to turn to Meredith. "Thank you," he said. She raised her eyebrows, puzzled. "For not having to attend every single network, studio, diva's party anymore, just the few you choose."

"Don't need to do it so much, myself, now, Raymond. The gossip and stories that used to come from those are now being chased by the TV shows—*Hollywood Tonight*, *Your Eye on Hollywood* and the rest of them. Thank God I moved into topical columns and major interviews before I burned out totally."

"Worse, wore me down," Raymond smiled.

"You don't look any the worse for wear. So, we're good?" she smiled. He kissed a forefinger then aimed it at her.

CHAPTER 19

Meredith planned her weeks carefully once Riley had entered their life. To the chagrin of some devout retro-femmes, her work remained of major importance to her and, with a great deal of discussion and organization, she and Raymond had established a structure and routine that gave them both time for Riley, time for work, and occasionally time for themselves. The additions to the house and that of the college student live-in helper, Lola, simplified life. Meredith's alcove now encompassed a small portion of the wide terrace, and a small but homey studio apartment beneath the stilted terrace high above the ground gave Lola a solid base. She went to classes two night a week and devoted a half day to the family five days a week, and otherwise made herself available when needed. The twenty-two-year old Guatemalan, raised mostly in America, was a graduate student in Education at nearby Pepperdine University. She felt fortunate to have landed in a situation where she had a most desirable place to live as well as a paycheck—and, a fascinating and considerate family to work for. Meredith and Raymond felt equally as fortunate to have Lola in the house. It had taken several attempts and helpers before Lola arrived in their lives.

A five-thirty a.m. alarm buzz started Meredith's day on Tuesdays and Fridays when she appeared on the *Morning Coffee* TV talk show produced by her former news colleague and friend Cassie O'Connell. Meredith's assistant Sonia continued to work in the Malibu home office two days a week. Riley's preschool drop-offs were shared between Meredith, Raymond and sometime Lola. From time to time Meredith couldn't help recalling the previous quiet, alone days at her long-time condo home before Malibu, Riley and Lola.

But on the schedule, this particular day, was an afternoon conversational

interview with the three backup singers in Las Vegas's current headlining star Tanya Meile's shows. Meredith had learned more about the murder case in Vegas through Raymond, Fred, even Sarah Freeman—the accused Sam Bethel's girlfriend. The week before, over an afternoon tequila at the Jingo's bar in Hollywood, Sarah told the journalist that Ben Salisbury had planned so many changes to his wife Tanya's Vegas show format that even the singer herself had balked. She felt uncomfortable with half-nude dancers with glitzy overt choreography, with the loss of the "harmonious" tone and style of the presentations including her side-kick crooner and three back-up singers in favor of a large Broadway-belting chorus. "It's not who I am," she had insisted.

But husband/manager Salisbury wasn't having any of her requests. He said he wanted to take her resident shows at the massive Vegas resort to a new and more contemporary level to appeal to larger audiences. The argument had spilled over in her dressing room after a late show with a handful of cast and crew just then leaving the showroom and privy to the words. Sam, Tanya's close friend and long-time loyal publicist, arrived in time to try to diffuse the explosive exchange. Sam claims the husband, flushed with fury and righteous indignation, was leaning toward Tanya with clenched fists. With a long-time association with both people, Sam tried to step in and distract what he thought was an inevitable assault. Salisbury told him to "Get the shit out and never come back." Sam stepped back and tempers eased. Tanya gestured to the publicist with her head to leave. He did, and in frustration walked around several of the neon-lit blocks of the gambling mecca, then went back to make sure Tanya was okay.

The place was locked up. He used his own key to enter and walked hesitantly around the dressing rooms. He called out, "Tanya?" All was quiet. He assumed both Tanya and Ben had gone home, so he returned to the stage door to leave. There, he ran into a security guard and his girlfriend, returning from an apparent smoke break, to the entrance where they should have been earlier. They smiled, exchanged pleasantries and Sam left for home, somewhat relieved. At six the next morning, in the dressing room, Ben's body was found badly beaten around the head and ribs, dead.

Sam was taken into custody on the word of two witnesses who remember him as the last person around the dressing room that night. Several others heard his earlier attempt to calm the tirade between husband and wife and mutter to himself as he exited the room that he'd kill Ben Salisbury if he didn't back off Tanya. Sam was out on bail in Las Vegas with life-altering investigations pending. His girlfriend Sarah was in tears by the time she finished telling the account to Meredith.

Two days later, Meredith sat in the atrium of The Gardenia, a frothy café in West Los Angeles with the "Bella Girls," Tanya Meile's back-up trio, near the recording studio where they were practicing. Meredith welcomed the threesome as they entered, all wary but curious. "I remember you from a week you spent with us a couple of years ago in Vegas—when Tanya first debuted there," commented a striking Black woman, tall and angular, her carriage causing immediate attention as she sat down at the table. "Verna," she commented offering her hand to Meredith. As the other two singers joined them, it was a notable sight—three eye-catching females all tall, wrapped in trendy fashions and well presented. Meredith smiled. It's like being the nerdy kid in high school but sitting at lunch with the prom queens. Verna, Budge and Sal. Budge more, or less, fit her name—slightly zaftig with an animated face and fashionably disheveled hair. Sal was a finely-tuned, pure as linen, beauty with fine coffee-and-cream-colored features and sleek dark hair pulled tightly into a bun at the back. Verna, her shining hair sculpted artistically in a braided art-piece atop her slender face with huge wide eyes, was definitely the Alpha Female and spokesperson. She regarded Meredith with palpable suspicion.

"What do you want with us? We can't talk about Mr. Salisbury or Sam or the case," she quickly pointed out.

"I know," said Meredith. "But you're cutting your first album. That's great news and a big breakthrough for you. Rare for a back-up group without someone breaking out as a solo act." The group talked about others who had tried, or succeeded, in such a break-out attempt, and told stories of the nuance of being the shadow of a super star. Meredith asked about how the trio met, began singing together.

"Tanya and Ben were auditioning for singers to fill out a background chorus," Verna explained. "Tanya was like a computer dating program. She heard us, auditioned each of us several times and then asked us how we'd each feel singing as a back-up group. Possibly permanently with her show." The conversation moved forward to humorous and troublesome incidents and anecdotes.

"Can you tell me a bit about the new Vegas show format," Meredith inquired without hesitation. "When Tanya's ready to return."

"If she does," sniffed Sal.

"Do you think she'll quit? Leave her career?" Meredith countered immediately.

"Doubtful, not that girl," said Verna. "She's always had total passion and love for her music. When she gets settled, I'll bet she'll weave her whole life around two things: her daughter and her work."

"Wasn't there going to be a change in the show format?" Meredith pushed onward.

"Well, not if Tanya—or any of us—or even her fans had their way," Budge piped up again. Verna speared a warning glance at her. She veered too close to the forbidden subject.

"Then tell me about this album you're recording," Meredith slid sideways. The waitress had arrived, taken drink orders, left to retrieve them. The conversation meandered around music and the song choices for the album. "When did you decide to try to go independent? You've been with Tanya for so long…?"

"Well, duh," snarked Budge. "We've heard the rumors about cutting us from the show for so long…." Once again she saw a tick in Verna's eyes and went silent with a shrug.

"It was actually the record producer Jimmy Bell's idea," said Verna. "He contacted us and then came up to Vegas to talk about it."

"That's great, Verna. Timing was perfect, too! How long have you folks been in the planning for this session?"

"Actually, us girls have been thinking about this for a while. We were gonna do it ourselves and had a whole session set almost ready to go. A couple of original songs, you know?" Meredith nodded.

"But, in fact…" Verna went on, "Jimmy was with us the night…well, that night. We had dinner with him between shows and he came to the late one. We all got together in his room for drinks after. We were ready to sign on the dotted line—did that a day later, but still...." Meredith mentally smiled. Jimmy Bell, popular rock singer, now an in-demand producer, was part of her own circle of acquaintances. He'd had a small but important role—and an impact—on the investigation of the death and drug mess four or so years before on Meredith's *Sunset West* investigation.

"Jimmy is Tanya's producer, right?"

"Yeah, but Ben wanted to set up their own recording business and produce her music, so..." Sal murmured. "So, it was nice that Jimmy, well...." She realized she was heading into forbidden conversation. Biographies of each singer were handed over to Meredith and she spent some time with each talking about backgrounds, training and future aspirations.

Budge looked at her watch and jumped up. "Holy S. I have a hair appointment. I gotta go. Anything else?" Meredith thanked her and set her free. Sal also then began to collect her belongings and stood up quietly, unobtrusively. "Me, too. Thanks for your interest, Meredith. Hope we can meet again— maybe under more pleasant circumstances." The singer's entire demeanor seemed to suddenly shrink into shyness.

Verna curled a little more comfortably into the table and looked at Meredith. "Well, it was nice of you to focus on us for a change. Odd as it seems, and as different as we are from one another, this trio gig works for us. But we have Tanya to thank for that. And as long as she'll have us, we'll be there because we get first class music, production, attention..." her voice trailed off. "And hope you understand that we're staying mum because we don't want to muddy the waters for Sam. He's been really fair to us as well. And I don't think any of us assume he was Ben's killer, but that's between you and me. Okay?"

"Absolutely," said Meredith. "But one question sits uncomfortably in my mind: Who was most pissed off at Ben? Tanya...right? What if...."

"Don't even think about it. He's done worse and she's always forgiven him. But more importantly, she was picked up by her driver while Ben was still alive. Ben always drove himself, but she had a driver—who saw Ben check to see she got into the car at the hotel and, watched her enter the house safely. The nanny confirmed her arrival time and that she was home for the rest of the night."

Meredith frowned and thought for a moment, then asked, "When are you going back to Vegas?"

"When the recording track is finished. Jimmy thinks three or four more days at the most. We all live there—easier to get to work on the shows."

"Well, Tanya's not performing right now, so it does seem a good time to branch out. Any idea when you'll all be back in the groove again at the resort?"

"None. The producer said probably six months, but well…." They stood up, shook hands.

"Good luck, Verna," the journalist offered. The stately entertainer smiled an unconvincing smile and said, "Yeah. Thanks."

Meredith knew, already, she had to talk to Jimmy Bell.

CHAPTER 20

"I'm so happy all of you came to visit," said the chipper white-haired woman, a periwinkle-colored long-sleeved pullover lighting up her cheerful face—artfully made up, heart-shaped sunglasses shading her from the sunlight on the small terrace of her retirement home apartment.

"You look like a cool teen," smiled Meredith knowing how it would please her mother-in-law, Elinor. The two women, plus Raymond, sprawled comfortably at a round glass table, sipped from tall frosty glasses of iced tea. It wasn't yet full on spring in Laguna Beach, but the day was bright and without a chill. The detective's family had arrived mid-morning at the California ocean-side area, collected Elinor then gone to lunch at a lush garden restaurant on the bluff overlooking the water. With naptime in place for Riley, the threesome finally had time to catch up.

Elinor explained her work with a local art event and that she was now in charge of the lobby flower arrangements for the complex where she lived. She commented on her own diminishing memory with a laugh. But both Meredith and Raymond had been alerted to the changing capabilities. Conversation rattled from one update to another until Raymond saw an opening which wouldn't seem obvious. 'Hey mom, you remember much about Malcom Odenato? Dad's ex-partner?" The older woman regarded him with a curious smile.

"What an odd thing to bring up. I haven't thought about those people for years. Not since the agency was sold. I remember Mal, of course, not exactly my cup of tea—a little too aggressive and obsequious toward your father as far as I was concerned. But it wasn't my business to interfere. Why do you ask?"

"His name surfaced recently in some conversation, and I couldn't put a face to him—just a bare kind of shadow in and out of the office in the early days when I was there. Any idea whatever happened to him?"

Elinor shook her head. "No. I'm not sure I ever heard. You know Ken and I moved here to Laguna a few years ago as he stepped back and before he died and the agency was sold. He only went into town about a few days a week for a couple of years—stayed at that lovely hotel up in the hills. Was home a lot of the time. I lost track of all his people when we moved. Even Ken wasn't very engaged with the group once we moved. Our life was here. He belonged to one of the yacht clubs and sailed, and we played bridge. Oh yes, and we were in London during the summer of 1966—nice consulting thing for your father. He called it his swan song. But it was wonderful—he was developing and overseeing the career of a wonderful singer establishing a European presence. She was introduced to Ken by one of his...."

"Mom...?" Raymond cut off her dialogue. "The agency people? Odenato?"

The gracious white head snapped to attention and a moment of thought followed, then, "Of course. Once the business was sold, I never encountered any of the old office again and I don't seem to think Ken did either. He seemed to retreat here, like he was glad to get away from the glitter. Such a different life from the former days in show biz. I do kind of recall Mal married some actress and they spent a lot of time in Palm Springs.

But...." She looked across the wide grounds of the complex, her eyes on some unseen picture with a mysterious unfolding story no one else could see. "Don't know."

"Who was the actress?" Meredith stepped into the conversation.

"Oh honey, you wouldn't have run across her. I certainly don't recall her name. This was so many years ago and she was some low-level extra or something. Probably married to Mal—or knowing how it works in Hollywood—someone else by now—figuring one of them would make her a star. And now is raising a houseful of kids in Van Nuys." Raymond veered the conversation in another direction and soon the tinkling voice of Riley broke in asking when they could go down to the beach. Meredith collected the beach gear and ushered the tot down to the sand.

As the door closed, leaving Elinor and Raymond by themselves, the octogenarian smiled lovingly at her son. "My how nice your life has turned out," she suggested. He nodded an affirmative. "Is Will and the family coming today?" she inquired about her grandson, Will—Raymond's only child. "How are they?"

"Not coming today, mom. And they're good, so far as we know. No explosions from the northwest and we talk ever week. They'll be down over spring break. We all know how independent Will and Sophie are, but maybe they'll come and visit. They always enjoy it and Kit loves seeing you. Hard to believe he's in school now. You should invite them."

She looked momentarily puzzled and asked, "They're on the beach aren't they?" Then shook her head as if to clarify and said, "Of course they're not." Silence ensued for a few moments. "I thought you'd be done with family life and fatherhood after the years you and Will raised each other," she quickly recovered with a chuckle. "So, I'm still so pleased and amazed how settled you—both you and Meredith—have become. I never expected it. Such cowboys and girls you were! You took the solo road after Lily died and I never expected to see that change."

"Road's a little bumpy now and then. But well, happily, Meredith is here to stay, and Riley such an interesting and good kid," he said upending his tea glass and gulping the dregs. "Life in the household can be noisy and chaotic, but once Riley's in kindergarten and then school, some of the extraneous activity and commotion can be tamped down a little bit."

Elinor laughed knowingly as a parent, and loudly. "Tucker," she admonished, using his family first name, "even you know better than that."

He half-sighed and half-laughed, then his thoughts shifted quickly. "Do you have any old picture albums from the agency days," he asked.

Regarding him curiously, Elinor answered, "I think so, but why would you want to dredge up those days? I look at them and all I do is miss Ken." The tall detective walked over to his mother, put his arms around her and hugged. "I know, mom. He was a big presence, but it's been a long time and I'm just curious." She took him by the hand and pulled him into the living room. Opening a cabinet at the bottom of a floor to ceiling bookcase, she pulled out two thick photo albums.

"Help yourself. I think I'll lay down and read for a while. Are Will and Sophie bringing Kit today?" Raymond was brought up short—again— by the out-of-context question.

"No, not today, mom...."

Elinor stopped, shook her head and waved a hand. "Of course not. How silly of me. I'm off for a nap." Raymond settled onto the couch and opened one of the albums. An hour later, Meredith came back with Riley who then quickly found a peanut butter cracker and curled up with her grandmother to watch TV in the bedroom. Meredith showered and dressed, then sat down next to Raymond, perusing the colorful pages in the thick books.

"Your dad was surely a handsome specimen, wasn't he? You take after him. Tall, that well sculpted face and deep eyes. Hair is getting amazingly similar to the gentlemanly silver in these photos." Raymond looked over at her and smirked. She ran her forefinger lightly over the contour of his cheek.

"Be careful," he smiled with a pleasant leer. "You know what that can lead to."

CHAPTER 21

"Donaldson moved to Spain," Sonia reported Monday morning. "Retired. Closed his business and left for Europe. Some very old woman in the union's library remembered him. Imagine that! And remembered when he left. Also remembered that he supposedly broke up the marriage of some young actress whose husband publicly threatened to kill him, which may be why he moved to Spain. Claimed it was a misunderstanding—he was gay. All of this mostly gossips and recollections. The librarian also dug around and found a little bit about him from an old newsletter. Moved about 1982."

"Any chance you got a copy of the newsletter?"

"She's faxing a copy of the article—didn't want to let go of the archive material. I'll follow-up. And I'll dig through the old regular newspaper archives to see if there was some press on the threat—maybe an old gossip column. We might even have something in our own files if I dig deep enough."

"Thanks, Sonia." Meredith hung up from the call, musing that her files went back in time so many years, amazed at how long she'd been in the celebrity news business.

At Raymond's office, Margot Flaherty sat on the edge of a desk in the open area and flipped through papers. "Marconi. That's the only Latin or specifically Italian-sounding name for any agent we could fine who was active in the time frame. But he was a kid—barely an intern at a couple of management or talent agencies.

Married a model. We tracked him to San Francisco where he's become a venture capitalist in high tech. Lives in Palo Alto, married with one young kid. And calculating years, would have been about 18 when Lindy Fuller's movie career was underway."

"Three possibilities so far," sighed Raymond. "Nothing very promising."

"Yeah but we're not finished yet," said Margo.

"Neither is Sonia, but I'll send off a report on what we have so far for the sheriff," said Raymond, "At least he'll have something more to work with. "All we know is the body was, in fact, that of Lindy Fuller. Belin had dental comparisons from — true story—a dentist practice in North Hollywood where Starsystem used to send its new contractees to get their teeth straightened or whatever other work needed to be done for good camera exposure. Oddly enough, they had files going way back and found x-rays of Lindy Fuller's mouth. They matched the one taken in the autopsy in the desert a few weeks ago. It's a start. Meredith's friend Fred had a contact who remembered that dental thing with the actors from his days working for the studio. Funny where these leads come from," he mused. "Belin also found a couple of off handed possibilities too. A couple of old bank accounts, long abandoned, one under the name L. Trandem but at the same address." He smirked.

He assembled his notes, wrote up a report for Belin, then added the photo of Odenato he'd slipped out, unnoticed by his mother, from one of the old agency albums. He'd already sent the faxed newsletter photo of Donaldson. At least he had bona fide images of a couple of possible links to Lindy Fuller. He faxed everything to the sheriff, mentally checked Desert Hot Springs off his list for the time being and moved on to other more pressing issues to handle. But he knew the house in the desert was still heavy in his mind.

CHAPTER 22

"This building, the Majestic, was the pinnacle of apartment living in is day. Joseph Kennedy supposedly kept one of his starlet ladies in the penthouse—at least that's the rumor. And other moguls besides Kennedy," a stocky, forty-something-year-old red-haired man explained to Meredith. They stood in front of a vintage white stucco, three-story building, uniquely charming amid the street-full of beige, mundane and faded apartment complexes seemingly built in the 1960s. "Still close enough to Paramount and some of the other studios and to downtown, Beverly Hills…the rest.

"The producer chose this building because, today, although it's pretty unique, it really represents the less expensive, lower-middle class neighborhood where it's located. And, that's the tone, the era and nature of the characters in the movie." Meredith perused a stack of materials handed to her by the movie publicity representative. She was researching her article on movie and TV locations. Interviews with production designers, some producers, property owners. Even actors who'd found some locations great to work in, others terrible. She already had material from numerous previous sets she had visited to cover more celebrity-driven stories. Most especially she had ample material from the *Sunset West* New Mexico location, the uniquely intriguing Ghost Ships from *Shadow of the Wave*, as well as New York, New Orleans and Anchorage-based TV series.

Some Mexican and European film locales as well. The Majestic was one of the filming locales chosen that was local L.A., in the midst of the greater Hollywood area. And not on the back lot of a studio, mused Meredith.

She glanced quickly at her watch and realized that very soon she had to leave to pick up Riley at preschool. On-set interviews had already taken place with the movie's main star, producer, production manager and set designer. "But you can't leave until you see the penthouse," implored her publicity host.

"Make it quick," she admonished. "I'm due elsewhere soon." She thought anxiously about the call she wanted to make to Las Vegas to find Jimmy Bell and set up some appointments with him and a couple of other back-up singing groups for her coming article about them. About Jimmy's take on the Ben Salisbury death—and the fate of her friend Sam, accused of the crime. She plodded up three flights of stairs alongside the studio rep to a dark, ornate wooden door, knocked and were greeted by a jeans-clad middle-aged woman, long well-tended greying hair and a wide smile on her face. She welcomed them heartily into the amply-windowed penthouse apartment. "They've made a few upgrades, of course—appliances and stuff in the kitchen, bathrooms and so on. But left the mahogany paneling, the vintage tiles like the tiny black and whites in the bathrooms...." As she showed them through the spacious rooms, Meredith's imagination slipped into retro and she could see the glamorous screen people of the 1940s and 50s lounging in their stylish casual clothes, or entertaining other glitterati in the then-opulent surroundings. They talked of the Kennedys, of a few other star names the manager had heard bantered about since she'd taken over her post four years before. Meredith made a few notes.

"Sorry to break off such a fascinating conversation," she apologized, "but I do have to run. Are there any clippings or documents that kind of tell the story of this place?" she inquired as they were leaving.

"Wait," the manager interrupted, went to a built-in cabinet on the side of the living area and rummaged around for a moment, assembled a few wrinkled, yellowed pages and handed them to Meredith. "These aren't much of anything, couple of rental come-ons, but they've been found over the years, fallen between cracks and vents and found only when they've been working on the place. There might be something in there. I didn't see anything much but you might." The threesome bid one another farewell, Meredith shook the hand of the studio publicist and walked rapidly to where she'd parked her car on the street. Her thoughts were already focused on Jimmy Bell and what he could tell her.

CHAPTER 23

"Oh no! The white board is up. Let me put on my glasses," snickered Raymond's partner, now chief detective for show biz crimes. Marty Escobar had ridden shotgun with his boss on celebrity and entertainment-focused VIP cases for more than a decade. He now ran that division. He also knew Raymond's reliance on well organized crime patterns and events and capturing them on a large white board in his office. The affable, athletic, squarely built Marty looked over at his corporate crimes colleague, Margo, and winced.

"At least we're making some kind of progress," she shrugged. Raymond glared at them both then grinned as he picked up the marking pen to outline their report.

"Tell us, Margo," he instructed. The blond glanced through her notebook. Then began to outline what they knew about ownership of the home so far.

"The small development was started about 1962, a few houses built but the whole development was never totally finished. When we get to about late 1964, the Elderwood house was bought by Canyonlight Partners but the documents we could find only showed one name as representative—apparently an attorney—from Riverside County. The law office only existed about six months, was closed with no further chain. The attorney resigned from the bar association that same year. Canyonlight apparently dissolved, belly up, and assets were purchased by Finance Incorporated, a Palm Springs based company who held the property for about five years and rented it out. We tracked down one of the former principals from Finance—now long retired and almost senile—who had no recollection of principals of Canyonlight. He seemed to remember they bought the house from the county in auction, in default. In 1975 it was sold to an L.A. real estate investment group and rented for years. The two principals left from that group say it mostly stood dormant, but the company felt Desert Hot Springs had promise and the land would appreciate. It kind of didn't and it was sold to an individual guy who owned it for about four years—also an investment and tax write-off—until he sold it to the current owner. A troubled history for the old place to say the least."

"Renovations or rebuilds, I wonder?" posed Raymond.

Margo shook her head. "Only thing that showed up in documents were a new roof about ten years ago and, of course, some appliance and plumbing pipes replaced or upgraded. Nothing structurally."

Raymond had stopped writing on the white board and the threesome in the room seemed mired in contemplation.

"My wife has a theory about houses," Marty spoke up in aside. "She says you have to treat them well for them to treat you well."

"Well, this poor place up on Elderwood is due some TLC. Hope the new owners do a decent job and respect it," Raymond murmured. Shortly afterward the group disbursed, and the detective stared at the notes on the board.

A few minutes later he was on the phone with the desert sheriff. "Sorry Ted," he said, taking a sip of coffee. "Not much from here. Margo asked about the names Oakley and also Trandem but no one recognized them and they showed up nowhere in her research."

The gravelly voice of the sheriff acknowledged the information at the other end of the phone. "Someone seems to recall a golf pro named Trandem at one of the courses but only fairly recently. We know now the actress died a ways back—probably long before Trandem was even around—maybe even born."

"If the driver's license is even remotely close to her age when she died, she would have been about 26 or 27, about 30 years ago," Raymond reminded.

"And don't forget, she had a kid. Autopsy confirmed that and so did Victoria, her former neighbor. Kid'd be about 28 or 29 now. But what happened to him or her and where are they now?"

CHAPTER 24

Dishes clattered as Raymond scooped them from the table, transporting them to the sink and dishwasher. His job tonight. He was anxious to give the kitchen counters the final wipe off and sit down with Meredith. He had news he wanted to discuss, and she was his most comfortable and trusted sounding board. She came down the stairs from the bedrooms, especially the lavender one with the animal mobile under which they both hoped Riley was now quietly slumbering. The vociferous youngster was an active, interested and seemingly tireless participant in the household. And never happy to call it a day at bedtime.

Meredith sunk into one of the loungers in the family area and let out a "Whew! I don't remember ever being this tired after a normal workday."

Raymond snickered. "Weren't we the ones who vowed to fully incorporate the kid into our everyday lives and not let it throw us off kilter?" Meredith waved a middle finger at him. She had to admit that as an "older" dad, Raymond was a good partner in the adventure—household, child management, schedule forecaster…and…and…. The detective lowered himself into the other leather lounger and cleared his throat, a dramatic call for attention. "We came across another possible name for the desert case…."

"And?" murmured Meredith.

"Interesting but of course, may have nothing to do with the situation at all, but at least...." He assembled his thoughts. "Margo has been chasing down the ghost companies and shell corporations that have held ownership of the desert house—all literally disintegrating into dust. But, this afternoon one of a couple of people she did manage to find called remembering the name of someone—he's not even sure which of the earlier owners—someone remembered he was a TV or movie producer. Not an agent at all. Margo linked it to an L.A. driver's license from more than a decade back. Name was Marcus Ladonna. Chasing him down, we're not sure who he married or when—but they moved to Miami. A contact in the Miami PD is digging there. The name ring a bell?"

Meredith shook her head. "There's a half dozen possibilities, yet nothing's landed on firm ground yet. Any connection with this guy to the desert except some long-time desert rat remembered his name on the corporation papers?"

"N-ope," sighed Raymond.

"Something will open up," she said confidently. "Or you'll suddenly see a connection somehow. If I can help, let me know." She settled back into the recliner then quietly added, "By the way, I'm planning to go to Vegas in the next couple of days."

Raymond turned abruptly and looked intently at her. "Why? For how long?"

She shrugged. "I'm thinking a day and night. I want to interview a couple of long-time back-up singing groups for the feature I'm researching on those kinds of musicians. Vegas has a lot of them around the big stars and even the lounge acts. And Jimmy Bell is working there for the next three weeks. I'd like to include him in the article since he's produced so many of the shows and music with the lead performers that the back-ups have followed. He's setting me up with three different groups and two of their star people."

Scowling at her, Raymond shook his head. "Please, don't tell me you're looking into Ben Salisbury's death and what's happening with your publicist-friend Sam. I don't even want to think about the dramatic consequences that could have."

"No, no," said Meredith. "I'll have to ask Jimmy what he's heard, but I promise not to put myself in harm's way. We both agreed on that when Riley was born. But I am a journalist and I'm at the tip of the discovery iceberg for a heavy current story." She looked at Raymond with open eyes and furled brow.

"I know you'll be as super cautious as you can," he conceded. "But…things just seem to happen when you pry open one or another Pandora's box when you're sniffing out a story…."

"I won't take any chances, put myself in danger. Honest."

Raymond gazed at her darkly, glanced away, then added, "You're not going to break and enter again? Get arrested?" A grin etched its way onto his face.

"Of course not," she murmured, barely audibly but stifling a chuckle. "But then, if it's necessary to the story…."

CHAPTER 25

The clatter of the Vegas airport terminal assaulted Meredith's senses as she deplaned mid-day on Tuesday, greeted by the cacophony of gaming tech, tourist trivia and general travel trauma. After decades of coming to the desertous gambling mecca, covering showroom specialty shows, celebrity gigs, other Vegas-centric stories, Meredith hadn't visited in a long while. She'd finished her Tuesday morning shot on the *Morning Coffee* show in L.A., wiped off her camera make-up, picked up her overnight bag, and headed to LAX. She'd be home tomorrow night in time for dinner as usual.

Off the plane, she hastened through the crowded, noisy terminal to the cab stand and hailed the first car in line. At the Silver Bullet Resort, she moved quickly to the front desk to check in. The perky young blonde behind the counter handed her a plastic keycard, a VIP welcome packet, and a note. Jimmy Bell had passed along his own schedule and how she could catch up with him. Her time here was limited so she knew she had to use it well. Vegas hotel management had a long memory and she was directed to an executive suite. She quickly assembled her belongings in the room, rinsed her face and sat down to plot out the short visit. Jimmy Bell in the lounge at four and a conversation with the first group of singers at four thirty, their performances on stage at six, sit down with the next group and then their nine o'clock dinner show. Sleep, a visit and quick conversation with another group at eleven o'clock morning rehearsals, flight home at two.

She had just enough time to call Sarah Freeman, girlfriend of Sam Bethel, currently under arrest for the murder of Ben Salisbury, now free on bail. Sarah answered the phone hesitantly. No doubt reacting to more than her share of difficult calls and phone demands. She sounded relieved when she heard Meredith's voice.

"I have about an hour. Can you two meet me here, in my room?" Meredith suggested, thinking about privacy and security for all. Her friend Sam came on the line. "Meredith, honey," his gentle southern voice sounded hard and unusually tense. "What I'd give to sit down and have a drink with you and just well…but I can't let you get involved in this. For your sake. And mine. It's the worst crappy script you ever read and I didn't ask to be, nor ever was involved, in the cast. Now I'm a key player. Listen carefully and you'll probably hear the Greek chorus in the background narrating the worst of things."

Meredith puzzled over it and then said, "Sam, will you come through this okay?"

"Don't know. Don't ask—It's fucked. But Sarah says she'll meet you in the coffee shop in ten. Please don't ask her to answer tough questions! And please don't print the answers to whatever you do ask! My attorney will be the first to condemn me! Love you." And Sarah was back on the phone.

"Ten minutes," said Meredith, picking up her bag, heading out, locking the door. Sarah grunted her agreement. Meredith settled into a table in an out-of-the main-stream coffee atrium. Silently, almost ghost-like, Sarah Freeman slipped into the seat across from her. "You look tired," Meredith said quietly.

The slender, tousled red-head smiled wanly. "Yeah. Well, I've been kind of locked away with Sam here and really don't get out much." She looked around furtively. "We've been kind of stalked by the media. I turned down a great movie project but feel like I'm needed here more."

"What can I do?" asked the journalist in a near-whisper. A crisply-uniformed, heavily-made-up waitress, brought two coffees.

The publicist waved a discreet finger near the tabletop. "Don't ask. Best way to help. Let the attorneys bicker it out." She gazed into a mug of coffee the server had placed in front of her. So, Meredith directed the discussion around general topics concerning movies and activities in L.A. For a half hour the two bantered gossip and news. Sarah's color brightened, her eyes came back to life.

"Meredith?" called a husky female voice, breaking into the hushed conversation. The regal imposing figure of Verna, Tanya Meile's alpha back-up singer. The tall performer plopped down in the extra chair at the table. "Oh hi, Sarah," she nodded dismissively at the other guest, then refocused on Meredith. "What bring you here? You should have mentioned you were coming when we saw you in L.A. a couple of weeks ago. We'd have rolled out the red carpet."

"I didn't know," explained Meredith. "And no need for the carpet. I'm just really digging into the story about back-up groups and other accompanying performers around the big stars and you all got me really interested. So, I'm here to follow up on the story. Jimmy Bell is helping me out."

The statuesque singer tilted her head, furled her sculpted eyebrows and looked intensively at Meredith. It made the journalist uncomfortable, like being accused of something. "Just filling in the blanks—adding more color and depth," she quickly added as a well built, darkly handsome man joined Verna.

"Oh," said Verna, a little surprised and apparently perturbed at the arrival of the guest. "Joe. I thought we were meeting in the lobby. Um…Meredith, this is Joe Domo, he's Tanya's duet partner."

Meredith, surprised by yet another member of Tanya's Meile's ensemble of whom she wasn't aware, stammered a "hello." Then added, "I'm sorry, duet partner?"

"Tanya and I sing a couple of duets, and I give her a short break mid-show by doing a set with Verna and girls," spoke up the arresting figure. Meredith felt a little spine-chill from his deep, dark eyes set under thick sculpted brows— seductive but dangerous—almost evil. "Sorry to surprise you, Verna. I noticed you over here as I was on my way to meet you," he said.

"'Kay. Well, have a good stay, Meredith," the singer tossed out as she rose, waved with a pinkie finger and swooshed away.

"What's that about?" asked Sarah.

"No idea," Meredith answered. Soon she hugged Sarah in farewell, murmured words of encouragement and then moved on to one of the lounges to begin the visit's work by meeting singer/music producer Jimmy Bell for a drink before interviews and show attendance. He arrived, slight but trimly built, and energetically businesslike. She thanked him—again—more than four years later for his help in the complex and troublesome case that started in a New Mexico movie set. He waved it off.

"What about Ben Salisbury's death?" she cautiously posed.

Again, Bell waved his hand but said, "Any one of a double-handful of people could have offed him. He wasn't a favorite around here and my opinion only—Sam got the short end of the stick."

"How so?"

"Ask anyone—just don't quote me. Ben was a bully to everyone. Most particularly to Tanya. And Sam."

"What are people saying around here in Vegas?"

"Oh, they're saying everything…Ben was linked to organized crime…he wanted to produce Tanya's show…Sam was having an affair with Tanya…the music director was having an affair with Tanya…the little girl wasn't his…Ben was hustling the wrong goof ball…Ben was hitting on the wrong guy's wife…Tanya did it…. The stories never end."

"How did Ben treat you, Jimmy—as Tanya's music producer?"

"I ignored him. Tanya and I go a long way back and she's one of the most compliant people I know. But she also had a very true sense of her own musicality and what, at this time in her life, she wanted to do with it." He took a drink of his beer and then changed the subject. "We'd better get going if we're going to have some time to spend with the Tone Poets, the backups for the early show. The group is really good, and approachable. You'll like them," he said, standing up and waving down the server for the check. "Between Tanya's group and the Tone Poets, you'll have some of the more permanent and stable groups. Later tonight and tomorrow, most members of the ensembles you'll meet make a living going from one show to another—always as chorus or back-ups. It's a category of its own and why many of these folks stay in Vegas. More jobs here."

"Didn't Whitney Houston sing back-up for several major stars?" asked Meredith, putting her pen and notebook in her bag, standing up.

"Yep. For Lou Rawls and Chaka Khan. So did Gwen Stefani."

And so, the work began as they made their way through the throngs of visitors, gamblers, hotel servers and employees, wide-eyed tourists, even a few pets on leashes. Meredith flinched at the twang of the lounge music, the gaming machines and slots grinding away, the subtle clink of cocktails and beverages on trays carried through the large room, and the human vocal excesses wafting about.

Twice that night she entered one of the town's massive showrooms, darkened for effect, the artificial A/C chill blasting her senses as she was directed to a front and center table. She reflected, appreciatively, that until the mid-1970s, smoking was allowed in the glitter-caverns, as entertainers sprayed their throats off-stage with hydrating solutions, and after shows, retreated to their hotel rooms where humidifiers pumped moisture throughout the night. Eventually, with pressure from the performers, musicians and others, hotels finally outlawed smoking in the showrooms. Still, the dryness of the desert air, the air conditioning in the massive rooms, and their largeness had a sensory personality all their own. And never seemed to change.

Looking forward to shaking off the din of the town, the next day, Meredith checked in at the airline ticket counter heading home. "So, what's the big story here in Vegas?" someone asked her. She looked up to see the familiar face of NBS TV's International News Correspondent Rick Santora. They'd shared an assignment and she'd come to know him well when she subbed for the cohost of the national NBS morning show from New York three years before. Although exchanging phone calls from time to time, she hadn't seen him since. The trimly built Santora, dark hair surgically and stylishly cut, was dressed in a polo shirt, blue blazer and grey slacks. His dark, penetrating eyes twinkled as he smiled at Meredith, reaching out to hug her, then stepped back to scan the view. "Looking great! I guess motherhood fits you pretty well!"

She laughed and asked, "What are you doing this far west?"

"Annual newsmakers conference," Rick answered, turned to introduce a tall, balding man dressed in an impeccable blue suit, a club tie and highly starched white shirt. "Meredith. Meet Woody Buchanan—the associate editor of the *News—New York*. Someone you need to know. Woody, Meredith Ogden is UAM's biggest syndicate star!" Meredith smiled and shook the man's hand, realizing the *News* as perhaps the most respected national newspaper in the country—possibly the world.

"Yes, I know about you, Ms. Ogden," Buchanan countered. "How about joining us for a drink and let's talk about the changing situation in the print syndication market. I think there's something good to be discussed."

Meredith was both surprised at his quick retort yet puzzled at his words. What changing situation? She wondered. Glancing at Rick, she saw no acknowledgment of confusion or question. "Good idea," he piped up. "Let's grab a table in the lounge...."

"Sorry guys, cannot," she simpered. "Got a plane to catch—heading home tonight. But I'd like to talk more. Can someone call me and let's talk. Or, let me know when you'll be in the L.A. area," she invited, handing a business card to both men before she trotted off to her gate, satisfied she'd acknowledged the weight of the interaction, but maintaining her independence. Rick pantomimed a phone call and winked. Curled into the seat of the small regional aircraft, Meredith worried the statement all the way to Los Angeles. As the flight bounced and jiggled into LAX she realized she had some homework to do.

Have I missed a step? I'm usually better focused, she pondered. And, did it matter? She collected her belongings from the overhead compartment and hurried from the plane out to the parking lot and found her Mustang. On the car phone, just before leaving the lot, she called home.

"Should I pick up something for dinner?" she asked Raymond.

"No need. I was planning to cook but well…Ito's here and he's taking care of it."

"Ito?" Meredith blurted. "What's he doing in L.A.?" They referred to the intrepid, buoyant, Japanese man, friend, accountant, MBA graduate, now financial specialist at her media syndicate, UAM, in New York. But she first met him as the "houseman" for her former boss gossip columnist Bettina Grant more than ten years before, cleaning, cooking, tending to bookkeeping needs. Ito had scaled the American career mountain from his early beginnings.

"I'm not sure," Raymond said in a hushed voice. "It's like he's on a mission—but don't know what it is, waiting for you—and you know how he is about cooking!"

"Where's he staying?" Meredith pushed forward.

"Here. Of course."

CHAPTER 26

"Where is he?" Meredith asked eagerly as she came into the house through the garage. She hadn't seen Ito in nearly three years. She tossed her lightweight overnight bag in the corner of the kitchen, dropped her purse on the table. Walked over to Raymond and kissed him quickly on the lips. Although also a friend and one-time accomplice of Raymond's, Ito had never met Riley. Their jubilant acquaintance was evident in the spirited voices emanating from the living room.

"Talk about instant attachment," chortled Raymond looking toward the sounds. Meredith hastened through the kitchen into the living room where their visitor knelt on the carpet, helping the exuberant Riley arrange small metal cars in neat rows. He looked up to see Meredith, rose from his crouch and walked over with a smile that seemed to say, "Whew. I'm okay now." They briefly hugged. Ito had never been one for much personal touching but had adapted to the whims of his close female friends.

"What's up math boy?" asked the journalist, using the name a detective had given Ito during the Bettina Grant murder investigation.

"Needed a strong dose of Southern California," he sighed. "New York is…well, New York. Exhilarating. High trend. High expectation. High energy. High pressure. I just needed to lay back, hear the ocean and absorb the sound of palm trees blowing. Ya know?"

"Um-hum," Meredith murmured, folding her arms in front of herself. "And what else?"

"I needed to cook a creative meal in a wonderful kitchen…and speaking of that I must look into the food." He turned, hustled into the kitchen and began busying himself with pans on the stove, in the oven.

"You didn't need to do this," said Meredith. "You're always welcome here, and you don't need to cook for your room and board. But I still suspect there's more than a culinary session, but…." Ito, his head stuck in the refrigerator, didn't respond. Raymond moved into the sideboard to mix drinks. Riley was busily picking up metal vehicles and putting them neatly away in their boxes. Meredith ran a weary hand through her hair, moved in to greet her daughter with hugs and a kiss, then quickly grabbed her travel bag and headed up the steps toward the bedroom. A quick face wash in the bathroom, glass of wine and dinner and conversation would be a heady tonic after the peripatetic day.

Later, dishes stacked in the dishwasher, Riley off to slumberland (Ito read her the nightly story before sleep), Paco the cat stretched languidly atop the refrigerator, the three adults settled on the patio with snifters of brandy—a special treat for Ito. He sipped at the liquor, took a deep inhale of the brisk breezy night ocean air, and sighed. Then, slumped back into his chair.

Following Ito's example, Raymond relaxed as well, savoring the quiet. "So how did your Vegas visit go?" he preemptively asked Meredith, obviously anxious to hear how her interviews and meetings had gone. "I'm glad you broke the mold and actually got home after only one day—distractions, detours—

and getting arrested," he chuckled. Besides her rumble with the Bel Air cops over Potty's passport, Meredith's work trips often extended or stumbled into trouble mid-way through.

"Who'd you interview?" probed Ito, his fascination with all things show business seeping out. Meredith spread both hands in front of herself and patted the air.

"Let's take a breath. Vegas was pretty mundane—everything went according to schedule. No super stars, just performing folks. I'll tell you more detail later but first, math boy, I know that something's on your mind. What?"

Clearing his throat dramatically, Ito sat tall and spoke in measured sentences. "As you know, I'm privy to a great many quite private goings on at the syndicate." Meredith nodded. "And we've been doing a great deal of audience and economic research on our various media offerings—the TV shows, the print columnists and packages, and so on." He looked at his companions to see they were listening and/or comprehending. "And, you know that some new very high up execs that came into the syndicate, Russ's bosses, a couple of years ago have been making subtle changes all along." He referred to UAM's managing director Russ Talbot, Meredith's long-time mentor and supervisor. "I have word that some dramatic changes are about to happen and you—probably even Cassie—lots of people—may be affected by them. I don't know the specifics or when or how they are looking at it. Has Russ said anything to you?" She shook her head but was reminded of the comments made in Las Vegas earlier in the day. "The changing situation in the print syndication market...."

"No, he hasn't. Do I need to go to New York and wrestle the problem?" she asked.

"No. don't. I think Russ will be on his way here before we all know it. Probably on his way now, which is why I leave on

Saturday morning. No one knows I'm here—but you of course."

Raymond looked carefully at Meredith. The inherent economic and political rollercoaster of big media organizations had been part of her life from the day she joined Bettina Grant's team so many years back. The business and political ride was never predictable, seldom thrilling or fun. And there was always a new downslope somewhere in the near future.

"I ran into Woody Buchanan from *News—New York* in Vegas," Meredith said, moving her patio chair around to face the other two. "He said something about the 'changing scene in in the print syndication market,'" she scowled, leaning into the conversation, elbows on her knees.

"Sounds like he knows something," Raymond replied. "I'm surprised you didn't nail him to the wall to get the story."

She sighed, sipped her brandy, then looked up at him. "I wanted to get home in time for dinner, like I promised." All three laughed. It was a new line. "Well, we left it open. I can always call him— or go and see him. He's still in Vegas, I imagine...."

"No," barked both Ito and Raymond. Ito spoke up, "Wait until you see Russ. I don't honestly know any of it except that things are very fluid and shaky around the offices. I can read the attitude, the environment, but not the reasons."

"Ito's right, Merri," added Raymond using her long-ago nick name. "If Russ is this close to a discussion, let him have it."

Later, after lights were turned off and everyone was diverted to their places of sleep, after Raymond made sure Meredith felt welcomed home and assured of his undivided attention, she laid awake, a smile on her face but turmoil in her mind as he slept. She had missed the indications of turbulence and rumblings in the central heart of her work—the media syndicate. That awareness was a skill she had learned two decades before from her former boss. And it was essential in the erratic world of the syndicated journalist. And now she had to catch up with the momentum, establish the source of the disturbance and try to move in front of it to secure her own footing.

It was almost always black ice—unforeseen slips, slides and dangers, requisite remedial choreography. Good shoes.

CHAPTER 27

As surely as the sun rose over the Pacific, the fax machine clattered in Meredith's office, adding to the scramble of life in the Malibu kitchen as she grappled with Riley for not finishing her orange juice, as Raymond pulled together his brief case and tapped his pockets for ID, glasses, wallet and side arm, and Ito drank his coffee, flipping energetically through the morning paper. Like an unwelcome visit from the local minister, the clack of the machine ignited overall anxiety prompted by the discussion the night before.

Raymond looked at Meredith. "Go," she instructed. It was his morning to drop Riley off at preschool. He narrowed his eyes at her. "Seriously." She reiterated, "It's probably just a news release about someone appearing in a TV show. Let's not make this media drama the center of our universe." Raymond nodded and soon was out the door with Riley in tow. It was Lola's day off. She was at the university. Meredith would be around all day long, writing mostly, and Sonia would be in for her twice weekly office work-day. Meredith poured a cup of coffee for herself and took a bite of an English muffin slathered with peanut butter. Not her usual healthy breakfast, but some mornings were more hectic than others. She sauntered into her office as Ito called out, "Let me know."

And, indeed, the fax was a press release. They both chortled with relief and she sat down at her desk. Ito quickly moved into the kitchen to make good on his offer to clean up. Fifteen minutes later, Sonia entered the house and shrieked in surprise as she saw Ito. Both were also veterans of the earlier Bettina Grant wars. As the conversation rang through the house on the seaside cliff, the phone rang and Meredith picked it up mid-laugh. Russ Talbot.

"Shit," she thought. The conversation opened affable and newsy. Quick updates on everyone's well-being then Russ casually mentioned he would be flying into L.A. on Sunday. He'd like to meet with her Monday morning. "Of course," she said. "What's going on Russ? You coming west is big news. Anything I should know about?"

"It's just that time in the workflow when we should update. I hate to ask you to come to New York with your household as busy at it is now," he explained.

Uh huh, she thought cynically. "I was in Las Vegas yesterday researching a piece about session singers—backup singers. Ran into Woody Buchanan—know him? He wanted to have a drink and said to get to know me. He was with Rick Santora."

Russ's usual deep near-bravado voice dimmed. "Sure, we've met. Did you do it?"

"No—I was on my way home. Should I have?"

"Well, he's a good guy to know. Pretty well seated there at the paper. But look, I won't keep you. How about lunch on Monday—maybe about one at Currents in Santa Monica?"

"Russ, you dog. Somehow you always know the hot dining places!"

"I have my ways," he laughed. "See you then." Meredith squirmed.

"Ito," she called out. Sonia came along too, sensing the gravity in the air. "And that's the plan," Meredith concluded the discussion a few minutes later, as though nothing was amiss.

Because she wasn't sure anything was—reminding herself not to allow conjecture to dampen the day. Her two colleagues had pulled up chairs close to the desk and listened with dogged focus. "I guess we'll see what he has to say on Monday." Sonia, wide-eyed and subtly suspicious, shrugged. Ito nodded his head silently and everyone retreated to separate quarters to individual speculation. Ito quietly finished his kitchen chores, put on sunglasses and slipped out the door to walk the beach.

CHAPTER 28

"Out 'a here," Raymond barked, resigned and impatient, to his colleague, Marty Escobar. He pulled on his jacket and grabbed the file containing details of the urgent case facing them. A rare one that demanded VIP police intervention—his own, the High Profile Division Captain. Domestic abuse ending in a homicide, and it was ugly. The live-in couple, caretakers for the large home of Larry Pinot, a popular producer. It wasn't the first time law enforcement had been called to the sprawling home because of the couple's fights. Pinot had been "spoken to" several times before. Raymond himself had previously tried to intervene, convince the producer to get help for the couple or get them out of his house before something tragic happened. He didn't. It did. This time, the wife got tired of being smacked around, took a kitchen knife and stabbed her husband in the heart.

Marty slid behind the wheel of the departmental car and headed to Pinot's mansion. As they sped down Olympic Boulevard and through side streets leading to Pinot's elegant neighborhood, Raymond multi-tasked and reviewed the telephone conversation he'd only just concluded with the Desert Hot Springs sheriff Ted Belin over the ancient death of actress Lindy Fuller. "We've got a longer list of potential residents or principals for the Elderwood house to look at," growled Belin over the phone to Raymond.

"Nice, Ted. Glad the info started to roll in. Tell me the names you have. Maybe one or another will ring a bell."

"The Trandem kid—Ray, the golf pro—didn't ever live there himself but his grandfather rented the place when Ray was just a small boy and visited a couple of times. Grandfather was with some agency like the Department of Ag and worked with the Valley farmers, and growers. Moved away after a couple of years. That was the name on that bank account we found. But it was about twenty-five years ago. Ray's thirty-two now. Granddad rented from one of the corporate owners. I'll send it to you. Lives in The Villages in Florida now and is pretty old but the kid says really spry. But had no information that was helpful." Raymond grunted his understanding.

"Then there was someone named O'Connor—Mat O'Connor—who we found through the construction guys working on the place now. O'Connor apparently did the first renovations and his kid, Billy, did a couple of remodels or probably more like upgrades—kitchen, baths, so on—much later. Original stuff about thirty years ago and then off and on with the younger guy over the last ten years until the new owners hired the group that's working there now. Mat O'Connor lives in Indio, down the road, now, and talked to him this morning. He did a few jobs on the upstairs plumbing—for one of the corporations about ten years ago. But had no knowledge of the actress or her husband. A dead end.

"By the way, the starlet had a kid. But no one knows what happened to him or her—just an infant the last time anyone saw them but the ME confirms she'd given birth. One more ghost to locate." The old man sighed.

Raymond cringed at the news. "Who else is on your list?" he pushed. He wanted to extract himself from the desert investigation. But sensed it wouldn't happen. Especially since his name "was all over it" from the start.

"Well, there's O'Donnell connection. You found out the guy moved to Spain. And Ladonna who your people say disappeared to Miami a few years ago."

"We're still following up on Ladonna," Raymond interjected. "And we're close on Odenato. He apparently lives in Mexico. That's another one we're chasing." He cringed again, knowing that Odenato was so close to home for him.

"Can you guys help us with the Miami guy. We don't have the resources to reach very far out from here? Seems like a lot of these guys were more linked to Hollywood than Palm Springs. Except for the two here. And we're on their trail."

"We're on it," Raymond said, trying not to sigh. "Fax me the information you have. Only a couple of these folks had any actual connection to the house, though. So, we're trying to find a connection to the actress."

The two chatted briefly, then promised to keep in touch as their various investigations proceeded. Raymond hung up and redirected his attention to the case outlined in the report before him. The ugly one.

Marty and Raymond pulled up to the electronic gate to the Pinot home, a uniformed officer waved them through. On the tree-lined street with the beautifully restored retro streetlight, media vans with transmission equipment and paraphernalia were crammed along the curbs, with several dozen photographers and reporters clogging the sidewalks. Raymond shut his eyes before stepping out of the car in the privacy of the driveway and hoped Pinot's PR person or manager was close by to handle the media. Some had to and it surely wasn't Raymond's job. He quickly reminded himself of the contact number for the Police Department's Public Information Specialist. She would be needed.

CHAPTER 29

A quiet Friday afternoon greeted Raymond when he returned to the office from the nearly day-long encounter with "high profile" law enforcement with a top Hollywood producer. The crime was in the employee cottage, the victim and culprit being tended to by various police, CSI and other specialists. But the drama was bounding through the overdressed main house as Raymond, Marty, younger and shrill Mrs. Pinot, and finally the public relations counselor and the manager of Larry Pinot grappled with the situation. Pinot, himself, was becalmed by a dose of white tablets his wife and manager seemed to have on hand, and a plan was carved out to meet the frenzied demands of the press, the mandates of the police, professional concerns, domestic eruptions and inconveniences…and the shrill Mrs. Pinot.

Raymond welcomed the still and emptiness of his office. He realized the quiet was because it was after hours and everyone had gone home. He had a call from Meredith telling him to meet her, Ito and "others" at the Sea Shack, their nearby go-to seaside restaurant. He rubbed his eyes, reached for his Rolodex and placed a call to an old military friend now working for the Fort Lauderdale PD. The hour was even later in Florida, but the dispatcher gave him a fax number and he sent off a quick note asking his contact to check out Darren Donahue and anything the local files and data records said about him.

Organizing his desk before leaving, Raymond noticed a long note in his in box from Margo. "Found Donaldson information—thank God for friends in the international network—went to Spain early 1970s, moved there permanently in 73, with his partner, James Ocre. Died of AIDS in about 76. Was a Hollywood agent, fairly well-known before his move. And known mostly then as a kind of lothario for his assumed conquests of beautiful actresses. Obviously, all fictional affairs. His actual partner was well fixed—family money—and apparently they decided to let go of the Hollywood masquerade and leave.

"Tracked down Malcom Odenato to about 1967. Was a partner in Raymond, Odenato, Schultz (!?) until he sold his partnership, left the company. Some really old legal docs show his address, a condo in Acapulco, but no record of him there now. Former neighbor remembered him and said he moved to Ensenada long time ago, kind of remembered he married, bought a fishing boat. Found Ensenada listing from a few years ago. Have address and other info if you want it."

Chewing his lower lip, Raymond left the note in the in box, turned off the light and went to his car.

A small trio twanged out country/blue grass music at one end of the Sea Shack patio. Friday night on the shore. At the other end, Raymond joined his friends' impromptu gathering, hosted by Meredith. Ito sat grinning and preening amid the group he'd come to know in his own days with the news team several years before—before he was elevated to professional status as a financial specialist with the UAM Syndicate in New York. Sonia and her hefty husband Art, Cassie unusually alone, without her swarthy photographer husband Bob—out of town on assignment, and George and Gloria Masner who over time had become part of the group. Meredith regarded Cassie, wondering where Bob's photographic editor job had taken him, and Cassie's less than usually animated face that had become constant over the past few weeks. Raymond slid into the seat next to Meredith, said hello and nodded to everyone—careful not to interrupt the conversational cadence. Meredith reached over and squeezed his knee, he leaned, brushed her ear with his lips then whispered, "Riley?"

"Baking cookies with Lola and Trey." She rolled her eyes. Raymond smiled as he imagined the bedlam currently abounding in their kitchen.

"Hear you got into a tussle with the police, boss. Arrested huh?" Ito's voice cut into Meredith's amusement.

"I was really stupid, Ito. I've never crossed over the law before—personally or at work—but I didn't think. Knew too much, assumed too much of an old haunt. Jay and Potty's house up there on Bright Leaf. Not theirs, of course, now. And, yep. I broke in and entered and got caught." All eyes around the table turned toward her, mirth stitching the airy sentiment. "Fortunately, I had my attorney next to me," she gestured to Gloria. "And a wise policeman on the scene," she looked to Raymond. "And I didn't go to jail—or even get written up. No smirch on my record. Whew!" Laughter skittered around the table as she told the story.

But Sonia slipped from her chair and went over to where Raymond sat. She squatted down next to him. "Meredith's friend Fred called while she was doing the morning show today, and left a message that his old buddy from Starsystem Studios—Meredith had lunch with him a while back—contacted Fred to say that the stable of actors that Lindy Fuller was a part of stuck pretty close together and were in a lot of movies together. Studio contract system. He seemed to recall one of them—Myra or Myrna, Madge something or other—I have the old posters, will look it up—was a roommate of Lindy's. And that Myra/Myrna was an outrageous character, so he remembers her and that she was dating one of the crew. Herb, Harv—something like that. Maybe she's still around. He couldn't believe he could even recall that much. We can check out some of the other secondary players. They must have all known each other and we might find one or the other of them who might know more about Lindy. Thought it might be helpful." She handed Raymond a piece of notebook paper with the names printed on it. He nodded to her and mouthed "thanks." Sonia straightened herself up and returned to her place, Art putting his arm around her. Raymond sat back in his chair, lifted his glass that glowed seductively with amber pilsner, to his lips and drank deeply, then assumed his usual silently observant place in Meredith's typically boisterous entourage.

The various seafood dishes served and consumed, friends moving around the table to nestle closer to their own conversational pals. Meredith's femme consorts gathered, deep in intense plotting, Raymond could tell. Together the group had unraveled more mysteries, problems and puzzles than most detective bureaus. Art, Raymond and George, sharing their commitment to the NFL, until Ito made his way over to the group. "What are they digging into?" he asked, watching the females interact.

"Don't know, but be afraid. Be very afraid," George and Raymond mouthed almost simultaneously.

CHAPTER 30

Meredith and Sonia huddled over the desk, carefully scanning papers scattered across the surface. "Madge Holden," said Sonia, adjusting her half-frame reading glasses. "The actress Fred's friend talked about must have been Madge Holden. She's there on two of the old posters along with Lindy Fuller and a whole bunch of other cast members, in small type, appearing in both movies."

"Now, to find her if she's still around," pondered Meredith.

Sonia picked up the phone. "Calling the library—they know me pretty well by now." Sonia's weekly show biz question and answer column syndicated across the country often required her to find out "whatever happened to…" any number of former celebrities. The various entertainment industry libraries were well accustomed to her calls and visits. Sonia chattered affably with a voice she obviously knew and when she hung up fifteen minutes later, she was beaming. "That was easy," she purred. "Madge Holden is still around but it took a while to uncover her whereabouts." Meredith abandoned her own work and perched next to Sonia on the front of the desk.

"She's Madge of Madge's Catering now. They service some of the studios! My library friend said there was an article in one of the trade papers only recently that featured her. She couldn't find the last name, but here's the number of the catering company. How easy was that?"

"Can't be that easy," smirked Meredith. "It's taken us months to land on that source. She reached for her own phone and dialed the number. Sonia locked her gaze on the interaction and felt more and more disappointed as she heard the short but clear conversation. "Madge is on vacation in Asia," sighed Meredith. "Won't be back until next week. Won't give me any more info than that."

"Next week is only a few days away. It's only Monday. Another week after twenty or thirty years ain't bad!" Sonia's persistence was always refreshing.

"No," Meredith agreed thoughtfully. "And anyhow, it would be best to pass this on to Raymond. Law enforcement hasn't started paying us consulting fees yet—there's nothing we can do with the information when and if we do get it."

"And you have a lunch appointment in an hour with Russ Talbot. Ready for it?"

Meredith muttered a cynical, "Sure. Always ready for the right angle turn in the road that comes without warning!"

CHAPTER 31

There's something almost ethereal about a high style restaurant in a trendy part of any town, especially in Santa Monica, California, the final stop at the ocean—the conclusion of L.A.'s daisy chain of modish west-side neighborhoods. Meredith stepped out of her Mustang, handed the keys to the valet who looked at the car with a mixture of respect and curiosity. "Cool," he said.

Adjusting her soft cream silk jacket and blouse, Meredith hoped she reflected the "I'm cool but don't give a damn" attitude she wanted to feel in this "Cool and don't give a damn" style of eatery. But she did give a damn, worrying that the meeting about to take place might represent her career future. Self-talking all the way down the hedge-lined walkway into the garden-ish entrance, she reminded herself she had a bigger life than her articles and columns. Riley was her number one focus and affection now. Raymond her number one and a three-quarters. Work/career a loud and demanding number two. And Paco the cat, always meandering through all levels.

The rationale evaporated into the ethos the moment she spied Russ sitting comfortably at a prime table near the window. He rose from his chair as he noticed her entrance. She waved and snaked along a pathway through tables of chattering lunchers. She was surprised when Russ reached out and vigorously hugged her upon arrival. He was normally more of a shoulder patter, she mused.

"The mountain comes to…well, all of that," she smiled, setting her bag under the table and sitting back in the chair.

"Kind of, but not like it sounds," answered Russ, shaking his head. "Came out to see a friend, play a little golf. The usual. But thought it a good time to catch up-update. What's good here?" he asked, redirecting the conversation. Meredith offered some suggestions and eventually ordered a Thai crunch salad for herself. Russ followed quickly with a salmon Caesar salad. Meredith eyed him closely remembering he was usually a meat guy. Barbeque ribs, prime rib sandwich, Reuben….

"Russ! That sounds positively healthy. And you've lost some weight. Hot new glasses. Looks good! Positively tony!" He grinned, shrugged and ordered a bottle of pinot grigio.

"It's the time of life to restore, resurrect and re-emerge!" he quipped. She winced. "Changes, changes," he canted. "Midlife changes, I guess. And speaking of that—look at you. Mother of a three—four-year-old. I thought Hollywood was the only kid you'd ever fret over." They both laughed. "Tell me about her," he went on, looking intently at the journalist. She recounted some of Riley's latest escapades and wins, pride and humor exuding from her words. She retold the story of getting arrested for breaking and entering. "Another kerfuffle," he murmured with a smile.

"And Raymond's still chasing down the celebrity bad guys," she snorted. The pinot grigio had arrived and was languishing brightly in their glasses. She recounted the case of the long-forgotten actress found dead under a house in Desert Hot Springs. And moved to the murder of Tanya Meile's husband. "Hollywood's still one big cesspool of crime and gossip." She paused a moment than blurted out, "we're not going back to daily gossip columns are we?"

Her mini-but-ever-so-cautious outburst surprised him. His eyes flew open and he fumfered, "No. My God no! None of us wants that! What would ever give you that idea?" he pushed.

"Sorry," she retreated. "Just that I'm always on edge, anticipating changes and not always good ones when you call a meeting." Russ raised his hands defensively and shook his head. "Or else," she pushed on, "you're leaving the syndicate—you're all shined up. Look ten years younger. A new job or a new woman?" She watched her mentor-boss blush. "Oh…a woman…."

"That's not what this is about, Meredith."

"No new woman? Then it's a new job! Shucks. I thought after the decade it's been since Marian passed, you'd landed a new hammock-pal in the tropics."

He continued to shake his head but finally said, "Well…."

"I knew it," Meredith grinned and thrust her wine glass toward him. "About time."

"Okay," he conceded. "This meeting isn't about just catch up. And although there may be a new female sparkle in my eye, we're here because there's a new sparkle in all our eyes and you need to know about it. You need to make some decisions and accommodations, hopefully some plans." He saw her shoulders drop and the liveliness on her face droop to troubled. She set her glass down and leaned forward on her arms on the table.

"Tell me," she said.

He set his own glass down and sat up tall. His was a serious announcement he hadn't quite yet intended to make. Lunch hadn't been served. "Okay. It is a serious subject. Believe me. But a good one. Yes, I'm leaving United American." He paused and saw her face fall even more. "Stop that. Wait until you hear the full story. At its best outcome, we're all leaving UAM because UAM is leaving the Hollywood business. Now don't get all snuffy. You probably should have taken the time with Woody Buchanan in Vegas. He'll be my new boss at *News—New York*. And, we hope you and your entourage will let him be yours." Meredith squeezed her eyes shut and tried to sort out what she'd just heard.

"More…" she stammered.

"'We,'" he emphasized, gesturing at her then at himself, "are now a 'package'—an entertainment industry bureau, operating much as we have been with even a little more resource, doing what you, Sonia and the others UAM has used mostly in a part-time project basis, are now invited to become 'staff.' Not much changes in the actual work except that from time to time we'd call on you to grind out a short breaking news story for the wire service. *News—NY* has a huge pool of subscribers all over the world. Beats UAM by miles."

"I can't move to New York, Russ. My life is more complex now and my home is here."

"No need. In fact, not a good idea. It would be life pretty much as usual. You or Sonia, if you prefer and she's available, would be the Los Angeles Bureau Chief." Meredith gazed out the window mentally putting the pieces in place.

"Money?"

"Better."

"Alternatives?"

"Up to you. There will be no UAM in the Hollywood business—at least in print journalism—after September 1. You're, of course, free to look elsewhere for a new berth. Or even stay home and freelance. But Meredith, *News-NY* is the most prestigious and powerful AND widely syndicated news source in the world. I don't know why you would not want to be a part of it."

Meredith took a deep breath. "I have to process this, Russ. One half of me is like a teenage cheerleader jumping joyful professional cartwheels. The other half has become somewhat resistant to a lot of change. I'm no longer the only one deciding to be the dog getting wagged by the tail. And what about Cassie and the *Morning Coffee* show? Ito, sitting there in New York, running numbers and figures and idolizing you?"

"We're working out the morning show now. *News-NY* produces and syndicates a couple of programs, mostly news. It's a new division and endeavor. We're still working out the details."

"Does Cassie know about it?"

Russ nodded slightly humbled. "Yes. And Ito—well, I'll find a good place for him. He really wants to come back to the West Coast, but we're working on that, too." The server arrived with two plates of food, approaching cautiously, noting the serious nature of the conversation. Well trained, obviously.

"Thank goodness. I need this," sighed Meredith, pulling her napkin to her lap and picking up her fork.

"Does anything ever curtail your appetite?" asked Russ. Meredith shook her head and reached for a roll.

Plates cleaned, glasses empty, Meredith folded her napkin and said, "Let me mull over this, Russ. I need to go back to Malibu and slather myself in my family and get some clear pictures in my head. Want to come out for cocktails at our house and dinner close by?"

"Two days," he said. "Wednesday?"

She nodded. "Call me tomorrow in any case. I'll have an answer by then." He acknowledged.

"And Meredith," he added as a footnote, leaving the table. "We need you."

Russ's words had stopped Meredith cold. She seldom thought of herself as a major cog in an important wheel. She always assumed there were a dozen or more qualified journalists ready and willing to step into her shoes…and plenty of publications, news syndicates ready to accept them. The idea of herself as a brand was intimidating.

She and Raymond sunk low in their living room chairs talking out the possible scenario ahead. Riley had reluctantly conceded to bedtime, tucked into her fluffy covers, Paco curled tightly against her and only the sound of the relentless surf in the background. Meredith rubbed her eyes and groaned. "Another crossroad."

The detective curled back into the recliner and folded his arms over his chest. "Sure. But it sounds like a total positive. I'm not hearing any threat or danger to your work—or your community or schedule—as they currently stand. Can you explain the negatives in the idea that concern you?"

Meredith was silent for a few moments. "Well, not really," she said seriously. "But no change this big comes bump-free. *News-NY* is such a heavy presence and we're—I'm—the face of it here in the L.A. core. I'm afraid what it might do to the balance we seem to be managing."

"It sounds like Russ is giving you more resources to build a stronger base. That should allow you to shore up the support staff and focus on your own work."

"Think about it. Even if Sonia is willing to add more days to her time here, who'll run her shopper newspaper? And, there'll be more and more people in this house daily. It's already filled up more than we ever anticipated when we, sorry—you, bought the place. There'll be less and less space and air for the family, for Riley. Less time for us like tonight. Probably more night events like there used to be." Raymond dramatically shuddered and thought about the tuxedos in the closet that used to get worn often but in recent years only a few times.

"See?" Meredith retorted.

"What's the alternative?" he asked. "You've played with that before and run into too many walls. Only the *L.A. Times* seems logical—although it's not a bad alternative now they're finally looking at movies and TV, music as a serious business, not just gossip or as critics. There're also the industry trade pubs—*Variety, Reporter*— but do you want that kind of schedule and rigor now?" Meredith shook her head.

Silence overtook the room and neither spoke for a while. Finally, Raymond quietly spoke up. "You could retire, focus on home and just freelance. You'd be highly recruited." Meredith sighed loudly. To her, the suggestion reminded her of all the reasons she had wanted to avoid the domestic scene—marriage, kids, etc.—since childhood. Now the same imagined scenarios were real and ingrown in her psyche. The tall, silver-haired detective unfurled his form from the chair, stood up, extended his hand to the whimpering blonde in the other recliner and murmured, "Let's sleep on it. You'll probably have better insight in the morning."

CHAPTER 33

Seven-thirty a.m. the next day, Tuesday morning. Raymond, still in his shorts and t-shirt from a quick run on the beach, was on the phone with Marty. "Hope you're up for a visit to the South," he opened the conversation. "You're headed ASAP to Miami. I've been on the phone already with Sheriff Ted in Desert Hot Springs and our venerable Chief here. They've agreed L.A. is picking up a short trip to Florida to dig there locally into the Fuller case and you're it!" Long-standing partner to the overly-enthused detective, Marty Escobar did a mental sigh and answered, "Oh joy. Sure. Get me the details." And hung up.

Riley watched her beach-run-clad father pace in small circles, phone pressed to his ear. He checked his watch frequently. The tot giggled and waved at him from her seat at the kitchen table. He waved through a scowl, argued into the receiver for a bit then said, "Yep. Marcus Ladonna. We've tracked him down. Moved to the house in Hot Springs about the right time. Former colleagues we can find say he was apparently married to a young actress or model but only stayed in the desert a short while before moving to Miami. We don't know if it was with or without her. But Margo has tracked him down. Went into real estate, but my contact at Miami PD is on a short leash with his superiors and can't really do much more than provide some paperwork. Ladonna has a couple of DUIs and one domestic disturbance on his record there. We need to talk to this guy in person." Raymond ran his free hand through his tousled hair and shook his head as he listened.

Raymond listened again adding "Uh huh," now and then.

"Thursday's fine. Roberta will set up your trip. Let her know your travel times and preferences. No emergency. Thanks, Marty. I owe you one," He concluded the conversation, hung up, then pinched Riley on the ear and bolted up the stairs to shower and dress for work. It was a dress-up day, he mused, using his daughter's words. A suit day. On his way up the stairs, he glanced to the kitchen where Lola was keeping an eye on the child while cleaning up breakfast. Raymond's next assignment was to drop Riley off at school and time was closing in.

CHAPTER 34

"Out!" The floor manager announced as *Morning Coffee* wrapped for the day and the cast. On Tuesdays, the cast included Meredith, who, along with the others quickly divested themselves of microphones and other technology. "Good show everyone," called Cassie as she swooped onto the studio floor from the tech booth. Her focus was distracted, obviously outside the TV studio, as she collected scripts, other immediate paraphernalia to be filed, reused or discarded.

"Cass," Meredith called from the set as she collected her own materials. "Can we talk? Let's get some coffee?"

Cassie turned her curly tousled short hair and said, "Sure. Next door?" She referred to a coffee shop down the block from the station. Ten minutes later the two old colleagues, friends and partners in journalistic adventures wilted against the Formica table and savored the first cup of good rich coffee after their show. "Today went well," Meredith quickly stepped in. "How do New York producers feel about our segments." She was dangling the bait for Cassie who, Meredith knew, was already read into the changing scene Russ had outlined. Cassie's daily show from Los Angeles was cut into NBS's New York based *It's a Good Day* twice a week with banter about Hollywood and show business with Meredith participating. It was a relationship that benefitted both TV production sources and was brokered through UAM Syndicate that owned *Morning Coffee*. Things were about to change, and Meredith wanted to know how.

Cassie toyed with the spoon in her coffee, stirring whitener around and around by saying nothing. "You talked to Russ," she finally murmured. Meredith nodded. Cassie looked up summoning the confidence she usually showed and said, "It's a negotiation. First, *Morning Coffee* on its own brings in great local revenues to everyone. Its remote cut-ins to *Good Day* have proven lucrative for NBS, UAM and given us all a strong presence. But the final numbers are yet to come."

"It's going away if you and Russ can't come to an agreement."

With a resigned shrug, Cassie looked at her friend. "This business is always twisting and turning. Look how many ways we've put it together over the past ten years. One day, while we're still keeping the hairdresser's grandkids in college with our dye jobs, and the dermatologists buying up Montana ranches, we'll finally realize, 'I think I'm looking pretty grisly in the camera lens. Maybe I'll retire!" They both laughed. "What about you?" Cassie asked Meredith.

"I called Russ at the break and told him we could negotiate." She took a long sigh. "It's too good to pass up, but there are conditions. My life is different now and I need to protect the balance." Cassie nodded in acknowledgment. "So, what else, Cass?" Meredith probed. The brunette producer looked up startled.

"There's more going on. I know you too well. What's amiss, what's not?" Cassie played with her spoon some more and fidgeted a bit in her seat. "Where's Bob?" probed Meredith.

Sitting up straight, gulping her self-confidence, Cassie answered, "Kuwait, Rwanda, Sri Lanka...it's hard to know anymore. He's such a big macho self and his life was always played on the edge before we met. Always in some war or skirmish, never on his own soil. Never had much of a real home. Then we met, he surrendered, and we dug in. But after the move here and the house on the hill and dog and all…my books selling so well, he had some kind of later-life crisis. The chief photographer role with the nature and travel magazines left him cold. Said he couldn't take one more picture of a lovely old tree suffering from bug bites, or endangered animals. About five years ago one of his old photo agencies called and asked him to sub for someone else who was recovering from malaria in some war zone. I've honestly forgotten which one. He pushed and I said yes, so he packed up his gear and took off for two weeks. Came back with fire in his eyes and the taste of danger on his tongue again. Since then, he's been gone a lot of the time. About two years ago he quit the nature magazine and accepted any assignment the agency offered. Six months ago, he took an apartment in Brussels." Tears formed in Cassie's dark eyes. The deep sadness there was something Meredith had never seen.

She stared in confusion. "You've never said anything. He's been around from time to time, but when he wasn't, I figured he was traveling on assignment with the magazine." Cassie shook her head. "So…" Meredith began slowly and carefully, "is it over or…?"

"'Spect so." Cassie picked up her napkin and dabbed at her eyes. "He tried to live the double life for a while. He's not a bad person. Oddly enough, he loves me and tried to find a way. Why you saw him sometimes. I kind of stopped crying a while ago but saying it out loud is hard."

"Wish you'd said something," Meredith whispered because her voice caught in her throat. "I want to help—would have immediately." She reached over and took Cassie's hand. "Want to now. What can I do? What's next?"

Cassie laughed out loud. "Who knows. Russ and I are negotiating and how that ends will determine a lot of things: work, income, location. Probably including any possible future around husband Bob. But that chapter may be written already."

"You planning on leaving L.A.?"

"Probably not, but don't really know yet. Hate to leave my house. I've loved it since we first saw it. But turning it from 'our' house to 'my' house isn't easy. Most days I do fine but then…."

"Drive out to Malibu and stay with us when that happens. We have room. Wish you'd done it sooner, might have helped."

Cassie snickered. "I did that once, but when I got to the street all I could think about was the red-hot nest of passion you and Raymond shared and I couldn't put myself into it. Went to a motel."

Meredith shook her head. "You know I always thought about the romance you and Bob started—in the war zone—the one you described when we originally met. Then the organic way you two took to one another. It was so seductive, and I was a little envious."

Cassie guffawed loudly again. Patrons glanced her way. "What a great story. With a bad ending. You had a better storyline."

"Don't know how I missed this. What can I do?" Meredith pushed. Then looked at her watch. "Come over tonight? I have to pick up Riley now, but…we can give you a good dinner, a comfortable guest suite, or I can lend you a bubbly four-year-old human or a cranky old cat to keep you company."

Cassie snorted. "Pass, but I guess I should tell you that I'm doing fine. Sad—devastated—about Bob and the marriage, of course. But I've had some time to live with it, and I have a shoulder to cry on and someone to keep me warm—for now at least. Unexpected. Other than the dog. But that's for another time. I'll call you later about the *News-NY* thing. There's a lot to talk about. When it's all worked through."

Meredith stood up, puzzled but amused, and walked over to her friend, hugging her tightly. "Yes, there is, and it will all work out."

"Miss optimism," snarked Cassie. "Thank God someone is!"

CHAPTER 35

Raymond tossed his suit jacket into the back seat of his car as he made his way out of the Wilshire Boulevard mirrored high rise where Larry Pinot's offices were located. The detective exhaled slowly to allow his mind and body to decompress. The gnarly producer needed someone to blame for the troubles at his home. His fight to defend the murderous actions of his housekeeper was, no doubt, demanded by his young wife who would otherwise have to interview and hire new household help. A task Pinot knew would be daunting to the somewhat inexperienced Mrs. Pinot—and a big bother to both Pinots. It was a vainglorious quest despite his rants and threats.

The day had carried its own bowl of frenetic activities at the west side offices of Raymond's Special Profile investigators. "You'd think every VIP in every field we cover has been struck with the crazies," gasped his administrative assistant, Roberta. A pro football star threatening to kill one of the cheerleaders for kissing an opponent on camera, a celebrity realtor pushing a client out of an open house because of her critical comments about the place, causing her to fall and break a leg. And Larry Pinot complaining to his state legislative representative because "how could anyone" blame his housekeeper for stabbing her violent, abusive husband to death? And, she should be exonerated.

Travel to Florida was on the to do list for his partner Marty, and likely to Mexico for Raymond. He winced at the thought—

and all it brought with it. Before wrapping the day, he had placed a discreet call to Reuben Alonso—an undercover DEA agent who had been deeply involved in the death and crimes Meredith had encountered on the *Sunset West* movie location in New Mexico a couple of years before. The two lawmen from such disparate agencies had become friends and collaborators. But Reuben was a "ghost" agent. One minute official "driver" for movie production personnel on southwestern or Mexican film locations, next, incognito among drug interaction participants, sometimes together with Border authorities exploring deep background for a crime. And occasionally doing a covert favor for good friends like Raymond or Meredith.

After the conversation with Reuben, home sounded good to Raymond, even the dinner scheduled on his own patio for Russ Talbot—with all the gravity and seriousness attached to Meredith's professional future. He slipped in the door from the garage and up the stairs unnoticed in the wake of the meal preparations in the kitchen—including the banter of a four-year-old napkin folder. He thought about the importance of the gathering to Meredith, decided to shave, mentally shaking off his own burdensome day, then stepped into the shower. The sting of the hot spray revitalized him. Casual beachside clothes felt so much more welcoming than business-like suits.

"And on the red carpet now…" Riley belted out theatrically as he descended the staircase, "…the world's handsomest detective." The words struck him as something her mother would have said—did say—in another time—only then more quietly and definitely more seductively. And at only four, Riley's reflection of Meredith amazed him. No question who's kid she was. Except, he flicked in last minute realization, for the OCD tendencies she shared with him.

"And the brave and stoic detective," smiled Meredith emerging from the kitchen. "Go put on your nice dress," she detoured quickly and instructed the youngster who smirked and started to pout. With a look from her father, Riley scuttled off to her own room.

"I already put on my nice dress," retorted Raymond with a mock curtsy. Meredith walked up to him and kissed him noisily on the lips.

"You," she said pointing at him, "please light the barbeque." He sauntered off to the patio to take care of grilling business.

The doorbell sounded a few minutes later. Meredith ushered Russ into the living room as Raymond came out to shake hands. "Great house," boomed the New York executive, as he scanned the layout of the living space that was punctuated by floor to ceiling windows out to sea. "Haven't been here in the past couple of years and I'm curious to see how you've remodeled it to accommodate the increased family size."

"It's noisier and busier now," Raymond chuckled then led Russ through the reconfigured house as Meredith returned to the kitchen to check on the menu. Lola had stayed in to help with the event, and as a blooming master's student, was invited to join the table to hear the plans unfold. "Lots to be learned about business and negotiation," the journalist had prepped the young woman

Dinner progressed with grilled steak and corn, a large fresh vegetable salad and garlic sourdough baguettes. Coffee and empty ice cream cups now sitting in front of them, Riley snoozing with occasional soft snicks from the living room couch, Russ outlined the final plans. "I've spent a long day of barter, bitching and negotiating with Woody in New York," he began in final summary. "So, what we've talked about has boiled down to this. The company will spring for an expansion of the space under your patio—or wherever it's best for you— Meredith. Maybe an extension of the space you now have for Lola under the veranda. There's still a lot of room across the oceanside front of the house there. But you may want to go back to external offices because you'll need more space for more activity. Sonia, if she agrees, will be in now for three and a half days—she'll have to explain how that'll work with her weekly paper she runs. But if you choose to stay in the house, you'll want to assure yourselves of privacy in your regular living spaces and allow for more technology and interaction in the office. The lawyers and accountants are arranging how to categorize this for future ease—and taxes.

"You'll file your own normal weekly long topical columns but feel more open to including your opinions, etc. And the once-a-week celebrity features. But you'll also be expected to file separately in the case of a major happening or an emergency situation—like the Manson stuff was—or…well, you know, murders, bombings, all the usual news fodder. And, there'll be a freelance photo editor who may need to use a spare desk in your new office from time to time."

Raymond sat stoically but internally grimaced at the words. He knew Meredith's choice for workspace would be at home, and began to calculate how much more work-related activity would soon fill the house.

"You may need some freelance help. Let me know," Russ went on. "There will be a big announcement to the industry and media at some point—soon."

Meredith sternly regarded her boss. "What about Cassie and the show?"

"Cassie's in this, too. Not much change in work pattern for her except that her bosses will be with *News—New York* instead of UAM. And we've negotiated larger office space with an assistant for her at the studio where you all tape."

"She knows about this?"

Russ nodded. "Yep. Met with her yesterday." Meredith sensed a niggling question in the back of her mind, wondered why Cassie hadn't elaborated the day before.

"You know about Bob?" Meredith persisted. Russ nodded and flicked his hand.

"Not my problem and she's handling it. At least says so."

"Salaries and compensation—we've already discussed all that." Russ continued. "Contracts are being drawn up now and will be delivered by Friday. I'll be here the rest of the week to hand hold."

"When?" asked Raymond quietly.

"Architect will call you next week, if you decide to expand here rather than take outside office space. If you want to use a contractor of your own, have him or her contact me. We need to be ready to go September 1." The moment his voice stopped, questions bubbled, with comments and "what ifs?" Soon Lola had excused herself to clean up the table and dishes. Raymond toted Riley upstairs and planted her softly in her own bed. She turned over and kept slumbering.

"How many times over the years have you outlined the future for these women? It must be like a déjà vu experience each time," Raymond commented to Russ as the evening came to a close. Meredith had gone to check on Riley.

Russ shrugged. "Laid out a lot of scenarios—made a lot of agreements and plans— for this group. But it's the first time without Meredith's old mentor Alan Jaymar. I miss his mellow voice and perspective. He calms the water. I'm just glad these powerhouse women decided to stick with us—me."

"Well," Raymond searched for the right words, "Meredith values family and home above all. And that's what this group has represented to her since Bettina died. You're certainly a part of it. And please honor that role. It means a lot to her. But…Ito. The little brother?"

"Not for other ears, but he'll come to L.A., work with Cassie in her new offices—part accountant/local bureau controller, and part-producer. I think he'll love it and he'll be great at it. Detail oriented and relentless in stats. And good eyes on the happening here." Raymond chuckled, and Russ called, "Meredith—come say good night. I need to get to the hotel and bed. It's late and a busy day tomorrow."

Meredith bustled down from the bedrooms. "A new chapter, huh, Russ. But I'm excited about the new affiliation—hope it's good for us all."

Russ reached over to kiss her cheek. "Lunch next week with Alan?" She smiled and said, "Would not miss it."

"Lots to ponder," Raymond said later, as he lifted his toothbrush and began the nightly cleaning ritual.

"I think I better get writing on back-up articles and columns," Meredith said. "Once this all kicks off, life will be a roller coaster. I hope you understand when I get demanding or stressed out."

Putting away his brush, he rinsed his mouth and then turned to her. "Well, Queen of the Hollywood Gossip world, first you have to understand that this affects me, too. Sometimes I'm not going to be willing to unearth the tux for some event, and will prefer to stay home and enjoy the quiet?" She nodded. "Then, I'm going to follow your advice on preventive things—and that means finishing off a couple of burdensome cases before all hell breaks loose around us. I'm leaving tomorrow for Mexico…I'll still drop Riley at school first, but I'll be on my way to the airport instead of the office."

Meredith looked at him with confusion. Concern troubled her mind and face. "Mexico—why and where?"

"Marty's off to Florida tracking down one of our promising desert guys. Another one is in Mexico. I'm flying to San Diego, renting a car and driving to Ensenada. We've traced Odenato there—from years ago, but someone's still living there with that name—doesn't sound local."

Meredith sat down on the bed with a flump. "Mexico," she shook her head. "As a cop. God it's had such a bad rep with crime, kidnapping and so on. Have you at least joined forces with the local gendarmes?"

"Look, this isn't a big bad arrest or even crime. It's just some research—investigation to find a long-gone 'party.' Nothing more. An interview for some details—or not—and a return trip home." He didn't mention Reuben.

"Sure," said Meredith, skepticism lacing her words. Few of the work trips taken by either of them ever worked out simply. She worried what was ahead for Raymond. It kept her awake much of the night.

CHAPTER 36

Reuben met Raymond at the San Diego airport and with the DEA agent's help, most of the paperwork hassle renting a car to take across the Mexican border was easily solved. "I'm staying in the copilot seat," Alonso told the detective. "I'm officially on a movie over in Calexico, but don't want to be seen with an American PD." Raymond understood. He drove through the crowded, scrabby border town surroundings of Tijuana and headed south along the coast. He hadn't been in that part of Mexico in years and was surprised at how much development had taken place—some havens beckoning tourists, some ticky-tacky retail and food establishments. He shook off feelings of regret that he'd taken on the assignment from Belin. The sheriff didn't have the staff, and Raymond's name was, after all, "all over" the homicide. He explained the situation to Reuben.

The two were relieved that the destination address provided him by his colleagues wasn't as far down the coast as assumed, but about half-way between popular Rosarito Beach and Ensenada. About a ninety-minute drive. After the commute flight to San Diego, renting a car, clearing through the border, the day was mostly over. The hotel reservation was at a nearby beachside "resort." In L.A. it would be considered a motel, but neither lawman was being picky about semantics, he reasoned.

Once checked into their room, they closed and locked the door and looked around. "Good enough," shrugged Reuben. A bed, a bathroom and a phone. "Let's take a ride," he said. They were back in the car and following the streets to the oceanside address they'd been given with the intent of scoping out the scene. The house was well designed with Mexico's traditional high surrounding stucco wall and locked entry gate. Behind it, a short, well-shrubbed, driveway up to a good-sized two-story house, nicely designed and kept up, but not opulent. The neighborhood itself was not new but homes were maintained and well placed near the beach but no advertisement of rich Gringos intent to live the surf life.

"This isn't a benign local family," Reuben began, instructional and in warning. "Don't kid yourself. The Odenato name isn't that known, don't know much about him. Maybe they decided living here was more fun and probably less identifiable for your guy. But his wife's family is a big one. Mexico City—oil, import-export and suspected underbelly operations of drugs. So, keep it subtle—low key. I wouldn't reveal the girl's death or any suspicion of Odenato's involvement. You're wily—those Hollywood crimes trained you well. So just be careful. The family tentacles extend long over the border. And I..." Reuben looked at Raymond with a wicked grin, "don't care to get recognized, involved or even killed. 'Kay?"

"Let's both avoid any of that," snickered Raymond. "But how about some dinner?" Reuben muttered, "Oh yeah."

Early the next morning, Raymond put in a call to his partner in Florida at an agreed upon time. "Well," Marty began, "Our Miami guy, Marcus Ladonna, has quite a history here with local cops. Two DUIs and one domestic abuse call by his wife. Never charged but some other complaints by neighbors of fights and shouting. He's a local travel promoter. I'm going by later today-hope to meet with him and the wife. Wish I had more for you—but neither of them are home-free or looking very promising at this point, T.K. Check in with me later today." The two agreed on a time when both would be at phones.

Then, as morning life began to move in the Mexican beachside resort area, Raymond and Reuben left their hotel and drove back to the nearby neighborhood they'd perused the night before. "Go around the other block," Reuben instructed. "I'm getting out and coming at the house from the rear alley. I've got your back, if you need that, staying under the radar unless I'm needed." He passed a small recording and transmitting device to his colleague who slipped it into his cargo pants pocket. Then, Raymond nodded, followed the route and by himself arrived at the gated home of Malcom Odenato. He parked on the street and pushed the intercom.

"Hablé!" came a throaty female voice. "Quién es?"

"Hablé Ingles?" Raymond returned, knowing just enough Spanish to get by normally in the heavily Hispanic world of L.A.

"Yes," said the voice. "Who are you?"

"I'm T.K. Raymond, a detective from Los Angeles. I'd like to spend a few minutes with Senor Odenato."

"About?"

"Just trying to identify a company that once owned a house in Southern California. Just looking for some background information he may have as a previous resident."

"I don't think he can help you." The voice was now more than just throaty. The Mexican accent was hidden behind perfect English, well-educated and articulate.

"May I speak with him?" The buzzer sounded and the gate slid open. A short beefy young man came down the driveway and beckoned to Raymond to enter. He took a deep breath and started toward the house, was unceremoniously ushered through a large, ornate glassed-in front door. The interior hall was cool and in keeping with traditional local décor: red tiled floor, high ceilings, stucco alcoves, shelves holding bright flowers or ceramic statues. The little man led Raymond into a dark parlor and indicated a stuffed chair for him to take. He did. Soon a tightly built, well-coiffed older woman entered and sat down opposite, facing him from a matching chair.

"Senora Odenato," Raymond stood up, said "T.K. Raymond," extending his hand. The woman patted it dismissively with a hand manicured in dark red polish, then waved him back to the chair. "Dolores," she said simply. The detective handed her his card. She regarded it with a combination of curiosity and amusement. "What has this got to do with my husband?" she asked.

"Senor Odenato once resided—may have been part owner— of a house in Desert Hot Springs, California. Near Palm Springs if you're familiar with the area at all. Some twenty-five years ago or more. New owners have bought the place and we've been asked to find the former corporate owners to clear the title and learn a few things about the original construction."

She smiled, amused. "Well, that will be a chore, detective. My husband died about four years ago." Breath caught in Raymond's throat. He struggled to keep his disappointment from showing, soldiering on. "Perhaps you can help me out with some timelines. That's all," he sought to keep the conversation going.

The woman stood up, dressed in fashionable black slacks and a low-cut black and white jersey top she cut a striking figure. Her long black hair was streaked with silver and knotted at the back of her neck. Silver hoop earrings hung from her ear lobes. Her age was evident in her facial features but remained striking with large dark eyes against her caramel skin. She waved at the short man who stood in the doorway, beckoning him forward.

"This is Pedro. He helps us out. Can you bring us some lemonade, Pedro?" He nodded, turning to leave as she unobtrusively handed him the business card, then sat back down.

"What would you like to know Mr. Raymond?" she asked, surprising him that she had paid attention to his identification. He was working to frame questions that were not threatening or challenging.

"How long did Mr. Odenato live here? Do you know when he moved here from Los Angeles?"

She shrugged. "Here, about twenty-five years. I met him in Mazatlán in 1965. We were married on New Year's Eve 1965 in Mexico City and he wanted to live here and buy a fishing boat. It took a couple of years because he had to travel back to California for work until his business was sold. He was mostly retired." Raymond nodded, doing mental calculations. He toyed with a small notebook and pen he'd taken from his shirt pocket as he reached for more questions.

"Sounds like he did buy the fishing boat?"

"Yes. And built it into a sizeable organization that partnered with one of the local canneries. He had a generous settlement from a previous work relationship, and then received more from the sale of the business. Hollywood. He hated it and was glad to be away from it. He built up a fine charter fishing business over the years then we expanded it into the commercial partnership. Our twenty-three-year old son Jaime now runs the charter boats—Mal was killed in a boat accident four years ago." She stared with laser-like focus at Raymond. "So, I doubt you'd find him involved in anything now in California."

"Well," began Raymond. "I'm sorry about your loss. We're only looking to any involvement he may have had with the corporation that owned the house in Desert Hot Springs. And can give us some information. It was at least 25 years ago, probably more. No repercussion today—nothing we'd be concerned about. Just some detail that we can't locate any longer in official records. Too much time passed. Do you recall if he ever mentioned the name of a company, Canyonlight Partners, from the old days?"

She shook her head thoughtfully. "No."

"How about the name Tad Oakley?" Again, a negative but this time with a miniscule touch of apprehension. At that moment a young man appeared unexpectedly in a door to the hall. He stopped and apologized for interrupting.

"My son, Jaime," the senora introduced him. Then briefly introduced Raymond. Jaime shook hands, then turned to leave. "Con permiso," he offered in apologies for the interruption, turned and left the room.

"Was Malcom married before, Senora?" Raymond continued his inquiries.

Her eyes hardened. "Yes, to some floozy actress. But he said it was a mistake—he divorced her quite a long time before we met or were married."

"Do you know where and when the divorce took place?"

"Yuma, Arizona, same place their marriage took place. That's what he said. Over before it was ever very real. Hardly a year, he said. Divorce was about a year before we met."

"Did they have a child?"

Dolores' nostrils flared. "No! Malcom's only son is Jaime," she spat.

"Ma'am, I'm not trying to suggest or judge—just unravel the past ownership of this house. I apologize if it seems anything other than that."

She looked down at her hands and rubbed her thumb over another fingernail. The two droned on about fishing and Ensenada, tourists and Mexican real estate, Dolores seemingly stalling serious conversation. Nearly thirty minutes later Pedro finally arrived carrying two sweating bottles of a popular lemon soda. He handed one to each, then a note to the woman. She held up a "wait a moment" finger to Raymond while she read the short script. He took a long swallow of the treacly liquid, surprised at the offer of bottled yellow flavored sugar instead of a glass of freshly made juice—which would have seemed more in character. Dolores looked up suddenly.

"What else, Captain Raymond?" She emphasized the "Captain," and he knew she'd received some intel on him. It chilled his spine. Maybe she just noticed it on my card, he told himself.

"Not much else, Senora Odenato. I wonder if your husband might have left behind any paperwork or archived files from his days before his life in Mexico. Perhaps about properties owned by his business. The years have eliminated most of the simple detail we could use to close this whole issue out."

The elegant woman looked at him, dark eyes glaring, mocking. "Perhaps. But let's strike a deal," she said, standing up, moving close to him, looking down without blinking. "I will provide you with whatever is in Malcom's files—it's very thin and you must accept that. And you will not approach my family again or focus any attention at all on our son Jaime now or from the past or in the future. Malcom doted on him. I won't have him threatened or mistreated…."

Raymond set the soda bottle on the floor, rose from his seat to face her without flinching, standing about a foot taller. "I have no intention—nor need—to approach you again, Senora. I'm sorry you took this visit and conversation as something threatening…."

"And one more thing," she spoke up abruptly. "You must cherish your adorable young daughter as much as I cherish Jaime. I think she's probably at her preschool about now," she said, looking at her watch. Raymond struggled to control himself and remain neutral. "So, that's the other part of the deal. I get a guarantee no one will come bothering me or Jaime—again. You get some old papers and a guarantee no one will come bothering your little one—from here at least. Deal?"

Ethical factions in Raymond's mind fought with each other. A cop now with what seems a good reason to know more about this illusory family tree and its connection to the young woman lying dead in the desert—or—a rational investigator with enough answers to frame the case he was working on, and protect the daughter and family he does, in fact, cherish. He pondered the confusing response for a few moments, then shook off what might have been a defensive retort.

"Deal," he said, standing tall, his face impassive, extending his hand across the scant foot between the two of them. Dolores smiled with both confidence and slight arrogance but shook it.

"Pedro will drop off a file for you at your hotel in an hour," she spoke, turning toward the door. "Goodbye, detective." Pedro gave Raymond a "Come with me," head tilt. The woman stood unmoving. Raymond followed the little man and feeling angry emotions and a myriad of dissenting thoughts, found himself in his car outside the closing gate. He absently wondered where Reuben was, started the engine and drove a block straight down the street when the DEA agent waved him down.

"Well," said Reuben, "That was…fun…or not. How're you doing?" He held out his hand for the small microphone/recorder in Raymond's pocket.

Raymond, smirking, mostly oblivious of the small machine, pulled it out, handed it over, shaking his head as if to clear the thoughts quarreling with themselves. "Not at all what I expected," he sighed loudly. "I need to get to the hotel and call home." His voice belied the panic he felt.

CHAPTER 37

Cassie stood at attention in the compressed, technology-humming control booth, anticipating the final wrap up on the morning show. The phone rang just as the last "goodbye" words were spoken and the camera went off. About to launch herself from the booth out to the studio floor, one of the assistants who'd answered the ring, called loudly, "Cassie—important call." She picked it up and heard Raymond voice and the urgency in it. "It's okay. We're wrapped. Hold on," she commanded and flipped the studio intercom switch and called out, "Meredith, need you here right now."

Meredith untangled her microphone from her blouse, tossed it on the table and walked quickly to the control room, curiosity spurring her on. Cassie handed her the phone. "Raymond."

"Hi," she began but the detective cut her short.

"Are you wrapped?" She murmured affirmative, puzzled. "Are you picking up Riley?"

"Well, sure," she asserted, amazed he needed to ask.

"Then do it quickly and take her to Gloria's. Trust me that it's important—very, very."

"What's going on?" she pushed.

"Nothing you need to know at the moment, but just to humor me please don't either of you go home. Go directly to Gloria's or somewhere you don't usually go." Meredith felt a knot of anxiety pulling at her chest and head, exacerbated by the pink telephone message handed to her at that moment by the assistant.

"Raymond, does this have anything to do with a maroon souped-up Chevy that pulled across the street from our house a couple of hours ago and stayed there with 'some Latin-looking guy' staring at the house? Lola noticed him when he arrived. She said his car rattled and then he left about twenty minutes ago." Pacing in the hotel room, Raymond lightly bumped his head against the door frame. Shit, he thought.

"The guy's gone?" he asked.

"I have to call Lola, but her message said yes. She called just before we closed the show. What's happening?"

"I'll be home by late afternoon/early evening. We're leaving now. But stay away from the house. If you can't go to Gloria's go out to Alan's place. Okay? Tell Lola to close and lock everything up. Close the drapes." Meredith started to stutter questions, wondering about the "we," but he intervened. "Meredith, just this once please don't stall. Trust me and do it?"

She grunted out, "'Kay—call me at Gloria's." the phone line went dead. She depressed the connection button quickly then called Gloria.

CHAPTER 38

For Raymond the day had progressed at warp speed, driven by anxiety and determination. He and Reuben took off from Ensenada in the promise of a brilliantly sunny day—perfect for the tourists—not so much for their state of mind. They had waited, fueling on food from a near-by drive in, for the hour forecast and indeed Pedro arrived with a manila envelope—predictably fairly flat with few documents. Reuben had collected license numbers from the automobiles by the Ensenada house, made calls to check and confirm the significant timelines—marriage, birth, other vehicle licenses—and then they'd driven in high acceleration all the way to the border. By two, Reuben was gone, the rental car returned in San Diego and Raymond was on a plane.

From the airport, he'd caught Marty by phone at the Miami PD offices and learned that Marcus Ladonna shouldn't be dismissed. "He didn't want to talk about this. Gnarly and grumpy," Marty reported. "Kept sniping at me and his wife. But, told me he had lived in Palm Springs—down the hill from Desert Hot Springs—for four years. Managed a night club. Can't remember the exact home address anymore. Says it was up a hill—and 'raw, raw desert.' He claims he'd married a local waitress who said she was an actress taking a break. Marriage lasted a couple of years. Divorced in L.A. in about 1965. I've got her name. Doesn't know what happened to her. He moved to

Texas for a year, worked in real estate but moved on to Miami, switched from real estate to being a concert promoter—back to show business—where he met his current wife about fifteen years ago. Constant bickering. Probably the whole time. Why the domestic abuse is on file. While he took a phone call, she told me he might be bipolar or something. Occasionally goes into a rage and takes it out on anyone or thing around. Said I should see the patched holes in the wall of their condo. I've got the dates, copies of marriage license. Roberta can check out the L.A. stuff next week."

Raymond cut short the conversation, telling Marty, "Great work. With the details you have, we can probably move forward."

"Taking the red eye home," Marty declared. "Not another night in this town—noisy, rude, not my idea of a pleasant night. Would actually feel better on a plane!" Raymond laughed and wished him a good flight. The detective hoped his own was good, worrying about his family and what awaited him.

CHAPTER 39

As Raymond boarded his plane that afternoon, Meredith arrived at the fulsome Bel Air home of Gloria Masner. Nanny/housekeeper Margaret stood at the door waiting for the arrival. She ushered mother and child into the elegant but hospitable mansion already a familiar second home to Meredith. In the guest suite, she changed into the yoga clothes she kept in her car, stripped Riley of her school uniform and put on one of Gloria's t-shirts. The vociferous child leading the way with news updates from school, they ventured into the gleaming kitchen and found some orange juice in the fridge and graham crackers in the pantry. Sated and tired from the change in pattern, Riley snuggled deep into the guest bed and for a nap, and was asleep immediately.

Her mind, still reeling for the tone of Raymond's call and all it implied for her normally cool and collected husband, Meredith poured a glass of white wine and stretched out on one of the plump chaise lounges under the terrace overhang. Worry and fear caused by the urgency and tenseness of the rapid conversation had grown exponentially since she took the call. Constantly reminding herself of Raymond's ability to assess and contain a situation she talked herself calm. After a while, she returned to the kitchen and picked up the phone, acknowledging that her best antidote for anxiety was to fill her otherwise skitzy mind with more challenging, nonthreatening tasks. And her feature on back-up singers was due in two days. She called Jimmy Bell at his studio office, doubting he would be there on a Friday afternoon. But he was.

"I'm trying to match up photos of some of these singers with names. Jimmy. I wondered if you could help me out. You know most of them."

"Sure," he agreed affably. "When and where?" She sighed silently forgetting that she'd have to leave Riley to drive the fifteen minutes to Jimmy's studio. Her hesitation prompted his own suggestion.

"Where are you?" he asked. When she told him he laughed. "I'm almost headed that way—dropping off some tapes nearby. I can make a quick stop and take a look at your pictures. I probably have a couple candid ones of my group that might be helpful." The plan was set, and Meredith headed for the kitchen for another glass of wine and her tote with a copy of the singers' story to edit. Grateful for the diversion from concern about Raymond, the "we," and her house, she settled at the patio table.

Forty minutes later, the tall solidly built singer/producer stood at the front door of Gloria's home and looked around almost in awe. He ran a hand through his curly brown hair and whistled. "I've seen a lot of splendor before, but it's all show biz plastic. This is pretty nice, isn't it?" Meredith could only chuckle.

"Yeah," she agreed. "But it isn't mine. Sigh." They sat at the patio table. Margaret brought them glasses of iced tea and some fresh croissants that seemed to materialize magically from the pantry. Jimmy slid the photos around on the surface and Meredith made notes of the names. Finished with that task, he brought out a folder with a few more images.

"I don't see the solo singer who sings with Tanya, Joe Domo, anywhere here. What's his story?"

"Pretty much a solo performer all the way around. Doesn't hang out much with anyone. Has been with Tanya for years and very close with her. You wouldn't find him partying with these girls or in many off-stage pictures with them. Domo comes and goes on his own. What I have for you are really behind the scenes shots. I've produced these girls' music and also sung with them and Tanya for a long time. They're…lively." Meredith perused the selection, her eye catching one where the trio and Jimmy were all sitting on the floor, laughing, with music scores scattered around them. "They do like to party," he mused, then added, "some of them."

"Sounds like it. Verna was telling me that you guys were in your room partying after their last show the night Ben was… well…you know." Jimmy looked at her quizzically, then squinted his eyes in thought.

"Not the way I remember it. But as I say, each of those girls have a totally different personality and idea of what's what. I asked them to come in for a couple of minutes to give them a different arrangement for the next night. I don't drink—'cept Pepsi. Budge will happily accept a gin and tonic once in a while, Verna does like her red wine—a lot—and Sal is a teetotaler and very serious about everything. Religious. We did get to catching up on each other's lives that night, and lost track of the late hour, but Budge was the first to leave, had to pick up one of her stage dresses to repair a small hem problem. Sal left shortly after that. Verna was the last to go—nearly had to throw her out, as usual."

"See how easy it is to misinterpret someone's words," said Meredith. "There wasn't any reason to write about that night, but glad I didn't try. I would have misunderstood it all."

Jimmy shrugged. "No harm. No foul—we're all used to misinterpretation, and it wouldn't have changed much." He left shortly after and Meredith trudged through the stylish hallways to the guest suite to lie down next to Riley and rest. Sooner than she thought, the house was alive. When Trey, the Masner's twelve-year-old adopted son, arrived home from school, Riley was on her feet, in one of Trey's discarded t-shirts rippling around her, traipsing after him. The lively young man was her favorite "cousin." Then Gloria burst through the door from the garage, taking an early leave from her office. She changed out of business garb into jeans and a t-shirt and joined Meredith on the patio. Wine appeared quickly in two glasses.

"Is this emergency drama part of Raymond's case about the dead actress in the desert?" asked Gloria as she sat down on a chaise lounge.

Meredith murmured an affirmative. "He's tracked a suspect to Mexico, one that's apparently "connected" and apparently Raymond has some concern for the family safety."

"Hmmm," Gloria responded. "Seems more intense than most of his work these days."

"Usually it's a lot less consuming—or threatening—but he's intense—uptight— himself. I think, because this dead body had his name buried with it, and the particular perp may have once worked with his dad many years ago."

"Perp," mused Gloria, sipping her wine. "Connection with dad?"

"Raymond says not. This Odenato, the suspect, is so vaguely involved that Raymond can't see any connection to the firm— maybe even no connection to the dead actress. Just a suspect in a much larger picture." Silence overtook the two old friends for a while.

"Quite a different life than we envisioned sitting on the lawn at college, isn't it?" Gloria snuffed after a while. "No kids, career and adventure full speed ahead."

"Well, we do have our adventures, Gloria," chuckled Meredith. "Like whatever is going on tonight. Scary. And yeah, it does look a lot different from what we pictured. But in a larger sense not so bad, do you think? Trey's a gem and if you were going to design a kid, he's pretty close to what you might design."

"And no miserable nine months of body pummeling," snarfed Gloria. "That was your adventure, but you did it pretty well."

"Glad it seemed like that. I kind of rued every moment and whenever someone said, 'Oh you're just glowing,' I wanted to smack them. The process was…well, not what I had envisioned in school for sure, especially the delivery. Ugh. But the results were perfect. It all feels right considering how well Riley has turned out."

"Yes, she has," mused Gloria, eying Riley as she and Trey built a Lego building. "I'm still surprised you went ahead with it all."

"Well," said Meredith ponderously, "It was kind of organic. Like everything was with Raymond and me. The reality of it all surprised us both, but I think we just threw ourselves into it as partners like we've done for so long—no formal declarations or expectations. One day at a time."

As twilight gave way to darkness over the hills of Los Angeles and George had arrived home, the assembled gathering was sitting by the pool when the sound of a car entering the driveway caught their attention. Rightfully assuming it was Raymond, George quickly poured a tumbler of his best scotch whiskey and the group rushed to the front door. The welcome caught the tall detective by surprise. He accepted the glass of scotch as George took his bag, Meredith his briefcase, and Gloria pulled him into the warm glow of the house. Martha double locked the door.

CHAPTER 40

In the darkness and late—eleven-thirty—the small family finally arrived quietly at their Malibu home. Raymond chastised himself for thinking that the curtain of night would shield them from the eyes and ears of evil. But he replayed in his mind the finality and seeming credulity of the "Deal" shared between the two players in the Mexican house. As both cars arrived in caravan from their friends' safe haven, they saw only a patrol car slow and creep by. Raymond waved. Opening the door cautiously from the garage, the house seemed empty and unsullied. Lola had arranged for a classmate/friend to pick her up earlier to take her elsewhere for the night.

Bolstered by the surprising change of pattern and events, Riley was tired but chattered away about her afternoon with twelve-year-old Trey. The little girl's borrowed t-shirt was covered in paint, chocolate and other assorted frivolities. They'd played a game on Trey's computer and watched a new program on TV, eaten ice cream sandwiches and later enjoyed Pizza. She'd picked up none of her parent's agitation and dismay. Climbing the stairs to the bedrooms with Meredith, the bouncing curls and animated face took one look at her bed, climbed on it and was fast asleep in five minutes. Her mother pulled the favorite stuffed rabbit next to her and her quilt up to the small, pointed chin. Moments later the large grey cat settled in as well. Looking in, silently, Raymond whispered, "Night Gup! What a team player you are!"

"Tomorrow, I want the full story on the 'team' you went to Ensenada with," Meredith admonished Raymond as they shook off their own day, preparing for sleep. He nodded, knowing that he owed her an explanation—especially after his own recent reprimand of her actions.

The small family straggled out of bed the next morning, one at a time. It was Saturday, which, in the world of law enforcement and in journalism, didn't mean much. But they always did attempt to honor a weekend when possible. This one was a mandatory honoring. It had been a high stress week and there was much to process and assess. The night before, Raymond had mostly unloaded the previous two days events on his closest allies and family. When the name Reuben Alonso was introduced, Meredith knew the Mexico excursion had been not only serious but dangerous. She didn't feel comforted. And had some words to share—but not then.

The next day as she began preparing breakfast, she saw a hand-scribbled note from Lola. All it said was "Lic #...." Meredith handed it to Raymond. In tandem they assumed it was the plate number from the maroon Chevy that house helper noticed watching the house the day before. "Lola's becoming us," moaned Meredith, thinking, suspicious and overly paranoid. Raymond went into his small office/desk area and started making calls. By the time breakfast was on the table, the almost-four-year-old was in her place and Raymond emerged from his den.

"Who was it?" Meredith asked between mouthfuls of scrambled eggs.

"Stolen—two weeks ago. Different plates. Probably in Mexico by now." He chewed on a crisp strip of bacon, then reached to butter a piece of corn muffin. "These are great!" he said after the first bite.

"And…" Meredith pushed.

"Bacon is so crispy and the fresh vegetables are a nice addition to the eggs," he smiled. "It's Saturday," he continued. "I'm suggesting we focus on some activities not associated with crime, star stories, death…well, you know what I mean. Later, we'll talk." Meredith nodded reluctantly, a scowl on her face, but picked up her coffee cup and said no more. Still bothered by what the inclusion of Reuben suggested in the previous day's activities.

"I know what would be fun to do," chimed Riley, swirling her fork in the yellow mass on her plate. "Can we ride the horses?" Both parents looked at her, puzzled. "You know. The purple and green ones—and lions too—that go up and down to music?" Her enthusiasm was so bold neither parent wanted to deter it. The Santa Monica Carousel was not far, surrounded by food and sights and not far from other opportunities. The plan took form.

"Maybe we should invite Cassie. She's all by herself and pretty down about Bob," Meredith suggested. Raymond closed the full dishwasher, Meredith wiped down the table and Riley arranged the condiments and paper shaker on the counter—in perfect symmetrical order.

"Cassie has all the company she needs," Raymond murmured. Meredith looked at him quizzically. "Believe it. I can guarantee it," he added. "Today's family day here. Okay?"

"You bet," responded his partner in cleaning the kitchen. "Yes!" shouted the other smaller partner, then added, "And can I paint my bedroom? I don't like that purply color anymore!"

CHAPTER 41

Monday morning and Meredith was closed in her office writing furtively, finishing her back-up singers' article to be sent off that afternoon—with photos. As she read through the text for the last time, and sorted through the photo selection, she hesitated at the image of Tanya's three singers relaxing with Jimmy Bell. It reminded her of the question that had formed two days prior and been lost in the happenings of the days since. She phoned Jimmy. "Quick question. Do performers at the hotel where Tanya headlines have keys to backstage during their gigs?"

He assured her most do so they can enter and exit dressing rooms, access costumes, etc. "Just curious," she said, thanked him and hung up. A vague, ethereal question was fomenting in the back of her mind. She thrust it aside to complete the task on her desk. Lola was returning today and would pick up Riley at preschool. Finally, as she started for the kitchen for a mid-morning cup of coffee, Meredith made a decision. Silly, she thought, but nothing is off the table in a homicide case, Raymond had told her years before. A kernel of wisdom she had kept tucked in her memory. She called Sarah Freeman, her friend Sam's girlfriend.

The publicist was at work, having accepted a short-term contract on a movie that was filming in Las Vegas. "I have something that's probably nothing, but you should put in the arsenal of information for Sam's lawyer," Meredith explained.

Sarah was amused but then realized how often Meredith's work took her into the inside hallways of just about every showbiz chamber, and how savvy the journalist was in associating facts to other facts. She welcomed Meredith's perspective.

"Verna, Budge and Sal were with Jimmy Bell in his room after Tanya's last show the night Ben died. They'd been in the room—in the hotel— talking, going over something for the next night, were apparently there for at least an hour and a half. But Budge left early to pick up a costume dress from her dressing room. I don't know times, but it seems like someone might want to check on that. So far, the security guard, who was not at his post for a while when Sam went in to check on things, says only Sam was backstage. But…anyhow. Probably nothing, but worth checking out."

Sarah snuffed. "I'm not sure anyone cares. They're so happy with locking Sam into this thing. But you're right, maybe Budge saw someone else there or coming in. I'll pass it to the lawyers."

Meredith felt better when she hung up. Like she had exercised an important duty. She learned in her late boss Bettina Grant's murder case never to ignore a hunch. To dig it out even if it's hiding.

She began to ponder Raymond's brief and somewhat nebulous explanation of his Mexico trip. She knew he was whitewashing the full spectrum of it—and the threat—but Raymond was a stalwart about some revelations or lack of them when he chose to be. The depth of the story would eke out gradually—and when she coaxed them from him. But the darkly obscure tale sat heavy on her mind as she went back to work.

CHAPTER 42

After a morning of intense management and negotiation with one of the VIP sports figures accused of a pedestrian hit and run, Raymond had finally been able to turn the situation over to the sports Special Profile Detective. Then, with his office door closed, he put up the white board on his office wall and began arranging names and detail from the Desert Hot Springs case in order of possibility.

Donato—"guess" from Victoria. Not valid.

O'Donnell—No trail, not valid.

Donaldson—Moved to Spain—no connection to desert or actress.

Marconi—Too young.

Trandem—Belin talked to grandpa in Florida—no connection.

*Ladonna—Miami, possible, violent past, desert, actress wife—check with Marty.

*Odenato—Possible—track down previous marriage, kid, before move to Mexico.

"Two possibilities," muttered the detective, uncomfortable that one of them landed close to home with Odenato.

The "Desert Hot Springs" file was now about 4 inches thick, every page and line of which Raymond knew by heart. His name associated with the murdered young actress had him spooked. It came to him at night, invaded his thoughts often. He was pestered by a sense of deep closeness with the whole scene, besides a name scribbled on an aging note, and he needed understanding or at least closure. He looked at the calendar and his stack of pending cases and concerns, set aside the desert file and turned to other pressing matters.

An hour later his door opened quietly and the slight figure of Reuben Alonso slipped in so amorphously that it seemed doubtful anyone outside of Raymond's office might have noticed him. "Get home ok?" he asked.

The entrance surprised Raymond, heavily concentrating on the papers on his desk. "Yeah, sure. Surprised to see you so soon. Here. What you got?" Reuben pulled up the side chair and sat down in front of the desk, handed over a sheaf of papers. "Some good news. Some troubling news. A lot of 'so what?' But first," he slid an official document across the desk in front of Raymond.

The detective picked it up and studied it, then with a slight grin on his face, eyes squinched, murmured, "We got it! Confirmation that Odenato was the spouse of Lindy Fuller and at our time frame." He took the pencil in his hand and banged on the desk. "Marriage certificate proves it!"

Raymond eyed the rest of the paperwork and asked, "What else?"

"The widow Odenato pretty much told the truth. She married him in Mexico City, moved to Ensenada area about a year later. Birth certificate for a son born in '69—Jaime.

Odenato purchased a fishing boat, already had a substantial bank account so also bought into family business, which included part ownership of one of the tuna canneries. Business fairly successful. Dolores owns the shares now, and the bank accounts except for one limited operational account in Jaime's name. Found the marriage license in Yuma, Arizona, for Malcom Odenato and Lindy Fuller 1965. But no divorce decree there. Or Calexico or any other obvious border town. No other associated birth certificates.

"Cars at the casa Odenato all registered to the family. Except for one that was parked on the road when we entered, and when we left, an outlier. It belongs to Jorge Nolo, a foot soldier for one of the drug cartels. Why there? Watching the house? Us? Just a heads up."

"And why watching us, in Malibu? Why the veiled threat from the widow? Shit," groused Raymond. "This should have been wrapped up and simple but like so much stuff these days, got tangled up with a cartel or two." He ran a hand over his face. "Let's hope it has nothing to do with my case…No divorce on record. Huh? Interesting."

"Do you trust the widow?"

"I'm trying. I guess we'll see. Want lunch?"

"'Course." They left the office headed for the grill down the block, knowing more dark surprises were likely looming soon.

CHAPTER 43

The week progressed. On Tuesday, Meredith made her usual appearance on *Morning Coffee*, telling some news about celebrities and other Hollywood happenings, discussing on-going local events with the two other members of the casual panel, and watching Cassie closely. She was still worried about her friend and the absence of a husband in what had seemed otherwise to be a grounded life. The two exited the studio to a quick, casual lunch and talk about the changing work environment.

"I know what it will mean in my world," sighed Meredith, biting into a BLT at the nearby diner. "But what about yours?"

"Well, the content of the show stays pretty much the same," Cassie answered, spearing lettuce from a large salad. "But the administration of it changes pretty dramatically. And relationship with the New York show. Russ is still working it out. Lots of threads that stream out from this TV platform—the L.A. station and studio, *Good Day* connection, and then the syndication rights and network to be set up. Complicated."

"You staying on?"

"I hope so. Still a lot of questions to be answered. But if it's produced here—by me. Probably."

"Doing okay, Cassie?" probed Meredith.

The brunette's lips turned up in a wry smile. "Yes, surprisingly. Things are fine—for now. You?" she countered.

"Good," shrugged Meredith. "We have three contractors visiting this week scoping out the expansion of the space under the veranda. We decided to keep the office at home rather than going into an external office. But I shudder to think of the chaos that construction will bring."

"But you're going ahead with it…?"

"Course. Hard to say no to the biggest powerhouse in the media business. And ignore the collapse of UAM's print media connection. There really isn't a better alternative. Russ is still in town, and I'll see him tomorrow with Alan. A social lunch—but nothing's ever totally social with Russ."

"That's true," her friend agreed.

CHAPTER 44

"So we finally got a break, a couple of them," crowed the raspy voice of Sheriff Ted Belin. Raymond, just returning from an appointment, pulled his jacket off, tossed it onto the side chair and sat down at his desk. Tossing his roast beef sandwich, still wrapped up, into his in-basket. "Found an older veterinarian out in Indio who's had a small practice for years—bigger now 'course—but remembers Lindy Fuller, Lindy Odenato. Brought her little dog to him years ago."

"He remembers her?" Raymond intervened, somewhat amazed.

"Says he couldn't help it. She told him about being an actress and that her last film, *Beach Caper* or something like that, was about to play at the Aladdin Theater in Indio the next month. She gave him an autographed picture. Her dog had cut his paw and the vet stitched it up. Lhasa or Chihuahua or something little. Expected them back in a couple of weeks to have the stitches removed but never showed. Tried to call her to follow-up but the number was disconnected." Silence overtook the phone as both men pondered the situation.

"What year?" asked Raymond.

"Hoped you could look that up, being out there in show biz," Belin snuffed a chuckle. "Aladdin closed/burned a few years ago. No real documents about movie schedules that far back. But if the movie was new, I'll bet there's something in Hollywood that says when it was released."

"I'm pretty sure we can dig that out," said Raymond, his mind already figuring where and how to look.

"Oh yeah, and one other thing," the sheriff added with a phlegmy growl. "The guy remembers her saying they were going to visit her family in—I think—it was Wichita—or—maybe Wilmington or Walla Walla—which was why it was so important to get the dog stitched up. She wanted him to board the critter—said he didn't usually do that then, but he gave in, taken with her sweetness and prettiness. Her bein' a movie star and all…."

"But she never showed up again?"

"Nope."

"He meet the kid?"

"Nope. Not with her when she brought the dog in."

Raymond thanked his colleague, hung up, immediately reached for his sandwich, unwrapped it, then snatched up the receiver and punched in Meredith's phone number. He knew she would find the release date of the old film—the newest source in the unraveling of the bothersome mystery.

CHAPTER 45

Lola could hear the remodel chatter taking place under the Malibu house veranda—the space next to her own comfortable studio apartment that boasted of well-secured windows looking out on the beach. Meredith had assured her nothing in her area would change since her small space only occupied a portion of the space under the overhang.

Working in the kitchen, she twisted her long, dark hair into a rough bun at the back of her head and thought about her role-model employer who seemed more stressed than usual. Lola sensed that domestic quiet and privacy had always been inherent in Meredith's life—and that Raymond filled the surrounding air with oxygen. She wondered how she could help alleviate the disarray she knew was en route with the coming changes, and worried that it might be chronic once it started.

Indeed, the household was in constant motion. And indeed, it brought anxiety and confusion to the residents. Meredith held on to the vision—belief—that the new media association would be a long-term one because the current disruptions to their lives were so profound that she couldn't envision the idea of undoing what had been such a burden to set up now and several times before.

With those feelings wrapped around her psyche, Meredith dressed to join Russ and Alan Jaymar at the tony Spago, celebrity restauranteur Wolfgang Puck's flagship eatery, and Alan's favorite. For him, it meant a trip into town from the bucolic retirement farm for senior agent, but he relished the visit.

The sparked ambience of Spago had all three charged, feeling like they were caught in the hurricane of vitalness. And they laughed about it. "Makes me feel important again," snarfed Alan.

"Makes me feel out of it," Russ countered.

"Just makes me hungry," Meredith contributed.

"When aren't you?" from Russ.

Meredith's former adviser and always-adored friend Alan arrived at the meeting tanned, reporting that the cruise taken recently with his partner Potty accomplished all they wanted it to. "It was such a pleasant time and everything Potty wanted it to be…maybe the last mission," he noted nostalgically. "He seems to be letting go—more distant…well, you know." The others could only nod with guarded sympathy. The conversation darted into the various activities, challenges and wiles of everyone until Alan finally stated his iconic position.

"Give me the outline. How's this new endeavor going to work and how will Meredith benefit?" Always the champion of the journalist from her earliest day as "legwomen" to deceased gossip columnist Bettina Grant.

Russ cleared his throat and began the narrative on the new arrangements. Alan nodded occasionally, asked the usual astute inquiries and played with his salad fork. "Will this work for your family?" Alan directed an iron-toned question at Meredith.

She thought for a moment, carefully considering how she would answer. "Well…I have to believe it and make it work, Alan. The connection with *News—NY* is as powerful as it can get, for what I do for a living. Think of it as protecting the investment I—we—have already made in this work, and I mean 'we' as my family, you included. I'm no longer a lone ranger.

Raymond and I have built the life we have as a wholistic partnership—part and parcel of who we are, what we do, how we do it. Riley came into that—not as an independent package functioning on its own. So…" she shrugged. "I think of it like a garden—us—that grows and flourishes because of everything and everyone that adds to the environment around us. The garden grows as it does because of the soil, other vegetation, the insects, the air. When one thing changes, everything changes—if only minutely. Riley has made a big change in our organic garden, but it's still the same garden. Does that make any sense?"

Both men nodded subtly and looked at their now-empty plates. Alan reached over and squeezed Meredith's hand. "Your work mode and choices remind me of those of Bettina Grant," he said, reminding them of the late gossip columnist who had brought them all together decades earlier in her home office.

"And Cassie?" Alan asked after a few minutes during which everyone finished lunch, drinks and made small talk.

"Think we have that worked out," sighed Russ. "A million tentacles involved with a TV show and the fledgling broadcast syndication endeavor. But I think we have it worked through now."

"I hope she's doing fine with the loss of Bob," Alan commented.

"She seems to have the situation corralled, but…." Russ's words tapered off as he signaled for the check. He invited Alan to join the entire group at Meredith's house the next day to finalize all details and make decisions about the facilities and personnel that may change. Alan heartily agreed. It was obvious that he was happy to be back in the game—even for a short time.

CHAPTER 46

Marina Azul Cristalino
Ensenada Mexico

The pleasant day waned over the shores of Ensenada, Mexico, and rows of fishing vessels in the popular marina. A soft orange sun dripped into the horizon. Jaime Odenato climbed aboard his 38-foot fishing boat he used not only to ferry tourists to the rich offshore sporting grounds, but as his office. He descended into the lower deck to close out the day, record income and file paperwork, ready for the process to start over again the next day. He was a slender, medium-built young man, curly dark hair and a slyness to his light cocoa-colored facial features, the combination of a Norte Americano father and deeply native Mexican mother. His revenue and lifestyle were fueled by not only his successful charter fishing business, but his use of it to traffic for the drug cartel that operated along the Baja coast. Jaime's uncle was a chief operative, the entire family heavily vested. Dolores, his mother, one of the organization's powerful doyens.

One customer from Chula Vista, CA, chartered Jaime's boat twice a month. The guest would arrive, a heavy duffle over his shoulder with his gear for a day on the water. He'd leave midday after a few hours on the boat, with a box containing his catch and a much-deflated duffle. Jaime took no other charters on that day and made a bank deposit in the afternoon.

Closing up now, after a full-day charter, Jaime caught the muted shuffle of feet on the dock, climbing quickly onto the boat. He looked around in surprise as he saw three large men standing on the steps to the lower cabin and felt the freeze of fear seizing his spine.

CHAPTER 47

With the help of some digging by Sonia, Raymond was able to call Sheriff Belin with triumphant news. "I think we have a time frame for Lindy Fuller's death!"

"Give it to me," Belin responded enthusiastically. "Maybe we can figure out who owned that house, it might lead us to who might have killed her. Tell me what you found!"

Raymond sat at his desk and pulled out his notes from under the pile of other work. "*Beach Moon Caper* was shot in 1964 but not released until the beginning of 1966. Two other B movies from that studio opened first. *Caper* would have hit Indio probably about the summer of 1966. The vet said the movie was due to open in a couple of weeks after Lindy was in his clinic. That puts the time when she visited him in early 1966. And she disappeared from his records at the same time. Ted, who owned the house then?"

He heard Belin murmuring to himself as the sound of papers shuffling filled the background. After several minutes of grumbling and shuffling, Belin came back. "I have Canyonlight Partners buying the place in early 1964. Finance Inc.—a local group, bought it from auction in 1967. Canyonlight actually owned the place only three years. It was rented after that, it seems, or empty, for a damn long time."

Raymond scratched his nose and searched his own memory as he dug around in his notes. "Canyonlight went bankrupt, and all the principals are gone."

"Well, Odenato married Lindy Fuller in Yuma, Arizona, in February of 1965, must have had a hand in the ownership, although he was in Mexico by late '65, marrying Dolores. Quick turnaround. We have to find out who was involved in Canyonlight. That'll give us more information."

"Nothing else from your show biz snoops?"

Raymond looked out the small window of his office, calculating dates and names and finally answered, "Not yet."

"Well, get to it boy!"

Later, evening tucked in around the house, Raymond watched a small amount of amber liquid swirl languidly in his glass, sniffed the woody fragrance of fine scotch.

"You're mellow tonight," mused Meredith, taking a sip of her Pinot Grigio and curling deeper against him on the patio chaise lounge, the purring cadence of the ocean around them. Moon shining with a celestial embrace above.

"We're finally getting some traction on the Desert Hot Springs body. Nowhere near a solution yet but getting some grist for the investigation mill."

"Mm,' she growled. "Articulate. Not a whine in sight."

"Well, we can hope. We have a time of death range, a marriage certificate giving us a cohabitation range for Odenato. And a couple of inconsistencies. But even though we think we have a light on that path, we still don't know whether Odenato was involved in the murder. He might have been long gone by then—already in Mexico—at least part time and married in late '65. Marty got a call today from his investigation in Miami. Now another, totally different possibility."

He proceeded to explain that Marty's volatile mark, Marcus Ladonna, in Miami, "...is raising loud hell about Marty's digging around in his life. Threatening to sue but no grounds for it. However, in his calls to Marty, Ladonna's threatening the family, Marty's job, and so on."

"Have you guys found anything about him that suggests he was around or involved in Lindy Fuller's death?"

"Well, he was living in Palm Springs area—he can't remember the address but described it as remote and on a hillside—married to an actress, Rachel Moder. Divorced but she's still alive and doesn't recall the address either. Never knew Lindy Fuller. He did have a connection to Odenato. Both in and around Hollywood at the same time, both played tennis at the same racquet club and had a connection to the old Starsystem Studios. But he claims he hasn't seen Odenato since they both left the L.A. area about 1966. Odenato kept a hand, however slight, in his theatrical agency until it was sold in 1970, but only came into his office a couple of times a month. Marcus Ladonna apparently wasn't around at all after he moved in 1966 to Palm Springs then Miami."

"You don't mention Odenato's relationship to your father and his company. Does that concern you? I wonder if it stresses you?"

"Puzzling. But I haven't found anything that links dad's company to the goings on in the desert, nor any association other than professional to Odenato after dad moved to Orange County. From what I can tell, Odenato was only coming into L.A. to work a couple of days a week and then monthly for quite a while as well, and already had established himself in Mexico by the time dad died.

"The deeper stress is my name associated with the murder, itself. I'd like to know why. I was in Vietnam at the time—prior to and after for a long time. No one is suggesting my involvement. Dad was mostly in Laguna and with my mother full time. They both always had a dislike for Palm Springs and I can't remember them traveling there in my adult life."

For a while, only the sound of the surf filled the air, then Raymond spoke up, "And frankly, there seems to be more questions about Marcus Ladonna than Malcolm Odenato. That's a thread we are going to pull and pull. We're still trying to solve the murder and he could easily have been as responsible as Odenato—we just don't have the full picture of connections yet."

"These names sound like an Italian opera: Odenato…" she began to sing softly in cadence, "Donatona, Donahue, Donaldson, Ladonna and Novato…and never forget Trandem!"

CHAPTER 48

Agreements were made and signed the next day at the Malibu house. It was a familiar assemblage with Russ, Alan, Meredith, Sonia, Cassie, an attorney and notary plus Lola watching whenever possible. The July day was sunny and warm. The new phase of operations to begin the first day of September. Raymond was at work dealing with one or another unruly celebrity peccadillo, Riley at preschool.

Once again, the group launched onto a new professional path—the cohesive personalities and skills still the foundation, but new directions leading them on. Meredith reminded the group of their first similar meeting at Bel Air Alan's house nearly ten years before, after Bettina Grant's death. Then the next phase four years ago when their individual stars rose but the glue among them remained in a solidly connected network. And now, an entirely new frame in which to organize themselves. Still their lives and work connected. The cliff and the mountain on which it was located was higher and more solid as *News—New York* became the core.

On Friday, Meredith rose again barely at sunrise and made her way to the TV studio for her usual second weekly appearance on the *Morning Coffee* show. Cassie's car was in the shop and Meredith offered to take her to it after the show, "If you'll ride first with me to pick up Riley at school." A no brainer for Cassie who totally enjoyed her time with the youngster.

"We'll be a little early," Meredith explained, "but that's okay. We'll get a good spot along the curb in front of the school and won't have to wait in the line-up around the corner." She pulled far forward, in first position, along the circular drive in front of the sprawling one-story brick school building, bounded by tall cement walls on both sides. Within minutes, other cars began to take their place along the curb as parents and child-tenders arrived. Meredith and Cassie chatted idly as children filed out of the door on the right side of the building, two teachers within the energetic ranks, keeping watch and making sure each small person found their correct ride.

Riley flounced out the door, curls bouncing, flanked by two other skipping youngsters. As she headed for the curb, about four cars behind where her mother was parked, the door to a dark colored station wagon directly opened and a swarthy tightly built man ran around the front of the car, grabbed a surprised Riley around the waist, lifting and pushing her to passenger side of the car. She screamed, remembering the lectures and practice she'd had about never going anywhere with a stranger or getting into a strange car. She twisted violently but he kept his grasp and carried her awkwardly to his car. She kicked and bucked but he was bigger and stronger and had her almost into the car.

Meredith realized how fast the abduction started, pushing open the door, yelling at Cassie, "911—car phone!" She rounded the bumper sprinting toward the fracas taking place. Meanwhile, Riley, taking advantage of an instant when she could swing her small arm—the one with the metal Star Trek lunch box attached—smacked her attacker in the chin, connecting with an audible thud. He staggered but kept his grasp. She swung and connected loudly again. By then, however, three other mothers had rushed from their cars and were almost on him. It seemed like the attack of killer ants to those watching as the parents protected their nest. And when Maribelle Davis flung herself toward the fray, all five-foot-ten, two hundred and seventy-five pounds of her, there was no contest. She crashed into the man from behind, knocking him sideways, stumbling, as Riley twisted away and ran toward her mother.

As the abductor grasped for his firearm, protruding in back from his waist band, relentless Maribelle fell on him. They both landed on the sidewalk as he grappled for the weapon as it scrabbled next to his leg. But Maribelle simply flipped over and sat on his back, his arm trapped under her foot. Everyone heard the grunts bursting from his lungs. And the police sirens.

Meredith ran to Riley, scooping her up into her arms, hugging her close and working to keep her own panic controlled and tears from falling. Riley was quivering and huffing and hugged her mother fervidly. Then let out a huge sigh. "I think I need more fighting lessons, Mom," she muttered, gulping the air.

The would-be abductor hung his head down, silently insolent, groaning in pain as the officers dragged him to his feet and secured restraints. As he was brought to his feet, insolence gave way to apparent disorientation. To some he seemed a little drunk. While anxiety and seriousness hovered over the front yard of the school, there were still comments of amusement and amazement about Maribelle's heroics. For herself, the hefty woman had brushed off her flowing bright orange tunic, shook out her arms, cricked her neck, and said, "I happened to be at the right place at the right time."

"What was that idiot thinking?" asked one teacher. "He's in a line-up of cars with kids, teachers and adults surging all around. Someone could have been hurt badly, but mostly he seemed impaired. Maybe drunk. He probably couldn't have pulled this off even without Maribelle."

"Yeah but he could've if he'd pulled the gun he had tucked in his waistband," countered a parent. "In that case he would have gotten away with whatever he wanted. Thank God Maribelle moved as fast as she did. He never had a chance."

"Just glad the damn thing didn't go off while I was sittin' on him…it!"

Raymond arrived after statements had been taken from most of the parents and teachers, and they'd driven off. Meredith and Riley sat in the library with two cops, the principal and bottles of soda in front of them, as they wrapped up comments. "He's an illegal," said one of the cops. "He probably wouldn't know how the school exit worked—and he seemed a little out of it, but it could have been a lot worse if he'd gotten to the gun." He shook his head.

"Debrief later?" Raymond proposed. The two agreed and he walked mother and daughter to their car where Cassie waited. "Can you drive them home?" he asked her. "I'll have someone take you back to your car." She nodded.

"Thanks. I'm a little shaken for sure," huffed Meredith, running her hand over Riley's hair. "You can stay for dinner and spend the night if you want, Cass."

"Let's figure that out once we get settled and safe," her friend replied.

"I hit the man in the head, daddy. He yelled, 'owee'. Just like we see on TV," said the earnest barely-four-year-old.

Raymond smiled, reached over and touched her cheek. "You were a hero, Gup!" The tall cop winked at Meredith. "Let's get you on your way and I'm going to go find out what I can about the bad man who bothered you."

CHAPTER 49

The two lawmen slumped over the table in an abandoned interview room at the Santa Monica Police Department, coffee cups and notepads strewn in front. "Not a word," said the local detective. "No comments, no expletives, not even 'Fuck you.' Not even the ever-popular 'lawyer.' I thought he was drunk at first, but once we had him secure, I'd say more like coke addled or worse."

"But I don't doubt he'll be bailed out by morning," sighed Raymond.

"Not a chance. Attempted kidnapping of a four-year-old—in front of about 20 people? I'd make you a bet, but you're biased—you got a kid in the mix."

"So, we only know he's illegal, seems to know his way around L.A.

and is driving a stolen car." The door opened and a young female police officer stepped in thrusting a slip of paper at her colleague.

"And," he crooned, "they've found a piece of a torn McDonalds receipt on the car floor with a phone number in Mexico." Raymond's countenance screwed into a tight scowl as a numbing realization charged his mind. Mexico. Why? He wondered.

"Check it out?" he asked.

"Doing it now. But takes some doing crossing borders."

"How about the license number? Anything on that?"

"Stolen. But it does track to the number you had in your notes on some car that perched in front of your house for a while." Raymond's stomach dropped.

"I think I know where that number goes," he murmured. He wrote down two names on his pad, tore off the page and handed it over. "Have someone check that out and let me know what you find," he instructed in a bark, standing up quickly, heading to the door. "I need to get home."

"Sure 'nuff boss man," his colleague mused, rising as well, leaving the room.

"And I trusted her. Stupid and naïve." Raymond muttered as he made his way through the building out to his car.

CHAPTER 50

"Couldn't have been anything I'm working on," Meredith insisted as she, Cassie and Raymond huddled at the kitchen table sorting through the facts they'd assembled about the kidnap attempt. Riley had fallen asleep in a thick, soft upholstered living room chair surrounded by stuffed animals and small metal cars. Paco the cat watched from atop the refrigerator. Lola had retreated to her lower quarters, and pizza was heating up in the oven.

"It's not you, Merri," sighed Raymond. "It's all me. I stuck my finger in a hornets' nest and erroneously thought the hornets were on vacation." He shook his head in disgust.

"It's usually one of you," chuckled Cassie. "Russ always said Meredith had the innate ability to stumble into kerfuffles. Now, Raymond, it looks like you've adopted the trait—by osmosis?"

Meredith bit her lip and held her comments. She wanted to say her instincts—which were so often accurate—had screamed that the trip to Mexico was dangerous, from the start.

"It's all unnecessary. I met with the glamorous Mexican doyen about ownership of an old house in the U.S. twenty or thirty years ago. She had a total out. She wasn't around and her husband who we were asking about has been gone for several years. Somehow, she took that as a threat to something."

The rich aroma of pizza wafted from the kitchen and Meredith rose, followed by Cassie, to see to dinner. Raymond quietly slipped into his private office and called Reuben. The furtive DEA agent was working the perimeter of a movie somewhere along the California-Mexico border and spoke in quiet but attentive tones.

"You're sure this attempt was initiated from Ensenada—from Dolores? Really?"

"Yep. People with better sources than I only took a few minutes to track the number on the crumpled scrap of paper we found discarded in the car. The would-be snatcher was such an inept foot-soldier. He won't have a nice future—whether it's here with the Border people, or Mexico with his employer."

"You may have spooked the widow with a question about a possible existence of another child by Odenato."

"Maybe she thinks ownership of whatever money or land Malcom Odenato left behind is subject to question. Maybe she worries Jaime isn't the rightful recipient of any trust funds or…that there's another offspring legally deserving?" The two voices were silent in thought for a moment. "Seems like a stretch."

"Let me make some inquiries. I have some deep-soil resources. I'll get back to you." Reuben hung up abruptly—disappearing as he usually did.

Pizza was devoured appreciatively but with more somber tones than usual. Riley awakened and came to the table sleepily. The afternoon's event had super-charged her for a while, but eventually the balloon of adrenalin fizzled and she could hardly get through dinner. Meredith walked her to the bedroom before the rest left the table— "…even before ice cream!" Soon after, with chocolate still rimming her mouth, Cassie heard the "honk" of the friend's car who was giving her a ride home. She hugged her two hosts and left.

Meredith wiped down the table as Raymond loaded the dishwasher. They cautiously took glasses of wine out to sip on the patio, both aware that although there was a police car sitting protectively in front of the house, nothing safeguarded them from the open sand and ocean.

"It was one thing when one of us dallied into danger," Meredith murmured. "The target was whoever did the dallying. It's another story when an innocent non-dallying short person is involved."

"I'm still mystified that this could have resulted from that truly innocent conversation a couple of weeks ago. I can't imagine what would prompt such a reaction."

"Whatever it was—it's kind of a lesson," she winced.

"Yeah, but for a Hollywood quasi-gossip columnist and a detective who functions mostly as combo law enforcer/handler/PR person for unruly celebrities?"

Meredith set down her glass and reached for his hand, pressing his open palm against her own. The feeling of his flesh was both familiar and comforting. "She's more than an independent third party right now. Riley's a blend of these two DNAs, and subject to whatever personality or behavior nuances they are, or misadventures they undertake. For a while. That's the magic and the miracle—and the mayhem. Also, apparently, the danger."

"Given her feminine DNA, it's no surprise she wants more 'fighting' lessons," he snickered, grasping Meredith's hand and ushering her into the house for the night.

CHAPTER 51

"Yell-er on line one," called Sonia. It was Monday and the activity in Meredith's journalism office was underway. While Sonia researched and wrote her own nationally distributed celebrity Question/Answer column and juggled Meredith's needs, a building contractor was doing the preliminary measurements and planning for the workspace addition. Lola was sorting menu ingredients for the week, and Meredith was editing her back-up singers' story. After the past week's bedlam and its continuing aftermath, she wasn't looking forward to confrontation of any kind. But she picked up the phone.

"This is Meredith."

"What the hell are you trying to do?" came the throaty voice at the other end of the line. Meredith couldn't answer. She didn't know what the question referred to or who the caller was. Silence responded. "Hey, I'm talking to you!"

"First, who am I talking to? And can you be a little better at explaining your question?"

"God you are dense, aren't you? This is Verna and thanks for hanging me and the girls out to dry!"

Meredith phumphered, trying to imagine what Verna was talking about. "Verna, I'm not sure at all what you're referring to," she acknowledged her confusion.

"So you just write stuff you make up. For effect. Or what?"

"Verna, I haven't written or produced a word yet about the

three of you and when I do, it's all positive. Where'd you get any other idea?"

"The police picked up Budge for questioning. We heard it was because of something you'd said."

Meredith suddenly realized what was happening. "Where'd you hear that it came from me?"

"Never mind but they said you told the police Budge snuck out of Jimmy's room the night Ben died and went back to the dressing room."

"No, I haven't talked to the police about anything, nothing. There were discussions and someone—not me—mentioned that fact. I don't know how the police heard of it or what they did with it. Is Budge in custody?"

"Not 'yet' but she can't leave Vegas."

"Did they talk with Jimmy?"

"He's in Japan doing a concert. But they took apart Budge's apartment looking for…evidence, I guess. Had a search warrant."

"Did they find anything?" The sound of profound silence was telling. "Verna?"

"Just her show dress but it's long and flouncy and she probably drug it through whatever—blood and stuff— was left on the floor from Ben's murder."

"Well, wasn't his body in the dressing room all night? Didn't she see him, if his blood was already there? Did she see anyone else who might have beaten him?"

"This is crazy," implored the angry caller.

"You told me no one cared much for Ben. How'd Budge feel about him?"

"No, you don't, writer lady! No more lies!"

"Verna, I haven't written anything yet."

"And believe me—you better not…."

"Or?" Meredith pushed, her heart pounding with unnerved

anticipation. Her answer was the sound of the phone disconnecting. She ran a hand over her mouth as she carefully replaced the receiver. She looked up and saw Sonia standing quietly in the door, eyes wide in question.

Meredith shook her head. "This is our week for punches and piques."

"You always use such big words," sniffed Sonia in jest, knowing none of it was really funny.

"I talked with Sarah," Meredith explained to both Sonia and Raymond later that day. "She says that there's not enough yet to charge Budge but she's 'a person of interest.' They're looking for any kind of witness that might have seen her at the dressing room—coming or going. And maybe the time she was there."

"Where'd they look?" asked Raymond, mentally mapping the layout of the large showroom and its surroundings. "There's more than one way into the backstage and dressing rooms."

"I have to assume they were thorough," shrugged Meredith. "The Vegas police surely know their way around a hotel venue. And, I don't have the clout to call and ask. You might."

Shaking his head vehemently, Raymond said, "Nope. Not my jurisdiction and no reason to introduce discord among cop populations. Besides, you're not a crime reporter Meredith. Remember the agreement." She nodded, acknowledging the pact to be cautious with work that could endanger the family.

"What did Verna mean—that you'd better not write about their group or Budge?" asked Sonia who'd stuck around until Raymond rolled in so the threesome could talk about the situation. It had been a long while since the writing team had been threatened for investigating or writing a story.

Meredith shrugged. "Verna's a hard-ass, kind of a blow-hard, which is why she's so often the spokesperson for the group. I guess I get it—since they've just cut their first independent album and don't need this kind of notoriety."

"I thought there is no such thing as 'bad' publicity?" Sonia commented in a sing-song tone. "And it's been a long time since we worried about a story causing threats. And from Vegas back-up singers, no less!"

"Well, we have security with the unmarked parked in front for now, anyhow," Raymond added thoughtfully, as though checking off a list of necessities. "And speaking of that, Sonia, while it's still daylight, you should get home. Call before you come in in the morning."

"And for you both to know," gulped Meredith, "my article was due this afternoon, I faxed it to the syndicate at 3:30."

"Did you say anything about Budge? Or the murder?" Sonia asked as an aside as she stood up.

"Only generically. You know, the trio is on hiatus while the murder of their mentor's husband is under investigation and, they themselves, have been subject to the usual police probes. Although one of Tanya Meile's colleagues has been charged so far, the official inquiry is on-going but no other arrests have been made yet…so on and so on."

Both Raymond and Sonia cringed. Meredith watched as Sonia collected her gear for the day and said, "Ciao! I'm outta here. God knows what's coming next!" She blew a kiss at them and headed to the door.

"Bye Son-ie," called Riley who focused intently on running her fleet of tiny metal cars around the roadways and track her father had built for her in a corner of the living room.

Raymond looked at Meredith, as if to ask "Why?"

She splayed her hands open and answered, "Because I'm a responsible journalist and I'd be white-washing the truthful story if I left that out." He nodded his head—it wasn't a new response—and went for the scotch bottle.

CHAPTER 52

Marina Azul Cristalino
Ensenada Mexico

Jaime slipped into his floating office well after the sun had set and darkness blanketed all the boats berthed along the rows of docks at the marina. He limped down the steps, aching still from the beating he'd taken a couple of weeks before. His bruises and welts had mostly healed but the deeper damage still reverberated. He unlocked the lower deck door and snapped on the pencil-point light over the portable desk. Now, just returned from his weekly visit to the bank to deposit the package from the California visitor, he opened the small safe under the single bunk, placing in it a thinly stuffed standard number-ten envelope. It was his own permitted percentage from the week's take. Locking the box, he reached in his pocket and pulled out a pack of cigarettes, extracted one and lit it. This was his private domain. Smoking was not permitted at home. And even with his responsibilities and stature as the head of the fishing fleet, smoking wasn't the only restriction levied in his mother's house. He felt squeezed, watched and judged by her and the rest of the powerful family.

"Ola. Que pasa? Good take today, Jaime?" came a low, theatrically melodic voice from the shadows deep in the galley. The young man turned quickly scanning the darkness. He could only decipher a figure sitting on the far back bunk, legs crossed, hands folded in the lap but not an ounce of skin showing anywhere.

"Who are you and what are you doing here?" Jaime blurted and reached for the pistol he kept under the desktop.

"Don't bother," came the reply. "You're already in my sights." There was a subtle Latin lilt to the near-hypnotic voice "All I have to do is pull the trigger. But why?" Jaime's eyes adjusted to the dark corners of the deep cavern under the upper deck. All he could see was a black enshrouded figure—black knit cap pulled down over the head and face, black long-sleeved turtleneck, jeans, black gloves, unremarkable shoes. And a shiny metallic shard of light reflecting off the handgun.

"Yes, why?" Jaime repeated, struggled to control the tremor in his voice. He worried that it was another visit from the enforcers his uncle had sent two weeks before.

"Tsk, Tsk," clicked the voice. "Don't you know not to take on a *captain* of a U.S. police department and expect no consequences?"

"What? What are you talking about?" The fervency of his voice suggested he really did not understand the statement.

"What did you tell mamacita about your beating?"

"That it happened. She couldn't miss it, had to call the medics."

"Who beat you up, Jaime? And why?" The slight glint of steel waved purposefully.

"My uncle's men—I accidentally shorted the cash delivery that week and…."

"That week or every week?" Jaime had no response. "Then how did your mother imagine the attack was directed by the American policeman who visited a few days earlier?"

Jaime shrugged. "Did she?"

"Listen," the voice growled as the tinny sound of a pocket-sized recorder scratched through the darkness. A weepy utterance, short but telling, said "I tried to take the child because Senora Dolores ordered it…I didn't want to. I don't hurt children. But senora said the Americans beat up Jaime. It was retribution, she told…." Hearing the scratchy but clear words, Jaime shuddered.

"That what you told Mama Dolores?" demanded the voice. Jaime stammered but had no words.

"Then here's what's going to happen, m'hijo, you're going to tell your mother the truth—tonight. About Uncle Basil's men and why they beat you. And that you lied to her."

"I cannot do that," Jaime stammered. "Uncle promised he would not tell her if I paid back what I stole. I have—and haven't anything left to pay you off if that's what you're after. She'll be very angry! She'll take very bad actions against me!"

"Better her than me," chortled the voice. "If I do it, you may not live to remember it…and no, I don't want your dinero. I want a little four-year-old child left alone to grow up. And that's up to you!"

Jaime was openly weeping. "You may be writing my death warrant, senor."

"Your mother or me? Want to gamble who loves you best— her or me?" Only the sound of Jaime nervously shifting his body in minute pacing in the small now-black space. "And as soon as you do that—tonight—make yourself and your mama available at the address on the date written on the card I placed on your desk. Wednesday at one o'clock that afternoon. No show, it won't be pleasant. Be very clear: you'll see me again. Or hear me—but not for very long."

"I can't see you now!" Jaime shouted angrily, whirling around dropping low and lunging at the dark specter. But his body struck air and he toppled against the bulkhead. Dragging himself up, he snapped on the overhead light. The small cabin illuminated brightly, but Jaime was the only one present. Even the bunk in the far corner where he'd seen the dark silhouette hadn't a single wrinkle in the cover, suggesting no one had sat there. The trembling young man scaled the few steps to the upper deck and scoured the rest of the boat, the dock and surrounding area. No movement, nothing changed since he'd arrived about thirty minutes before. He went below and snatched a beer from the small refrigerator and pondered his options. The only one viable was his most feared one.

CHAPTER 53

Riley charged out the door, pulling her father by the hand, anxious to get to school on "music day." Raymond complied with feigned enthusiasm, waved to Lola and shut the door. Meredith had left much earlier for her first appearance on the *Morning Coffee* show for the week.

Arriving home after lunch, Riley following closely behind, fumbling with her purse and school bag, Meredith set out to make the afternoon productive. Once settled in the fluffy bed in her room, the little girl went into nap mode immediately. Meredith changed into casual jeans and a sweatshirt and headed down the stairs to the business part of the house. But her attention returned quickly to random thoughts that tumbled through her mind all morning long. Ones she really didn't want to deal with.

A short news release about the murder investigation of Tanya's Meile's husband triggered questions. Long-time reporters have a kind of sixth sense about their stories, she reminded herself, and intuition was saying there's more going on in Vegas than was declared publicly. She poured herself a cup of coffee, said "hello" to the workers under the veranda, and Lola studying in her own enclave. Then, sat down at her desk as she pondered the complex layout of the showroom and backstage that Raymond had mentioned, wondering how many unseen ways there were into the dressing room area. Remembered the odd interchange between Verna and Joe Domo whose name had never come up in any of the discussion about the murder even though he was said to be very close to Tanya. And Budge, returning to the dressing room—unobserved—how? A security guard was at the stage door, had returned only a short while before. And the blood spot on Budge's dress?

And she thought about her agreement with Raymond not to meddle where there could be dangerous repercussions to herself. She debated, with herself, the next moves. So, she called Sarah, Sam's girlfriend. "I can't investigate this right now but I have some questions."

"Okay. Ask and let's see where it goes," Sarah answered, puzzled but engaged.

"If Budge went back to the dressing room the night of Ben's murder and the security guard didn't see her, how come? Did she enter through another way? Through the showroom? Last I heard there were no witnesses, only the report she was headed there to pick up a dress. And the police found it—with blood on it."

Sarah muttered her understanding.

"And where has Joe Domo been all along? Isn't he supposed to be so close to Tanya? Is he comforting her? He's like a ghost in the whole discussion. We know he wasn't with the girls when they were with Jimmy in his room that night. Anyone know where he was? These are just disconnected thoughts that I'm passing along. I ask because Verna called me and was livid. She'd heard I was the one who had mentioned Budge's going back to the dressing room."

Sarah hung up with the promise to ask some more questions. Meredith still felt a little cautious about pursuing the Vegas story, but somewhat assuaged that she'd followed up and someone else would be the messenger. No doubt others had those thoughts and questions and had already answered them. But…. Sonia arrived and the two sat down to review the upcoming schedule.

In Raymond's West L.A. office, the detective listened to Reuben's voice crackling in a vacuous echo from his phone deep along the border in Southeastern California. "Tomorrow. One p.m.—Coastella Restaurant in San Diego. The Widow AND Jaime. And you. I'll be around." Raymond took a hard breath and thought about the possibilities of meeting with the Mexican family doyen. And her protected offspring. How many ways can this go bad? He thought to himself. And am I putting my family at even greater risk.

"It seems smarter to have this on the U.S. side of the border. I think this whole issue will resolve itself, T.K.," Reuben had suggested. "I'll have ammo for you—not firearms but video admissions. Let's meet an hour earlier—I'll call later and tell you where."

"I just want to close this book. There's nothing that needs to be done now. And if so, it'll be someone else's problem. I'm just the investigator—not even my jurisdiction."

"See what happens when you do police-type favors for others?" And Reuben hung up.

CHAPTER 54

Chief Bernie Bristow lifted the beer glass to his lips and drank deeply, finishing with a guttural sigh. Sitting in the retro confines of the Los Angeles Men's Club, he set his glass down and stared at Raymond who nursed a tumbler of iced tea. "I just have to walk a block," chuckled the weathered chief.

"I don't," Raymond pushed back. "The I-10 is a mess any time of the day and especially late afternoon."

"And you think I don't know it?" teased Bernie. "Remember, I live in Playa Del Rey now. Every day—Santa Monica Freeway both ways."

Raymond nodded and then grinned at him, "Except those days when you're in my West L.A. office."

"Told you the promotion would cost you," beamed the grey-haired, grey-mustached gentleman. "So, how's it going. What's the update?"

Raymond filled him in on the on-going cases and activities of his division—a veritable pie of "high profile" investigators in several different industries: entertainment (his own), real estate, sports, and others. Bernie chomped on a hamburger and listened carefully, offering comments from time to time. Raymond picked up his own BLT and bit into it at the conclusion of his prepared report, then put down his half-eaten sandwich, wiped his hands and looked intently at Bernie. "I think we need to talk about this Desert Hot Springs homicide. I should recuse myself since it's now become personal, but that's also why I need to stay on it, too."

"You sure about that?"

"Personal or staying on the case?"

"Well, pretty sure if they tried to abduct your kid, it's personal. And it's your personal. But can anyone else parse this case well enough to help the Sheriff down there? Or follow the breadcrumbs left around the situation?"

"I don't think so. But I'm learning where and when to draw lines, but it's becoming harder and harder with my own family in the crosshairs."

"Remind me," said Bristow. Raymond recounted the entire case from the three a.m. call to come to Desert Hot Springs to the meeting with Dolores Odenato to the attempted snatch of Riley. Bristow wagged his head. "Should'a left the situation down south to the Mexican police."

"There wasn't a need," countered Raymond. "We weren't investigating anything but a chronology for Odenato's time in the desert with Fuller, the actress. Not even a mention of the homicide. There was nothing said or inferred that his life with Dolores—or his son with her, Jaime—had anything at all to do with the one fact we were trying to establish."

"But she assumed there was more? Another kid who might be an heir to...what? Fishing boats? The money? And she ordered the idiot to take Riley for...? What? Get you off Jaime's back?"

"That's the only link we can come up with. Now, there's a face-to-face with Dolores in San Diego on tomorrow. On U.S. ground. I have the whacked-out abductor's recorded mini-statement that she ordered the grab. All he said."

"What do you hope will result from this?"

"She'll drop the whole thing. But how she ever got any idea we were actually threatening her domain or that it was the point of the original meeting, or that I had done anything to violate the agreement we had at the end of that session, I don't know."

"You need back-up. I'll call folks in San Diego."

Raymond anxiously shook his head. "No. I have backup. I need clarity. A swarm of American law enforcement won't make this discussion any more candid than keeping it personal. With a recorder…."

"…and the ghost man for backup. And here he is again," snickered Bernie at his lunch partner. "Well, son, you'll have backup—as undetectable as the ghost man but also probably closer. Just in case, but keep me updated— and don't contradict me. You know better."

"Don't call me son. I'm too old to be your son, Bernie."

CHAPTER 55

Raymond stood up at the kitchen counter working on a hasty breakfast before heading out. He buttered a bagel, took a deep gulp of a thick protein shake, and finished off the truncated meal with several big gulps of tepid coffee.

"Remember that Friday we have that fancy network dinner—honoring their returning series stars for the new TV season," Meredith reminded him. "Black suit or tux. Your choice." Raymond cringed, then shook his head.

"Be careful?" Meredith eyed him from the lunch she was preparing for Riley. "Want a lunch sack to take along?"

"Yes and no," he answered as he collected his jacket, brief case and made sure he had the small transmitting recorder. "I'm covered. Between Reuben and Bernie...."

"...but are you carrying?" she persisted. He nodded, holding up the shoulder holster that he'd strap on once he arrived in San Diego. He turned to her, smiled a little distantly, touched her cheek, and then left. She watched the kitchen door close, stood without moving for a moment until she heard the garage door lift and then retreat. These days, she always felt a small sinking loss whenever Raymond headed out to case work. Especially this journey. She understood well the ramifications of the various outcomes. And they frightened her. And was reminded how difficult it was for either of them to live up to the agreement they'd made to exercise caution in their work.

She dressed to take Riley to school—followed even now by an unmarked PD car—and then to MGM for a sit-down interview with a TV series star. Her columns for the week were already filed to New York and Sonia would soon arrive to follow-up on any errant detail and to work on her own column. An easy, simple day with an interview, then lunch with Gloria and an afternoon workout at the fitness center while Riley was home with Lola. It was one of those rare days light with work and deadlines.

But the activity taking place with Raymond in San Diego was not far from the journalist's mind, heart, and emotions. This whole thing is like a scene out of a very bad movie, she told herself. There's some kind of compulsion pushing him forward on this old murder and when all is said and done, it'll probably be nothing concerning Raymond after all. She hoped. She took a deep breath and started the day.

Later, at the small bistro near Gloria's office, the two friends leaned in over the small, white-clothed table. "You gonna be okay?" asked the well-appointed dark-haired lawyer Meredith had known for decades. "This Mexico thing isn't something that's going to follow your family around for years, is it?"

"Hope not," answered Meredith. "Can't help but wonder how Raymond's name scribbled on a piece of paper on a twenty-five-something-year-old dead body has opened up the gates of hell. And it's possible that the freaky family south of the border isn't even involved in the situation."

"Well, I think all of our instincts that say, 'there are no coincidences,' can't be far off."

"M-hm." Meredith agreed. "Doesn't mean we like it."

"So, what's with Cassie? She doing all right? She going to come out of this transformation to *News—NY* well?"

"I think 'yes' to it all," said Meredith, chewing on a piece of lettuce, "because Cassie is so driven and confident. But this has been chaotic for her. Marriage disintegrating, job morphing, new infrastructure and requirements. And Ito. Once he arrives and is installed in her new offices at the studio, I think she'll have a lot more support and a landing zone."

"Where's Ito going to live?" Gloria inquired of the slight numbers-smart Japanese man who had been such a part of their lives for a decade. "Back to Venice Beach?"

"Nope. He'll stay with Cassie for the short term while he finds a place. He's thinking of either Hermosa or Manhattan Beach or the Hollywood Hills. Driving—commuting—isn't something he's done for the past few years. The beach is about twice as far as the hills, but he loves the water."

"Well, he still has Bettina's old Jag, doesn't he?"

"Yeah, and the repairs for an old car and the poor gas mileage it gets!" They both laughed.

"But Cassie," Gloria picked up the conversation. "She must be lonely and grieving."

"For sure," said Meredith, "but she has someone else to absorb the time, she says." Gloria looked over quizzically. Meredith shrugged. "I have some suspicions but no evidence...."

"Anyone I know?"

"Maybe."

CHAPTER 56

The line to the car rental counter was short and Raymond studied every face, plus gazed outside of the rental center wondering if he would find Reuben. He didn't see anyone familiar and hoped his backup was nearby. He also wondered if the widow Odenato would actually show up.

He strapped on his shoulder holster, slipped in his firearm having retrieved it from the carry requirements of the authorities, shrugged into his jacket, adjusting his visible silhouette. Then started the car and followed the stream of cars leaving the airport. Arriving at the restaurant, perched elegantly over the water on Harbor Island a few minutes' drive from the airport, he questioned his own decision leaving the car with the valet, but wanted to make sure he was on time. He took a number of deep breaths as he adjusted his posture and walked tall and confidently through the restaurant and out to the terrace.

Hair loosened and tumbling around her sharply structured but attractive face, Dolores stood up. She wore white soft silk flowing trousers and a soft lavender silk long-sleeved blouse. She looked directly at Raymond and extended her hand. Son Jaime, sitting at the table stood up as well, clumsily and with hesitancy, his hands in his pockets.

"Senora," said Raymond his hand out, with confidence, disallowing any idea of trepidation.

"Dolores," she corrected him, with a seeming flirtatious smile. "Good to see you, Captain."

"T.K.," he said, following her lead, and sat down. A wait person arrived and asked what he'd like to drink or eat. He asked for coffee and settled into the chair, reaching easily into his cargo pants pocket to snap on the transmitter/recorder, the dramatic skyscape of San Diego city spread out across the bay behind him. He looked at Dolores, his face flat, devoid of emotion or movement. It was her move.

"I believe I might owe you an apology," she spoke up boldly with no intended demurring.

"I think we know what prompted this meeting. My four-year-old certainly does. But maybe you can enlighten me on why that happened?" He glanced purposefully at Jaime.

"Miscommunication," said the elegant woman.

"Was there something you wanted to communicate to me— about our previous conversation. Maybe Mr. Odenato's past life? Children? I'm totally puzzled. None of that was intended for anything other than trying to identify any former owners of an old house in the California Desert. And for that—you hire an assassin to kidnap a four-year-old girl?"

"My sincere apologies, T.K. I stand by my word and I stood by my agreement. But well, Jaime why don't you explain to us why the little girl was terrorized as was her entire school and family."

The young man looked down at his hands, and seemed to pale as attention shifted to him. Raymond noticed several other diners on the terrace. None looked his way but any could be law enforcement. He focused on the reticent Jaime.

"Start at the beginning," his mother instructed with a tone that suggested there wasn't another option.

"I like to bet on the dogs—the greyhounds— at the Tijuana track," Jaime began in a small voice, clearing his throat after the first statement. "I am not a very good gambler and lost more than I could cover." He again cleared his throat. Dolores' stylish fingernails silently tapped the table. "I take the proceeds from the fishing charters to the bank each week and shorted the amount to cover my debts. My uncle's money. I thought I could pay it back before he noticed it."

"He was wrong," interjected Dolores.

"It was a lot of money. One night a few weeks ago, uncle's soldiers came to see me. They beat me up and since then I have had to scrap around to repay him. But I didn't want to tell my mother what I had done." The young shoulders were hunched forward and the boy was mildly shaking. "So, when I got home and was so badly bruised and beaten, I told her you had sent someone to silence us." He stopped speaking and stared at his hands.

"And I believed him," sighed Dolores. "I was the fool. He's only twenty-three and I had bigger confidence in his ability to maturely run his operation. His life. Obviously, I was wrong."

"And you unleashed Roberto, the drug-addled kidnapper? And to what end? What did you plan to do with my daughter?" countered Raymond, tamping down his growing fury.

"There was never any intention to harm her. Just send a message to you over what I assumed was the assault on Jaime we believed you instigated. We intended to release her safely two blocks away in the large shopping center."

"You've heard how badly that went?" Raymond said, his distrust of her words still burning the back of his throat.

"Oh yes. We've seen videos. Apparently one of the parents had a video camera poised to shoot their child coming down the steps. It's all over the air waves. Wherever Roberto is now, between the U.S. and Mexican authorities, he'll never see the light of day," she vowed, her tongue clicking. She reached into her bag and pulled a thick manila envelope, pushing it toward

Raymond. "For all the trouble and trauma for you and your family." He could see it was stuffed with bills of large denomination. Without a breath, he pushed it back.

"Money won't make up for the distress or trauma. Our family will handle that. It's what a good family does. Money can't buy forgetfulness or forgiveness of the four-year-old or for that matter, her mother. But worse, for me, is the sense of disappointment and surprise that comes with the now forced distrust of someone who seemed trustworthy and honest and assured me of her best intentions. What should I do about that?"

Dolores started intently at him and said, 'You understand that she is deeply sorry, that she owes you whenever you might need her, and that the perpetrator of this ruse will be punished. As you Americans say, 'you can take that to the bank.'" Jaime looked down and hunched further forward onto his arms, scant tears brimming in his eyes. He quickly blotted them with a napkin.

Dolores looked up regally and said, "Would you like some lunch T.K.? Jaime, why don't you go home." Two patrons from the bar appeared and stood next to Jaime as he rose from the chair. They left quickly without a word. Raymond pondered the invitation and decided it was time to fold the tent. He shook his head and pointed at his watch.

"So, we still have our deal? And you'll make certain those around you will honor it?" he asked. She nodded and offered her hand in agreement. He took it with a subtle shake then turned to leave. A few steps away, she called to him, "T.K.!" He turned.

"The wide woman. Heavy-set. In the orange fluffy blouse at the school?" she called.

"Maribelle," he murmured.

"Tell her if she wants a job, to call me." Dolores winked.

"She has one," he called back. "She has five kids."

CHAPTER 57

The TV set in the family room clattered away with a kid's cartoon show as Raymond sunk into his recliner and dropped his head back with a sigh, a glass of scotch in his hand. Meredith kept an eye toward the family room but focused on the exhausted detective. "Reuben?" she asked.

"Popped up from the back seat of the rental five minutes after I was in it headed to the airport. Heard it all, told me, 'well played.'"

"And how are you feeling about it, besides wiped out?"

"I think fine. I think it's over. Amazing what a stupid unthinking kid can do. But the fact that she made him confess to me and is punishing him, especially for making her out to be a liar and cheat, is promising. No doubt the kid's powerful uncle has a hand in this as well. Dolores grumbled something like, 'Jaime will be working in the cannery now. Where we can keep an eye on him.' Poor guy."

"What's the old saying, 'trust but verify,'" murmured Meredith, still doubtful whether to trust the situation.

"We'll keep the unmarked outside and on Riley and you for another week," he said.

The unmarked stayed around until the network's series kick-off party on Friday evening. Meredith wondered what the two officers thought when the couple, dressed in fashionable party wear, piled into a limousine waiting at their door.

"Think they're snickering?" asked Raymond, wrapped in a striking black Armani suit instead of a tuxedo, and fidgeting with his black silk tie. Meredith slid into the luxury car, adjusting her soft aqua calf-length sheath, simplicity in design and color rich against her copper blonde hair.

"I'll bet they're salivating—wishing they were going with us."

"They kind of are—going with us," he smiled.

When the sleek elegant car pulled up to the entrance to the Beverly Hilton, what Raymond considered a typical charade began: Meredith wending her way through clumps and gaggles of well-dressed TV people—network executives, producers, series stars, publicists. She knew many of them and comfortably stopped to chat with them. Raymond trailed along for a while, shaking a hand, accepting the introductions Meredith offered about him. After a while, he spotted a quiet corner near the expansive buffet table which he slid against, behind the array of foods waiting for the celebrity crowd to devour.

He leaned against the wall and watched the crowd unravel from being stiff and overly-aware of their own importance to settling into the conversant chatter of colleagues and working friends. As always, his glance fell on Meredith by whom he always felt amazed. Striking, confident, laughing, and incredibly hot. Well, to him, anyhow.

"Hello. Can I serve you something?" a raspy throaty voice pulled him out of his reverie. Standing in front of him was a staunchly built middle-aged woman, bright red-orange hair, a black and white caftan and a total sense of control. "I'm the caterer, Madge Meecham," she explained but then looked at him and squeezed her eyes. "Do I know you?" she asked.

He stared at her for a moment and then chuckled. "Other than the worse come-on line I've heard…yes, I was on the scene when the columnist 'broke and entered' your property. Looking for the former resident's passport? T.K. Raymond," he smiled, offering his hand.

"Oh, my gawd, yes! Of course. I call that episode 'Harold's folly.'" Her grip was firm and thick.

"I didn't know you ran these kinds of catering…" he stopped for a moment, something eking its way out of the back of his mind. "Madge…we've been trying to reach you, but didn't know there was a connection to your house up on Bright Leaf Lane and your catering business…."

"I was away for about a month and still haven't caught up with all the backlog yet. Sorry to be so slow to respond. What can I do for you?"

"We're trying to track down some information on an actress who we think you knew in the early days in movies. Lindy Fuller? Someone told us you two were roommates?"

The apple-cheeked face under its barrage of red hair blossomed into a huge smile. "Oh, my gawd," exploded the expressive woman. "Yes! Three of us lived in a one-bedroom apartment in Hollywood in those days! Lindy was sweet as apple cider and so caring. But not too smart, loved to party and none of us were very good actors. We did those three bad movies but nothing ever again. I started my own business. Our other roomy became a paralegal. Lindy didn't need to. She fell into a sugar daddy relationship—big muckety muck studio chief or producer or something. He rented her a penthouse apartment in some high rise somewhere in L.A."

"Who was he? Do you remember?" Raymond asked, focusing in on the conversation.

Madge shook her head. "She wouldn't tell us. Said it was a secret just for 'now,' probably married. We never did find out. But I think he finally married Lindy and at some point, moved to Palm Springs or some place around there."

"We're just tracking down ownership of an old house in the Desert Hot Springs—a few miles away from Palm Springs. I tried to find a marriage certificate but couldn't locate one."

"Well, Fuller wasn't her real name. She was…oh my what was that name…Lynn…Freeman? Fielder?" Madge walked around the table in thought, checking on the food display, then rushed back over. "Lynn Feeley—when she arrived in L.A. We used to laugh about how suggestive it was. She changed it for the studio. Wanted a stronger name for the screen. Her marriage license was probably under that name."

"Did you ever hear that she had a child?"

The electric red hair swished side to side. "We never heard anything else about her. I guess whoever her mogul was, he closed off her past."

"Any idea where she was from? Her hometown?"

Again, Madge screwed up her face in thought, reached down and picked up a gherkin, crunching it in her teeth. "Wichita. She used to sing this silly little song about Wichita! She was cute and funny if not too bright or maybe just too trusting." She stopped and thought again. "Lynn Feeley is not her real name either—I mean her maiden name. She was apparently married for a VERY short time in Wichita and kept his name—Feeley. I don't know what her maiden name is."

"Madge, you're terrific. Thank you. What you've told me is a big help."

"Then you can continue to stand there, leaning against the wall, looking like Gregory Peck or James Bond—and adding great flair to our table."

He laughed and immediately looked to Meredith to see whether she might be ready to leave. But the food laid out on the table did look good. Following Madge's lead, he reached down and picked up a gherkin. He motioned to Meredith that he was ready to leave if she was. She apparently was not, so he stood up very straight again and posed against the wall. No one ever told him before that he reminded them of Gregory Peck or James Bond.

CHAPTER 58

The fax machine whirred against the quiet of early morning at the beach. Raymond was sending to Ted Belin the information he'd garnered the night before about Lindy Fuller's names. He asked that the sheriff check county records for anything under the name of Lynn Feeley. As he wrapped up the project and put his home desk in order, he heard the clatter of Saturday morning coming from the kitchen.

"Eat your breakfast, Riley. Aunt Gloria and Trey will be here in a little while, and we want to clean up your room before you leave, don't we?" "Combination whines and chattering debate responded to Meredith's commands.

"Where are you all headed?" asked Raymond, pouring a cup of coffee.

"Riley is going to the Griffith Park Zoo with Gloria and Trey and another friend from Riley's school." Meredith poured the thick orange mass of a fruited smoothie into two glasses and handed one to Raymond,

"And that'll certainly give you a calm break from the day-to-day world," he chuckled with sarcasm.

"Oh, I'm not going. We decided this will be a good field test to see how it goes without me. Riley has stayed with Gloria and Trey before and does fine. And, she's been begging to see the zoo."

Raymond's skeptical look didn't need words, but he spoke up. "Want me to go?"

Shaking her head, Meredith said, "Has to happen, sooner or later, Raymond. Worse case, we drive over and pick her up. But I don't anticipate that."

"If you say so," he muttered. "I'm going to have breakfast then take an achingly long run on the beach. I'm overdue."

"And once this ragamuffin heads out on her safari, I'm off to the fitness center for a strenuous aerobics class and maybe some weights."

Returning from his strenuous beach workout, Raymond took in the stillness and calm of the house as he came through the garage door. No voices, clatter, sound of numerous bodies moving around on three levels. Lola was away for the weekend, Riley with the animals at the zoo, and Meredith working out the tension knots in her muscles to the solid beat on the fitness center's aerobic dance floor.

So, a still house. He reveled in it. It reminded him of the years spent in the cocoon of Meredith's former townhouse in Brentwood. There, small sliding glass doors gave scant views of the thick, surrounding trees and foliage. A contrast to today's bright and sunny wall-to-wall vistas to the ocean. But those were days of pure quiet, intimacy and self-focus. Wow, what a change, he thought to himself. Will, his son, and girlfriend Sophie, then married and produced Raymond's grandson Kit. Then, Riley arrived. The larger house on the beach became central headquarters for every branch of the Raymond-Ogden life. Including people, employees, and even contractors now. He reminded himself that over-fifty was the time of peak manhood. He winced and thought of the added responsibility he now held, but with it came the added joy and pleasure that responsibility brought to his life these days.

He stripped his running shorts and t-shirt off, dumped them into the bag in the laundry room, took a moment to enjoy the rare privacy around him. Imagine being in the living room stark naked!

He made his way up the stairs and into the shower—happy of its open design with no doors or curtains. The sting of the spray refreshed his body, sticky and worn after a two-hour run. He languished in the numbness of it, going meditative. His ennui was subtly interrupted by a set of fingertips gently kneading his back, moving around to his chest. Fingertips and a firm touch he recognized so well. The touch moved lazily down his chest as he turned to the woman to whom the hands, arms and alluring body belonged. Meredith smiled wickedly, then focused with a slow grin on continuing the journey with her hands—meandering down his chest, over his stomach and into velvet exploration beyond. He settled into the knowledge of what the afternoon would look like—just before he totally surrendered to that reality.

Pressed against her body, water still spraying down, he looked into the grinning face. "Sneaky," he murmured, almost gasping. She nodded grinning. Then he straightened up, doused himself quickly, took her by the shoulders and turned her out of the shower. "Game on," he whispered urgently pushing her toward the bedroom.

"Quid Pro Quo?" she asked.

"Of course," he said as they fell onto the king-sized bed, grappling with each other hardly before landing, Raymond already reaching to make good on his quid pro quo promise.

"Yay," she whimpered.

Meredith lifted herself onto an elbow, extricating herself from the jumble of pillows, covers and Raymond. Shaking the sleep from her eyes, she squinted at the clock on the nightstand and gasped. "Oh no! It's after three. Riley and Gloria will be here any minute. God, where'd the afternoon go?"

"I can tell you," yawned Raymond, but she was already off the passion pyre and headed into the shower. Less than two minutes later, she was back pulling on underwear, shorts and a t-shirt.

"That's too bad," sighed Raymond.

She glanced at him, smiled broadly and said, "Get up. Your daughter will be home shortly, and I don't think she needs to see her dad unflagrant." He followed instructions while she straightened up the bedroom which was showing all the evidence of reckless debauchery.

Downstairs they pulled out a package of crackers and a giant round of cheddar, munching greedily, and drinking rich chardonnay from overly-large goblets which some studio had gifted Meredith promoting something she couldn't remember. They'd missed lunch. "Been a long time since we had a household to ourselves and our own depraved needs," he laughed. "Takes me back to…well, a while ago." Paco the cat sprawled on the top of the fridge and eyed them languorously.

"We should do that more often," she mused as the front door opened with a clatter and flourish and the zoo-stragglers marched in.

"Is there more wine?" asked a weary-looking Gloria.

CHAPTER 59

Monday morning Raymond was in his office early, placing a call to a contact in the Wichita, Kansas, police department. "Looking for anything you can find on a Lynn Feeley, or Lindy Fuller. Marriage license, driver's license…." The officer at the other end of the line was rattling paper and humming out loud.

"All these years, T.K. and you're still beating the bushes for perps."

"Not perps. Trying to tie down an ID on some property out here. Tracking down an old actress. But names are tough to come by after so many years. We're told she married someone in Wichita, her hometown, named Feeley, then divorced him before running off to Hollywood."

"Sounds intriguing. Let me see what I can find out. Call you back."

Out came the white board and Raymond set about organizing the new timeline:

February 1965—Lindy Fuller and Malcom Odenato
marry in Yuma Arizona

February 1964—House in PS bought by
Canyonlight Partners—Odenato a partner?

New Year's Eve 1965—Odenato marries Dolores in
Mexico City

March-June 1966—Lindy Fuller disappears from desert

1966-68—Odenato part-time with L.A. agency—per Dolores

1970—Business sold. Odenato full time Mexico—Ensenada

Marty wandered into his former-partner-now-boss's office, hands shoved into his pockets, and gazed at the timeline. "Still chasing down the actress?"

Raymond muttered, "Yeah but she's elusive. We know a lot about her except who killed her and when and where'd the kid go?"

"Sure there was a kid?"

"Pretty. The vet in the dessert says he saw him or her. So did one of the neighbors."

"Wasn't killed and buried someplace else?"

"Could've been. But we've no line on the child anywhere. Not even a birth certificate."

"Take a break? Lunch?" Raymond stood up and said, "Good idea."

The break became an all-day issue when a sports agent with too much lunchtime imbibing punched out a parking attendant at a tony restaurant and the two high profile officers were called in for VIP help.

Raymond headed home and the end of the day without a cursory glance at his inbox—or the fax from Ted Belin waiting for him there.

Meredith was wrapping up her own desk as he arrived. Riley watching a video about horses and waved at Raymond as he entered. He went into the family area and picked her up, struggling with how big she had gotten. "Pretty soon you'll have to teach me how to punch and defend myself," he joked.

"Oh, dad. I haven't had my fighting lessons yet!" He winced.

"Please don't encourage her," Meredith growled, but thinking in contrast that it would be good for all young girls to know how to defend themselves.

Raymond smiled thinking about how much the two females were alike. "What are you working on today?" he asked Meredith.

"The movie locations article. I researched it a while ago and have been holding the material. But it'll make a good interim piece if this office thing gets too intrusive and I can't get something out one day." She stacked the paperwork on the desk, shuffling through old and yellowed clippings and a couple of wrinkled ancient photos.

"What're those?" he asked.

"Just some discarded stuff from the retro apartment building in Hollywood—The Majestic—where they were shooting that movie a few weeks ago. This stuff apparently slipped into crevices and under cabinets over the years. They found it as they renovated not long ago. Almost threw it out but held on to it, thought it might be useful for my article. Probably not, no one I recognize, but nice to have it as a reference."

"How about I put on the grill?" he asked, "and we have a martini?"

"Up for it," Meredith agreed, closing down her office for the day.

CHAPTER 60

"Whoa! Tell me again," Raymond spoke energetically into his phone, making his way around the desk to sit down. He picked up a pencil and his notebook.

"Marriage license. Lynn Marie Oakley to Gerald Feeley. Wichita 1960. She was eighteen. He, twenty-five. Divorce decree one year later. Quick trip through marital bliss, I'd say."

"I'll say," retorted Raymond to his colleague in Kansas. But his mind was reeling. "Any address on the bride or any idea whether Oakleys are still around?"

"I can check it. Call you back."

"Thanks," mumbled Raymond, his mind fixed on the name Oakley. Immediately he began to work out a trip to Wichita—he shuddered—to find out more about this woman. He asked himself why, after all these years, he should care about a cold case homicide that probably had no solution to the murderer. But, he realized again, his name was with her when she died. As was someone named Tad Oakley. What, he wondered was the connection?

He called out to his administrative assistant, Roberta, and asked her to check air schedules into Wichita, Kansas. Then he phoned Chief Bernie Bristow, his own boss. "I need some time away to follow-up a lead on that murder in the desert." He heard Bernie chuckle.

"Tell me more," said the venerable Chief. Raymond explained the entire set of details that had come in so far. He outlined the timelines and explained, "I don't see a right way to follow-up on this except in person."

"It's your case. Go after it, T.K. But keep me in the loop." The permission struck him with slight trepidation. He wondered what he would find in Wichita and if whatever or whoever might be at the heart of it had any idea the fate of the young woman.

For two hours, he set about organizing the projects and issues on his desk and being dealt with in the office. As he was packing up his briefcase to leave, Sheriff Ted Belin from the desert called him, "I'm on the road to Oregon for a few days R&R, but my gal at county records is faxing you a copy of a birth certificate that might be important. She thought maybe. Should be along shortly." Raymond heard the fax rattling outside his door, and as he packed up his briefcase, he picked up the several current contents of his inbox, and the fax—now lodged in the background of his mind. He shoved them all into the case and headed to the car and home to pack an overnight bag.

At home, in Meredith's realm, tension hovered over her and Sonia as a slight, nervous, huddled figure wrapped in an oversized grey hoodie, shuddering in her chair. Sonia bustled quickly from the kitchen with a glass of ice water and Meredith squatted next to the trembling figure, holding her hand.

"Sal, what's going on?" the journalist implored. "Why are you here and how did you get here?" She gently pushed back the head covering of the young woman and looked her carefully in the eye. Sonia handed her the glass of water. "I can see you're frightened but you need to tell me why. What we can do to help."

Meredith turned to Sonia and explained, "Sal is one-third of the back-up singer group for Tanya Meile—the group I wrote about a couple of weeks ago." Sonia nodded.

"I didn't know where else to go," sniffed the thin young woman. "You were so fair and complimentary toward all of us I thought you might understand my situation." She was close to tears.

"What situation, Sal? What are you afraid of?"

"Everything," snuffed the vulnerable young woman. She breathed in sharply and began her tale. Hearing the first few words, Sonia slipped out and put a call into Raymond. When he wasn't in his office, she dialed his car phone.

"Raymond, you better get here," she commanded quietly. "We've got a situation and it's way over our heads." Her words shook him immediately. And he asked for more information. When Sonia told him the little bit she knew, he sighed.

"You're right. Do me a favor? Call Marty at the office and ask him to meet me here. This is above all our heads." He hung up, pulled over and phoned Bernie again.

"This isn't a regular celebrity issue and not one in our jurisdiction," responded the Chief. "I'll call Vegas Homicide and get them involved."

"But please be careful," Raymond implored. "This kid apparently believes that if she's discovered, they'll target her. How she ended up seeking out Meredith."

Bernie snorted, "Our Angel of Mercy!" And hung up. Raymond continued his journey home wondering how he was going to juggle competing emergencies. At least Riley wasn't involved this time, nor had Meredith been accused of breaking and entering!

As he entered the house, a serious air hovered over the three people sitting at the kitchen table. Sal Andover, the normally bright and smiling singer, seemed shrunken and spent. Her hoodie now shrugged off, she seemed gaunt and sickly in her terror. As Meredith introduced Raymond and explained how he would help her, the woman seemed to shrink even further into herself.

"This can't be," she murmured. "I can't talk to cops. They'll know and I'll be next."

Raymond spoke calmly and softly, telling her he had no reason to disclose anything to anyone—yet. That they needed to hear the full story and decide the best plan of action—and safety for all involved.

"How did you want me to help?" asked Meredith gently.

"By telling the true story. If it's in the news, someone will have to investigate it," countered Sal.

Meredith, Raymond and Sonia all shook their heads vehemently. "All you're doing is adding one more person—Meredith—to the list of 'their' targets—besides yourself. Let's sort this out," Raymond said. "Start from the beginning."

Sal took a drink of water, folded her hands and began. Tanya Meile was managed and basically controlled by husband Ben. Ben had been approached by several individuals who represented some of the larger music and show production unions who would like to see the resident shows in Vegas using as much production personnel and labor as possible. Tanya did not use large casts of performers. Her shows were mostly around the orchestra, the backup trio—Sal, Verna and Budge— and the solo backup singer Joe Domo. Tanya resisted the pressure. Her shows were stylized to her, suited her fans and centered on her own hits and music. The representatives who approached Ben offered him a great deal of incentive money—upping the show's budget and his and Tanya's salaries. But it also eliminated much of the content that included the backups and Joe Domo.

"Ben and Tanya fought about it all the time. But you know about this, I'm sure," said the young woman. Meredith acknowledged they knew about the changes in the show format but not about the money incentives or reason for Ben's interest in changing formats. "It was about to go down," Sal explained. "We were told that Ben was signing the contract in two days. Well, Joe engineered a coup with…well, us…the girls. We met with Ben and tried to talk with him, but he laughed at us, called us old hacks and to get a new life." She stopped for a minute. "I'm not even old yet."

"That didn't go over well with the group?"

Sal shook her head. "Verna and Joe made a quick-witted decision to stop Ben before he signed the contract. The night we were all meeting with Jimmy, one by one everyone—but me—split off and met under the stage after the staff and crew had left. The security guard was always off smoking with his girlfriend about that time and there was hardly anyone ever left in the show room…."

"What did they think or say about you not joining, Sal?" Meredith asked.

"I said I'd go along but not participate. And never say anything to anyone about it. I'm a good Christian girl and could not, in any kind of good conscience, take part in an actual murder. They all said, 'fine' but swore me to secrecy—OR else…. Joe Domo has a lot of strong Vegas ties to all kinds of organized crime. He's been performing there for years and owns a couple of bars. When he threatens someone, better believe it."

"So, Joe, Verna and Budge all descended on Tanya's dressing room late after she'd left but before Ben did?"

"Budge and I waited in the coffee shop across the street from the hotel. Verna went with Joe who took a tire iron and snuck into the dressing room then left—back the same underground way they had come in. Joe's the one who beat Ben. Budge had to go back because she remembered that her dress was torn and had to be fixed for the next night's show. Someone saw her."

"And Sam the publicist wandered in and out just before it all went down…?"

"And got accused because the security guy saw him leaving late."

"What do we do with this, Raymond? Where does it need to head?"

The detective sat with his chin in his fist for a few minutes and finally answered, "I think the FBI. It's now across state lines and it's bigger than schlepping it to our unit. I can see your concern for bringing in the Vegas cops—but it's a disaster for everyone and needs to be revealed and managed. Otherwise, Sam'll be tried for a murder he didn't commit, Tanya's show will restart but the pressure will never be off her to changes formats. And eventually no one wins." Sal began to cry quietly.

"How will your colleagues feel about your coming here?" Meredith asked gently. Sal shook her head and squeezed her eyes shut. "Sal also needs to be protected," Meredith urged.

"Yes, and she will be," said Raymond. He sighed deeply, hoping Marty could and would run interference on this for him. He had a flight to make in two hours.

Like clockwork, Marty arrived, puzzled but focused. After a half hour of discussions and phone calls, Marty escorted Sal to his unmarked car. She looked terrified but compliant. "We'll get you to a safe place with someone watching over you until this is all laid out with the proper authorities here and in Vegas." The young woman only nodded, looked over her shoulder, questions and hesitancy in her eyes, at Meredith who nodded back at her and said, "We'll keep an eye on you."

The household was silent in thought for a few moments. "And that's how a gossip columnist falls into a dangerous story without trying," sighed Meredith.

"And I have to leave for a flight very shortly to Wichita," shrugged Raymond, worried about the safety of Meredith and her colleagues as well. He would talk discretely with Marty on the way out to make sure there were eyes on the house and its inhabitants—again. Raymond stooped down to pick up the stack of yellowed photos and notes from Meredith's location story which he accidentally knocked off the desk, a vague sense of curiosity and karmic familiarity prompting him to jam them into his briefcase for later perusal. Meredith was staring wide-eyed at him, stunned by his plans and asking, "Why are you going to Wichita?"

"I'm running too late," he deflected. "I'll call you from there tonight and tell you all about it. But if I don't leave right now, I won't make my plane." He'd already dashed upstairs, packed a hurried overnight bag so was ready and out the door before any question delayed departure any further. And before he had to unleash a lot of questions and concern over how the complex daisy chain of details about the dead actress in the Southern California desert was leading him to Wichita, Kansas.

CHAPTER 61

The six hour, one-stop flight from LAX to Wichita wore the detective down to exhaustion, after the frantic scene and emotional interchange with the young singer before he left. He hated rushing out without seeing his daughter or settling the schedule with Meredith. But he had to bring closure to the emotional weightiness of the murdered starlet case. And new information he'd found along the way was debilitatingly unsettling.

How, he wondered could a twenty-five-year old dead body of an actress he'd never heard of, in the wind-swept isolation of the high desert, turn his world so murky. After a night in a roadside motel, he was relieved to get a call in his room just as he was dressing, from his police department contemporary who had offered to help with his investigation. The two met up at a local diner and caught up—on each other's lives and the case at hand.

"I can't promise any of these addresses have any value to your investigation at all," the local cop told Raymond as they finished off breakfasts larger than Raymond ever ate. "Three Oakleys are listed, one isn't spelled exactly the same, one seems to be a young family, the last one is an older guy. But that's all I have."

"I'll start with the older guy," the L.A. detective said. "Everything about this case is old—the body, the story, the house. But I need your discretion, Glen. This whole thing has been shadowed from the start. Who's the girl? Who's the husband? Where's the kid?" He explained the undulating path the investigation had taken. The local cop shuddered when Raymond told of his experiences from Mexico.

"Well, I can tell you that Malcolm Odenato is not listed in any way, any data base or licensure here."

"That's probably to be expected," said a slightly timorous Raymond. The documents he'd read on the plane had shaken him a bit and slightly rerouted his expectations. "Let's roll," he said, dropping some bills on the counter and picking up his case to begin the upcoming probe into an older gentleman's world.

"Call me if you need anything," Glen, the local cop told him as they left. "I mean it. Let me know what's happening."

Following the map he'd been given, Raymond found his way to the quiet, suburban neighborhood where the older Oakley lived. He'd called ahead and the man agreed to meet with him. The house was an older single story reminiscent of so many neighborhoods in smaller towns from the early 1940s and 50s, but well kept up and cheerfully painted white. A simple but nicely manicured yard led up to the front porch and a screen door. When he rang the bell, indeed an older gentleman answered. He was of medium build, slightly square, and probably in his seventies. A mop of greying hair fell slightly over his brow. His face was full and apple-cheeked, his eyes were smiling and his demeanor welcoming. He wore old style horn-rimmed glasses, a blue and yellow plaid sports shirt with wide khaki trousers. Raymond felt relieved and somehow comforted. "Ed Oakley," said his host, extending his hand.

Raymond took it quickly and smiled, "T.K. Raymond."

"Coffee," Ed offered, ushering Raymond into a well-ordered living room with older furniture but immaculately clean and preserved. Raymond accepted the offer and followed him into the kitchen—also reminiscent of 1960s modern but updated appliances.

"Nice house," he commented.

Ed smiled and replied, "My wife Alice was a neatnik. She passed about six years ago and I try to keep the house like she loved it." Back in the living room Raymond saw family photos on every wall, including glamor shots of Lindy Fuller as well as everyday scenes of picnics and holidays. He noticed the inclusion of a younger boy, probably a brother, and then an entire panorama of another boy, seemingly much younger.

"Lynn?" Raymond asked pointing to a glamorous shot of a young woman.

Ed shyly nodded. "She was something. Her mama's pride and joy! A little wild early on, she married a loser right out of high school but we helped her get rid of him within the year. A bad decision, but she went on to Hollywood and made three big movies!"

"I know of them," said Raymond with a certain amount of awe.

"Why are you here again, Mr. Raymond?" Ed smiled as they sat down.

"I'm working with the sheriff in a desert town in Southern California to try to track down ownership of a house there we think Lindy and her husband lived in. A long time ago."

"It must have been," sighed the older man. "She passed so long ago. Broke our hearts." Raymond tamped down his surprise.

"How'd she pass, Ed?"

"Pneumonia. Always had some allergies and apparently the desert sandstorms just plagued her. She caught a bad bronchial infection and they couldn't stop it." The hurt was evident in his eyes and voice even after all these years.

"That must have been so hard. How'd you find out? And what happened then? We understood there was a child."

"Yes. There was. Her husband, Malcolm Odenato, brought her home. He was broken up. Also brought the little boy, Taddie. He was only two at the time." Ed's voice had dropped low and sad. Raymond hated to bring up the tragic past.

"When was that, Ed? And how'd he bring her home?" Raymond kept seeing Lindy Fuller—Lynn Oakley— shriveled in the desert sun from years of hidden burial.

"Oh," he said, pausing to take a drink from the china cup on the table. "She was cremated, and Malcolm came here— November 1966. Never forget it. He brought her ashes in a beautiful copper urn. Small and dainty like she was but lovely bright blue enamel engraving on it. We kept it on the mantle until her mama died a few years ago. Lynnie and her mother were very close, so I buried the urn with Alice." Raymond kept silent, allowing the moment to ground.

"What about Taddie? Did he return to California with Malcolm?"

"No. That's the saddest part of it. Mal said he just couldn't care for the boy. Wasn't equipped with the fatherly impulses needed and was a big-time producer or something like that. He said he would never be able to raise the boy properly. He asked us to please take in the child and raise him as our own. The boy would have a better life." Ed paused in thought, the conversation obviously swelling with memories not visited in a long time.

"That was asking a lot, though, wasn't it?"

"Well, under the circumstances, not really. At the time it was the only right thing to do." Ed furled his brow in the recollection. "Alice and I were both young enough. Our son— Lynnie's brother—Sid was also young enough to help us a little. So, we had to say 'yes.'"

"It must have put a significant financial burden on you—to start over. Did Malcolm offer to help?"

"Oh, more than offer. He had already set up a bank account at a local bank with a lot of money in it for day-to-day support of Tad. And, set up an educational trust for him when it came time for college. Tad was a really smart little guy and by the time he got to university, he had a pretty full ride in math at Stanford in California," Ed's voice swelled with pride. "But the trust fund helped a lot. I was still working, was the local postmaster and Alice was a teacher. So that money helped us give the boy a very good life. Allowed us to retire as we normally would have. All in all, the whole episode—tragic and sad as it was to begin with— turned out to be pretty good." Even Raymond was closed down and drawn in. No one spoke for a few moments. The detective looked around the room at the pictures and the evidence of a stable, contented life. Little league, picnics and school honors— everyone proud, smiling. With the added glamor of Lynn, the actress and outlier in the family.

"Did Malcolm bring the birth certificate for Tad?" Raymond ventured cautiously. Ed rose and went to a cabinet along one wall of the family area. He rummaged around quickly and brought out a file folder, extracting a document.

"Sure did, but sent it a few weeks later. Originally forgot to bring it. You can have a copy if it helps. We kept extras—seemed like someone always needed it." He handed a sheet to Raymond, closed the folder and returned it to the drawer. The detective took a quick glance at the paper and withheld a grimace. It showed the mother as Lindy Fuller, the father Malcolm Odenato, from a small hospital in the San Fernando Valley. Raymond knew it was a phony.

"Ever hear the name Canyonlight Partners," he asked, again with a focused tone of caution and hesitancy.

"Those were the folks who originally set up the trust funds, transferred them into something closer to home here. Malcolm said he was one of the partners."

"Malcolm check in on updates about Tad? Visit?"

That's when sadness set in for Ed. Shook his head. "No. We never saw or heard from him again. He signed off on adoption papers and a name change from Odenato to Oakley. We thought it was easier. Malcolm's California attorney executed whatever needed to be done and paid for the legal services. The last we ever heard."

"Who was the attorney?"

Ed thought for a moment, then recounted a name with which Raymond was familiar. The one they'd seen on the Canyonlight purchase contract for the desert house—the attorney who'd dropped completely out of sight years before.

Raymond nodded subtly, feeling some kind of kinship with Ed. Wondering what life was like growing up in such a traditional grounded household. And feeling guilty because of all the lies and deceit Odenato had perpetrated on the Oakleys and that he, himself, knew the real story. But integrity aside, Raymond decided he didn't want to disrupt the life that had played out and the foundation on which it was built.

Ed offered to refresh the coffee. Raymond accepted and again followed him into the kitchen where they sat at an island counter and talked casually for a while. The detective spoke of his work, his own family, his own two children that spanned multiple decades. Ed laughed and said he could relate. Then said he might be visiting Tad where he worked in a high-tech company in Irvine, California. "I was out there a couple of years ago and maybe I'll go next year." Raymond did a double take. "If you're ever in Orange County, why don't you look him up," Ed suggested. "I'm sure he'd love to meet you. He's a smart boy but a little shy."

"I just might do that, Ed. I feel…grateful and comfortable talking with you. You've been so open and helpful. I'll bet you've been a good dad." The older man blushed a little, slightly embarrassed. "Do you need anything? Will you be okay by yourself?" Raymond persisted.

Ed smiled. "My son Sid already has it worked out. When and if I need taking care of—he's built a little father's suite on his house. I'll move in there." The detective nodded.

As he left, Raymond felt like embracing Ed for the role he'd played in his family's life, but he suspected Ed would never know why the sudden affection. Once in the car, several blocks away, Raymond pulled over and put his head against the steering wheel. Out of Hollywood, away from the cacophony of greed and hype, there were good people. He wondered what it was like growing up in Ed and Alice's world.

Jumbled visions of fatherhood filled his mind, first his own role with Lily, his first wife, deceased long ago, and their son Will. Daughter of working-class parents, a nurse herself, Lilly brought grounding to the young Raymond. His own military service in Vietnam, the birth of their son and then Lily's death when Will was 10 created a rarified and equitable father-son relationship that Raymond had no regrets about. While the photos in his mind weren't as plentiful or poignant as what he saw in Ed's living room, the experiences had been there as Raymond played dual-parental roles—often without cameras. And minimally resurfaced in his fulsome current life.

But his thoughts were strongly jerked back into recollections of his own young years growing up with sophisticated show business parents and as the only child. He thought of the family pictures in the Raymond living room: formal portraits by well-known photographers, a photo here or there at a graduation, one professional shot of himself with Lily and very young Will. He recalled his father's office where only two photos included the young T.K.—one on the lap of a popular actress, Rita Hayworth, the other with his parents and famed director Alfred Hitchcock at the entrance to the legendary Grauman's Theater in Hollywood. The Hollywood of his childhood was a different world, one of a glittering town lined with cabarets—restaurants even drug stores known for being frequented by celebrated faces and names, spotlights circulating over film and club openings. The stuff of the myths—now only myth in today's diminishing town. But hardly remembered by Raymond who seldom saw the glitter.

His mother was always the one who accompanied him to any sports events—little league, swimming, tennis, birthday parties. There were no father-son fishing or camping trips. A few large vacations abroad, graduation days, then some "mature" lunches as T.K. was entering the work world and the elder Raymond was lobbying for and pushing him into the world of high-placed show business agency and management, his father's world. The pressure sure didn't take, he winced, scanning his own background: soldier, law student and lawyer, and finally, cop.

And yet, Raymond recalled how he had revered his father and felt strong love and connection if only in those infrequent times when the elder was present and engaged in the household. And the detective also knew there was something deeper than loyalty between his parents.

Still, his thoughts wandered back to the warmth and simplicity of Ed Oakley's simple Wichita home, and he felt unexpected hot tears trickling down his cheeks. Not just for his own lean father-son relationship, but because he was seeing the tragic truth in front of him, and he wept not only for himself, but for Ed and Alice, Lindy and Tad. Just about everyone involved in the situation.

CHAPTER 62

A marine overcast hung above the retirement residence where Elinor Raymond lived, and her son scowled at the tiny amount of oppressive mist. It was mid-afternoon. Raymond had hurriedly left the Oakey household about ten a.m., rushed to the Wichita airport and found flights to Orange County, California's John Wayne airport. With the earlier time zone on the West Coast, he had time to make the mother visit he could not put off.

He was told by the front desk at the residence center that Elinor had just returned from a group outing to South Coast Plaza, the large fashionista shopping center where the gaggle of senior women had enjoyed a chic lunch and saw a movie. Raymond knew that his mother would be tired, and he hoped that would allow her to be honest and open. Not closed and defensive. Or mentally and emotionally distracted from reality.

"Oh, goodness," she crowed as she opened the door to him. "I didn't know you were coming to visit. Come in. If you'd called, I would have planned lunch or dinner."

As he entered the comfortable unit, he explained, "I didn't know, mom. I was flying in from the Midwest, and I had some time." She fixed iced tea for them both and invited him to sit on the deck. Settled in, he steeled himself for a conversation that he had to have but knew would be difficult.

"Mom. I wanted to talk a little more about the actress we mentioned a while ago—Lindy Fuller." His mother's gaze turned blank and flat.

"I didn't know her," she said "She was in Malcom's life, not ours. They went off and married and I never heard about her again."

"Mom?" Raymond goaded. "Isn't there more to it?"

She looked at him with a steely gaze and said, "No, Tucker. There's not. Not now, not then and not ever. I'm very tired and the girls will be here for brunch any moment." He stared at her, totally nonplused. He realized that she had just left "the girls" and it was late. No one was coming over. He recognized that the always steeled character and presence of this elegant woman was fracturing a little every day. So, he gently nudged the subject a little further, then more.

"But mom," he urged, "any memories of when Malcom married her? Was she involved in his business at all?" he probed hoping to unravel more information. The question ignited thirty minutes of incendiary discourse that went by in a flash, laced with wrath and indignation. Raymond shrunk against the sofa back. He struggled to mentally capture as much of the detail buried in the venom as possible because taking out his pen and notebook would be an afront to his mother's candor.

Then, suddenly, the dignified woman, now shrinking in her exhaustion and sadness, stood up. "Mother? Can I help you with something?" He rose and went to his mother, helped her from her chair and hugged her.

She cried into his shoulder softly. "Don't think about these things. They had nothing to do with us, Tucker. You were always perfect." He wasn't sure his father felt that way, but it was what it was. And he thought again of Ed in Wichita.

He could see she was mentally leaving the current reality. He walked her into her bedroom, held her hand as she lowered herself onto her well-appointed bed, handed her some tissues, and kissed her on the forehead. "I love you mom, I do and I'm grateful how hard you worked to keep me happy and focused." Elinor smiled and closed her eyes, then asked him when Ken was coming home, and was soon snuffing in deep sleep.

Raymond satisfied some vague curiosity and pulled out the photo albums they'd looked at during the visit weeks before and hurriedly thumbed through other documents he could find, none of which were organized or plentiful. A lot of years had passed. Then, he called down to the central residents' station and requested a caregiver, surprised when a young woman arrived at the door only minutes later. He told her his mother had experienced a difficult time just before napping and could she keep an eye on her for a while. She said, "Of course. Elinor does this sometimes. Sleep seems to revive her a lot."

He felt emotionally and mentally disjointed by the Wichita visit as well as his mother's rantings and the story behind them. He desperately wanted to talk it out with Meredith—for his own sanity. But the story wasn't complete yet and he needed closure. He sighed as he headed into the worst rush hour time of the day and in his rented car, doggedly plugged his way home to Malibu.

CHAPTER 63

When Meredith saw him entering from the garage, his eyes darkly circled, ragged countenance and weary stance, she fixed him a scotch, hugged him tightly and sent him to the shower. A few minutes later he arrived in the kitchen looking slightly refreshed, better groomed but still tired. Riley ran to him and hugged his legs. "Where have you been?" she insisted. He sat her on a stool at the counter next to him and chattered for a few minutes, then set her back down to return to her games on the floor. Bedtime was looming and he knew it would not come easily with her renewed energy at seeing him.

"Have you eaten dinner?" Meredith asked. He shook his head. She went to work putting together a reprise of the meal she and Riley had shared earlier. Raymond took Riley to her bedroom, convinced, cajoled and finally corralled the tot into bed, quickly into sleep.

"Fill me in," Meredith said as she placed a plate of pasta and salad on the counter along with a short glass of scotch. "Sounds like a tough two days, but I want—no need—the whole story, Raymond. And you need to tell it."

"Well," he began, clearing his throat first, "the trip was successful—in some ways—but yes, tough." Then he fell silent, not sure where to go next.

"Maybe dinner will help?"

He laughed. "Home helps."

Later, with Riley and Paco tucked solidly away in the lavender room, Raymond settled in on the sofa, Meredith tucked into his side, waiting for his story. He deflected and asked about the Vegas murder case and the young singer, Sal.

"Status quo," Meredith answered with a shrug. "Out of our hands and all I know is that the feds have her in tow and working the situation through. I've been told to stay out of it until there's something to write about. Anything else might jeopardize—well a whole lot of things. You might get more info when you're back in the office. But now tell me what the last two tough days have handed you. You have to admit, I've been patient in the midst of Reuben's involvement and the Mexico dramas, attempted abduction of Riley, Wichita, your very unusual confrontations with your mother…I haven't butted in or made demands about it. It's time to tell me the whole story and why it has you pulled in so many different directions?"

"For many reasons, this is a story with no real ending because the perpetrators—at least of the homicide—are all dead and gone. No one left to punish. Was probably Odenato who pulled the trigger, but well…so much more." He was quiet for a short time then began the whole story, starting from the beginning, in apology explaining, "I need to hear the whole rundown myself," he said. "It gets too complex." He talked about the body in the desert, the struggle to find possible family to Lindy Fuller, husbands, time frames. And how the smallest details—from the vet's recollections to Madge-the-caterer's insight—shed light on the journey to Wichita and the Oakley family he met there. Meredith had heard bits and pieces of the investigation but was hearing the whole chronology for the first time. "I have one last stop to make," Raymond sighed. "And, a report for Belin before…well, it's mostly complete."

The detective was quiet for a while, then spoke up, "I want to know the whole story before I try to tell it. Right now, the details are so sketchy and scattered I can't put them together. And I'm not going to let the tragedy of it cloud the life Ed and Alice gave to Tad in any way. Maybe it started out in loss, deceit and sadness, but what resulted was a robust and healthy life for an entire family. There's no sense in unraveling that at this point."

"I'm here when you need to tell more, when you feel like you have it together. I'm worried for what this is doing to you, my stalwart defender and crime stopper. But I'm also worried about leaving your mother alone after that tough session," said Meredith, circling back to the tearful discussion with Elinor.

Raymond sighed, ran a hand over his forehead and answered, "Merri, you might not even realize how much she's lost after our visit—what—a few weeks ago? She hung in there all the way through the conversation. Lucid, knowledgeable, really angry much as she must have been forever. But when I walked her into the bedroom and helped her lie down, just before she went to sleep, she asked, 'When's Ken getting home?' I don't know if she'll remember the conversation. And if she does, it'll be very stressful—but apparently like so much else involving those days. But me? I had to get home before I lost it, myself." His body had caved into Meredith's, slumped like a worn-out sock.

"And here you are," she soothed, circling his body with both arms. "What can I—we—do to help, make it better, solve the mystery?" They both laughed.

"Maybe…" he smiled, standing up offering his hand.

CHAPTER 64

Thursday morning, Raymond waved 'bye to his vociferous daughter as she met the teacher and other students in front of the school and bounded up the steps. The preschool would be taking the month of August off and closure was coming very soon. And, the detective reminded himself, Meredith had invited the work gang to a casual dinner at the Sea Shack the next night, Friday, celebrating the new affiliation, so he wanted to be caught up with his week's to-do list so he could let go for a totally social evening. He needed to get to the next item on his case list, check it off so he could close the story.

Checking his directions, Raymond headed for the 405 south toward Irvine, calculating the best route for traffic at the early morning drive time. Ultimately, he found his way to the 705 to I-5 and punched along with the throng of other drivers. Two hours plus later, he pulled into the modern business park along the freeway at Irvine.

As Raymond wended his way through the steady stream of vehicles, Meredith brought a coffee and bagel into her office and sat down to review upcoming articles and columns. As she checked her calendar to see what screenings, interviews and other events were planned for the next couple of weeks, she answered her phone to the call of Sarah Freeman. Just the sound of Sarah's voice put her on edge. So much had gone down in the Ben Salisbury murder case in Las Vegas and Meredith's encounter with Sal, Tanya's back-up singer who had come to the journalist in a confession of sorts. The situation still hung out in the air unresolved and precarious, as far as Meredith knew. "What's up?" she hastily asked Sarah.

"Sam's been released," blurted the women on the line, Sam's girlfriend. "I don't know all the particulars, but apparently they have the killer in custody."

"Oh my God," huffed Meredith. "Tell me what happened."

Sarah stumbled through her dialogue but proceeded to tell the skeleton details as she knew them. "Some stubborn police detective decided to learn more about the byways of the big showroom, how they bent and twisted through the stage area backstage into the dressing room areas. They found a janitor who'd been working the big room and saw Joe Domo—Tanya's solo back-up singer—walking quietly along, ducking behind some of the equipment. He was heading toward backstage. When the detective started pulling back-of-house staff together, the janitor told him what he'd seen. And…well, someone confessed…something about a group decision to kill Ben…I'm not sure who the 'group' is but I can guess. Anyhow, the crime seems to be solved."

"How's Sam?" asked Meredith, knowing something about the confession, herself.

"Trying to get focused, the change came so fast and without a lot of explanation. He sends his love, and we'll get together soon, but I have to go now. Just wanted to let you know."

Meredith murmured "Bye" and immediately called Jimmy Bell, who, rarely but fortunately happened to be in his office. She asked for any more details—if he knew them.

"True, your friend Sam is off the hook," he acknowledged, "out of his ankle bracelet and free to go, as they say. But—well life for some of the rest of us is screwed. Well, that's harsh. A lot of momentum brought to a halt and some futures just dead for now."

"Could you explain a little more?" she probed.

"Cops dug deeper into who was around in the showroom and the back hallways into the dressing area the night Salisbury was killed. They had the blood on Budge's dress—which had to have happened after the murder. And, of course, they had a participating witness to the real story. Guess the police originally figured Sam was the easy mark."

"There's more to it, isn't there?" Meredith pushed. "What else have you heard?"

"Well, just idle gossip—okay? Seems the trio and Joe Domo were mostly enamored of Tanya as their main meal ticket and saw it disappearing. Domo's been a 'connected' guy around Vegas for a long time, sang with back choruses in the early Rat Pack days of Sammy Davis, Sinatra, and so on. Did a lot of gambling and had a lot of good buddies. He apparently coopted the trio, convinced them the only way to keep their role was to eliminate the problem—Ben Salisbury. They must have all bought in, trusted him. He might have gotten away with it, too, but for—well, you probably know—one of the backup trio, and her turning on them all. Once they were in the interrogation room, they were singing more than Tanya Meile's back-up tunes."

Meredith sat stunned by the rapid and absolute turn of events. "So, finished?"

"Not quite that easy—never is. Attorneys at play for sure now. But one thing we know: There won't be any new album for the girls."

"What about…well, the one who confessed first…?"

"You'll have to ask the Vegas prosecutor, although I doubt if she's talking yet. No way to know. I sort of know who it was, but no one's singing that song either."

"I think I need to say I'm sorry. I was right in the middle of it, but I did try to keep out of the cross hairs, Jimmy. I seem to have stumbled into being a catalyst in this."

"I know. Me, as well. But you've got a great story now—better run with it while you can."

"Substantiation? Confirmation?" she posed.

"Call this guy in Vegas—a friend and one of the investigators. He won't talk on the record but…you have a way." Jimmy gave her a name and phone number then said his goodbye and hung up.

Meredith immediately called, talked with the Vegas investigator and a few other carefully guarded contacts, and then began to write, as always challenged over neutrality when reporting a story that included someone she knew and cared about.

CHAPTER 65

Raymond parked the car and walked almost cautiously up to the front entrance of the steel and glass high technology company. He stopped at the airy reception desk. A slightly disheveled young woman, dirty blonde hair clasped back but straggling around the face, and large saucer-round eyeglasses, pointed down the hall. "Through the double glass doors at the end." He'd called ahead and made an appointment.

He followed her direction. Nervous, above all, and anticipatory, he made his way down the starkly white and empty hall and pushed the glass doors open to a wide room filled with workstations placed at strategic angles. The occupant of the nearest to the door looked up at him and pointed toward a glassed-in office at the back of the room. He found his way through the maze of workers on computers and phones. Arriving at the door to the transparent office space, he knocked. A tall, willowy young man stood up, wire rim glasses and slightly longish light brown hair. A polo shirt with jeans, beckoned him in.

"I'm Tad Oakley," he said.

Raymond swallowed hard, introduced himself and explained, "I'm investigating a case near Palm Springs and think you might have some insight. And there's a story that goes with it."

"Let's take it downstairs to the coffee shop. It's pretty rudimentary but the coffee's okay and it's quieter," said the younger man as he turned to his desk and switched off his equipment.

"We call this our industrial strength coffee bar," he told Raymond. They helped themselves to the dark steaming liquid from the commercial beverage machines and found their way to a Formica table, settling into two white plastic chairs. "It ain't elegant but it's caffeine," smiled Oakley. "So, tell me about this crime case and the story," he smiled. 'Hope I'm not implicated in something illegal," he added.

Raymond took a drink of the hot coffee, flinched, then began, "It's not a pleasant discussion I'm bringing to you, I'm afraid. But I feel like it needs to be aired and I keep thinking if I were in your place, I'd want to know about it. I hope I'm right about that." Oakley scowled deeply and looked intently at the detective.

"Sounds serious."

"It is," answered Raymond and clearing his throat out of nervousness, he began the story, starting from the daylight discovery of the body of Tad's mother in Desert Hot Springs. Forty minutes later, concluding with the story of Odenato in Mexico. The young man said nothing, listened intently and occasionally took a sip of his coffee.

"Wow," is all he said at first, then added, "Interesting. Intense. Let's walk." The two stood and silently walked for about a block. Raymond intuited that the silence was important to the younger man. Walking seemed to be as well, the detective thought, noting his tall, firm and fluid build. Questions had begun from Oakley—deep, detailed inquiries. At the end of the meander through the entire business park and back to the steps of Tad's building, he said, "Let me process this, please. I don't know what to feel—there's a lot of consider."

"I'm sorry it's a story that had to be told, but I felt it was only fair for you to know the truth," Raymond explained again.

"I agree, T.K. But make me a promise. This story will never be told to my grandfather—Ed—or any of the family. It's not their story. It's mine—and yours now—and there's a lot to process and a lot I want to know more about. Deal?"

"Yes," Raymond acknowledged, then opened an opportunity for more discussion at a later-but-soon date. Oakley bought it immediately.

Leaving the business park, Raymond thought about driving over to Laguna to see his mother again, but then decided against it. Too much input too soon, certainly for his mother, but even for even-tempered mild-mannered T.K. Raymond. He headed back north to L.A. and his office.

He settled into his desk to clean up the work left over from the previous day. Then called Marty in and the two debriefed over their various projects. "You can let go of the Marcus Ladonna investigation in Miami," he told his colleague. "Everything I learned in Kansas pretty much tells the story of the actress found in the desert. No absolutes but given the timing and Odenato's actions delivering the young boy to the grandparents, and the ashes, well, there's the unhappy ending we've been hoping against." They commiserated for a few more minutes.

With a great deal of thought, Raymond then wrote a long and involved faxed letter to Sheriff Belin, eliminating much of the tear-driven diatribe—and its story— from his mother. "We know all I can dig out, Ted. I've personally made the calls and visits. And this is what it is. No doubt Odenato pulled the trigger. Timing and his marriage to two women at the same time—one of which he stuck with—kind of tells the story for me. Ed Oakley spelled out the rest. But there's no indication that anyone from Kansas even knew that Lindy Fuller was murdered. For them, she died peacefully of pneumonia and was buried in Kansas with her mother—that's been the family's reality for the past 27 years. Mexico knew nothing about a child and cares less about the rest of it—until Jaime tried to foist his own crimes onto it. But that's resolved and put to rest now. I'm stepping out of it at this point and leave it to you to handle how you guys down there in the desert think best for your purposes. Why my name was all over it? No answer except my father was a partner in Canyonlight, the investment company that bought the house originally, and was in business with Odenato in many endeavors. Maybe my initials jotted down mistakenly instead of his—T.K. instead of K.T.

"Come and visit us soon. The ocean feels pretty good after the scorching heat you're having this summer. Nice working with you, old friend. Keep in touch.

"T.K. Raymond, Captain, High Profile Industry Unit, LAPD."

CHAPTER 66

His office never seemed as stable and welcoming as it did to Raymond Friday morning as he arrived after the stress-filled day he'd plunged through the day before. He reported in by phone to Bernie and worked through the pile of projects on his desk and in-basket. At lunchtime he and partner Marty caught a quick hamburger down the street and moved through the current cases and issues facing the celebrity section of the unit. It now seemed normal and calming to him.

"Gloria and George—and Trey maybe—Sonia and Art, Cassie and even Ito will meet us at the Sea Shack in about an hour," Meredith reminded Raymond as he walked in the door a little earlier than usual and looked forward to casual friendship and socializing after the long investigative road over the murdered actress. Riley ran up to him and he scooped her up for a hug. Then set her down and sent her off to Lola for a treat.

"Ito staying here?"

"No. He's staying at Cassie's until he finds a place of his own. They're going to be working together in the same office again—at the studio. And she's got extra room right now plus appreciated the company."

"Good. Because I have a family friend who will be visiting for the weekend, arrives tomorrow afternoon. I hope you don't mind. It's just for the night."

She regarded him mildly perplexed. Then chose to move past the questions. "Sure. It's your house, too, Raymond. Remember? Although these days it seems to be everyone's house. But who's the guest?"

"Just a family friend. You'll meet tomorrow. Part of the long story."

"'Kay," she said, sensing not to push him at the moment.

CHAPTER 67

She let the shower cascade over her back and took a deep inward breath. Someone told her that breath strategy helped find focus. Between Raymond's stress-filled week, Sal and all the drama around the Vegas case, its surprise outcome and story filing, and a morning TV appearance, Meredith needed a moment of calm. She dried off and put on a pair of white jeans and a bright turquoise silk blouse. A quick brush to the hair and a swipe of makeup here and there and she heard the door downstairs open. She heard Gloria's voice and Trey and Riley greeting each other as Lola came out of the kitchen to take control of them.

"I don't know the full story yet. He just says a family friend—but it's unusual for Raymond." Meredith discretely explained to Gloria before they joined the group sitting around the wooden table on the terrace at the Sea Shack. Gloria nodded and winked. "Not a word—to Raymond or anyone else," Meredith admonished her. Raymond, Art and George, had gone up to the bar to order a new round of drinks.

"Where's Cass?" asked Gloria. "Isn't she coming tonight?"

"Yes—and Ito who's staying with her while he finds his own place." Meredith answered. "She said they'd be here just a little late." And as she explained, she caught sight of the brunette coming through the restaurant, followed by a grinning Ito and...? "Who's that?" Meredith wondered out loud.

"Is Bob back?" asked Sonia. Meredith shook her head. "Not built like Bob." The threesome threaded their way through the bustling restaurant, extra busy on the Friday night in summer. Arriving at the table, there was an unspoken surprise gasp among the group. Russ Talbot greeted everyone jovially and said, "Tonight's on me." He turned quickly to join Raymond and crew at the bar. Ito smiled mischievously. Cassie sat down with a thunk and said, "So...?"

"So?" Meredith repeated. "Coincidence, item, or...?"

Cassie smiled artfully. "We journalists never believe in coincidence, you know."

"So?" repeated Meredith again.

"Right time, right place. It's good." The gaggle of men arrived bearing drinks for all and the subject was closed off, but new topics quickly took flight as conversation erupted across the table, down the table and into the night air. Meredith looked at her longtime colleague and friend, Cassie O'Connell, and realized what all the years had meant to her. Her bouncing short brunette curls had dramatic streaks of silver, her eyes were solid and grounded with the confidence she'd gained in her work as an L.A. TV producer. Mostly Meredith realized Cass was nearly a decade older than Meredith herself. And that the fresh-cheeked young professional image she always attributed to Cass was always a little skewed. They'd seemed like partners in the stories they had pursued, equal and evenly matched. But Meredith was always years behind her, reminding that Meredith, when she joined Bettina Grant nearly 20 years before, had replaced a decade of Cassie in the legwoman role. Did she deserve a solid, high-powered romance?

You bet. Good for her. Good for Russ.

"Here we are again," Russ mused. "Another new endeavor, with the whole freight train along for the ride. Thanks for inviting me in for the fun." He stood and offered a toast to the new venture. The assembled group all joined in. Meredith noted that Cassie was blushing.

"This is almost too much surprise," whispered Gloria to Meredith. "I can't wait to hear more about it all—Raymond's family friend? Cassie with Russ Talbot? Oh my God. We've all been beamed up to another planet!" The food servings arrived then and conversation darted from subject to subject, balance sheets to gossip.

"Lots to talk about," said Cassie as she prepared to leave the diner with Ito and Russ.

"Wine day at my pool soon. I'll call you all," Gloria spoke up.

"Me, too," interjected Sonia. The women all agreed.

"Danger, danger," mused George to Ito. "This intrepid group in motion can catch, flay and lay you out on the plate before you know what happened."

<h1 style="text-align:center">CHAPTER 68</h1>

Saturday morning Meredith and Raymond sat over breakfast later than usual. Riley was busily drawing in her room. Meredith spoke up quietly.

"You need to tell me the whole story now. For days, you've been nerve-rackingly circumspect, Raymond. You've had some time to process it all and now's the time to talk about it before this mysterious 'family friend' arrives. I'm not just asking—I'm insisting—that you tell me the rest of the story? What happened with your mother?" He tone had taken on a familiar demand. She was serious.

Raymond took a deep breath, toyed with his scrambled eggs and began the narrative. "I asked her for the truth about Lindy Fuller, the actress."

"'Didn't know her. She was part of Malcom's life, not ours,'" Elinor had insisted.

Raymond then pulled two documents from his briefcase, both he had examined for the first time on the plane to Wichita. Feeling badly about forcing the subject and the discomfort it was bringing, he nevertheless laid them on the table before her. One, the original birth certificate from a small Riverside County hospital: Mother listed was Lynn Marie Feeley; Father, Kenneth T. Raymond. The child: Thaddeus Oakley Feeley. Lindy had used her pre-Hollywood name which was later changed. Feeley was undoubtedly the "other" name—the one that was torn off—

on the yellowed slip of paper in the woman's buried purse. Tad was the name written next to his.

The second document was a wrinkled yellowed photo—snatched hurriedly from Meredith's "location" story stack—of a handsome, silver-haired middle-aged man, grinning, sitting comfortably on a chintz chair in a well-appointed room, the youthful, glittering red head Lindy Fuller on his lap, his arms around her. "It was dad," said Raymond, "no question."

"Mom cried and snarled and snapped. 'Harlot,' she kept calling Lindy."

"I begged her so gently for the full story! I'd chased around half the country and parts of Mexico to find out why she was murdered because I kept thinking about Sheriff Belin's initial summons: 'It has your name all over it.'

"Mom finally blurted it all out. 'Your father got himself entangled with the hussy. She chased him—even called him at home—couldn't get rid of her, but then I knew he was already involved up to his…well, you can guess. I knew something was up, but you know how busy he was. Always at evening and out-of-town events.' And she explained to me that her family brought the money in the marriage, had established dad in his agency business. She said she threatened to divorce him and take everything. Of course, he didn't want that—and I think he loved mom—us-but just," Raymond stammered, "…men…" he shrugged self-consciously.

"I had to bring mom back to the current subject a couple of times. Her mind would just wander off. But she managed to barrel back and onward about Lindy.

"She said dad set Lindy up in that fancy apartment in Hollywood—the Majestic—in the penthouse, and spent half his life there with her for a couple of years. It's that building where you were researching a story. It was one of the photos in the stack you brought home. It's what clued me in. That's when mom insisted they move to Orange County. After that, dad went to L.A. only a couple of days a week—semi-retired. Mom thought it would end the affair and it might have, but then Lindy got pregnant!

"She wouldn't give up the baby. Wouldn't be bought off. I'm only guessing she figured dad would give in, divorce mom, and they'd make a new home. She was a little unrealistic, I've gathered. But she didn't know my mom. Dad apparently cared about Lindy and the child, but just wanted out of the mess by then. So, he made a deal with Malcolm Odenato, his business partner, to marry her, raise the child, and remove the whole drama. My parents sold their beloved Balboa Island house and moved into a condo in Laguna. Mom still resents that. Malcolm got the money from the sale as his first down payment. The whole sordid affair seemed to disappear when my parents went to Europe for several months over the late summer and fall of 1966—dad had a project there. It was kind of the end of it. Mom said 'it was totally over. The subject never again came up.'

"After she went to sleep, I dug through the cabinet where she kept pictures and papers. In the back of a small drawer, buried amongst a huge, wrinkled stack of documents, I found a simple manila folder labeled, "CL." It stood for Canyonlight. And all of the signed and notarized documents were there— mostly signed by the attorney who was apparently made a partner in CL but ultimately disappeared. There was a hand-written note dated October 1966 from Malcolm Odenato, a month before Tad was delivered to the Oakleys in Wichita. It simply said, 'Desert Hot Springs issue handled. Contract executed in full. Delivery to Kansas in one week. Final payment due.' I'm assuming it referred to delivery of the mother and child to the Oakleys. But it was hardly the package I'm sure my dad thought it would be. When dad's business was sold, a larger than equal part of the profit also went to Odenato, again. I suppose, as security and resource for the child. At least Mal did pass some along to the Oakleys."

"Did your father or mother ever hear about or mention the child or the woman again?" asked Meredith.

"NO. That was the deal. Odenato married her, moved to the Palm Springs area—the company even bought the house for Mal—and then the child was born. But there was never any more information passed along about him. Again, part of the arrangement."

"You don't think your father actually…" she stumbled to find words.

"Killed Lindy Fuller?" he added and shook his head. "In all his missteps in this situation, I know my father was not an evil man. And he wouldn't go that far. My mother was strong and a fighter, though, and if she'd probably let up, we might have lost him." Silence filled the space for a few moments before Raymond spoke again. "And, my parents were in London during that time…which may be why Odenato felt free to move on Lindy. I doubt my father ever even knew about the murder. He probably figured Malcom Odenato simply passed Lindy off to her family along with Tad and the problem was solved." Raymond was quiet for a few moments, then continued. "Dad already had one mini stroke by then and a big one took him about eighteen months after he got home. I think the stress had him tied in knots by then and he couldn't deal with it." The stoic detective was silent, listening to the surf. Quietly saddened, he said, "Yet, of course he was the hand behind her death—maybe not directly or even intentionally. But he's where it started.

"Mom thought Malcolm moved Lindy and Tad to Mexico. She said, 'Mal always liked the Latin spirit!' She was glad that she and dad built a life in Laguna until he died. But Lindy and Tad were never part of their world. She said I should be grateful!"

Meredith took a deep breath as she listened to the story. "How did you leave it with you mother? How's she handling it?"

Raymond pressed his hands together. "When I took her to her bedroom, she thanked me for bringing the family over and asked me when Ken would get home. I called her the next day and she was lively and excited about going to lunch with her friends. Said she hoped I might come and visit soon. It'd been ages…. Soon, we'll have to talk about…well elder care, I'm afraid."

"How are you doing with all of it—the murder and the realities of it, your mother…?" Meredith asked softly, knowing how strong Raymond's ethical grounding had always been and how hard for him this duplicitous situation had been. It was a rare time when the stolid detective emotionally wilted. She was, herself, unusually challenged by the need to bolster him—a turnabout from the usual.

CHAPTER 69

Meredith freshened up mid-afternoon, anticipating the arrival of Raymond's guest. She'd fluffed up the guest room and made sure the kitchen was stocked. Heading downstairs as she heard the doorbell, she saw a twenty-something, tall, slightly rangy man, his hair light brown, a little long with a swath hanging over his forehead. He wore wire rim glasses, and his angular features were somehow familiar to her. She assessed that he was about the age of Raymond's son Will.

"This is my wife, Meredith Ogden," said Raymond as she put forth her hand. "Meredith, this is my brother—well, half-brother—Tad Oakley."

Meredith clasped the hand even harder but couldn't find words. It was the first time anyone had used the words. She'd already been told the truth, so it should not have been a surprise, but she worried that her mouth was hanging open. "Um," she finally pushed a sound out. "It's a real pleasure." But she looked at Raymond with wide questioning eyes. Oakley smiled, seemed a little awkward and uncomfortable, himself.

"Actually, it's my pleasure," he said looking around. "This is all a little surprising and well, overwhelming, to me, too." He smiled.

"We have so much to talk about," Raymond said. "It's important to me that you two get to know one another, but right now, let me take Tad to the guest room and get him situated."

As afternoon waned, the three sat on the patio and talked about their lives. In even more detail for both Meredith and Raymond, than they usually revealed or put out to one another. Tad talked about his youthful time in Kansas, his pastimes and school days. He talked lovingly about Ed and Alice but there was a note of sadness in his discussion.

"There's no point," he added, "in alerting my grandad Ed to the fact that my mother was murdered, and her body cooked in the desert sand for nearly 25 years instead of reposing in a delicate urn snuggled with her mother. Ed has his reality—the one the whole family believes and grew up under—and at this stage, I don't want to upset his view of the world. It was hard enough for me to do it when T.K. called and came down to talk with me." The young man was quiet for a while, then added, "I kind of knew the story never held up well. No father would just drop his kid at two years of age and disappear. Even more, look at me. I'm six foot three. My mother was a tiny thing—about five feet, according to my granddad. Malcom was only about five feet six. And there's not one thing about me that's Italian or Sicilian—everything about me is in the Irish-European vein." Silence for a few minutes.

"What will happen to the real body?" asked Meredith cringing. "I mean someone will want you or someone else to take care of it."

"Ashes over the Pacific," whispered Tad. "Something I can do that I think would honor her love of all things California. I'd sprinkle them on the Hollywood Sign, but I think it's illegal." Raymond quickly acknowledged the truth in the statement.

"One day before he retires, I'll have breakfast with Sheriff Ted Belin at his favorite diner in Hot Springs, and finish the story," Raymond added. "Doing it now accomplishes nothing, we won't know anything different about the actual murderer than we know now. Occam's Razor—the shortest distance between two points and all. Odenato's hand was in everything and then nothing. He engineered the story for Ed and Alice, had control of Tad and arranged the break when he left—to return to the woman he was already married to in Mexico."

And, thought Raymond to himself, on that future day, I'll show Ted the birth certificate that he never saw because he had it directly faxed to me while he was on vacation. That could have been a bombshell—especially for my father, for me—if I hadn't been able to clarify everything, contain it first.

At breakfast the next morning, Meredith, Raymond and Tad worked on omelets and biscuits. It was a quiet conversation, away from the small but often busy ears of Riley who was watching a TV cartoon. "We've agreed that for a while, there'll be no mention openly of brother or half-brother—yet. But I wanted you to know," Raymond said to Meredith.

"We all know it," mused Tad, glancing at Raymond and Meredith "And for now, that's enough. One day..." he shrugged.

"...when Ed isn't in the picture and the whole issue has calmed down...." Raymond added.

"Know that you are family here," said Meredith affectionately to the young man as he prepared to leave. "You are always welcome—and expected—if you can't get home for the holidays, you have a home here. If you just need a quiet place to veg out, or decompress, we're here."

Heart-felt hugs wrapped up the visit. Riley weaseling into the mix. "You can be another favorite cousin, you know," she chimed in. "Trey is the other one. You have to meet him."

"Thank you," murmured an emotional Tad Oakley. Raymond put his arm around the young man's shoulders and walked him out. Meredith thought that some of the crisp veneer and stalwart edges of Detective T.K. Raymond had worn off with lots of purpose. She found herself calculating the delicate balance of the family and the legacy of Raymond: Son Will, grown and almost in his thirties with a five-year-old son; daughter Riley with an entire life ahead at four; now a brother half Raymond's age also with a full adult life ahead. Boy, she thought, if that doesn't keep him on young toes, nothing will. When she met Raymond, he was a solitary figure, already in his forties, seemingly happy to tread a solo path that she coopted. But she, too, had been a singular figure, having bid a sad farewell to early-deceased parents, on a singular journey given over to the arrival of Raymond. There would be some healing needed, some emotional rebuilding and story constructing to see the drama transform into life's real-time manuscript.

Also, Meredith knew, a lot of supportive understanding, forgiveness, love and affection would be needed for the man she always knew to be the pillar of stoic strength—now on somewhat shaky ground. She reminded herself that family-engaging support would be a new role. She silently gasped "whew," but had no qualms about stepping up to it. There is no "normal" in active adulthood, she mused to herself. Just flexibility, commitment and love.

CHAPTER 70

Later in the day, a brisk brilliant summer sky over the never-ceasing surf, Meredith and Raymond sat on towels in the sand watching Riley play with two neighbor kids, Lola watching over the lot, interacting with her own youthful vigor.

"Ever miss the condo days?" she asked.

He laughed raucously. "Really? You dare to ask?" She nodded. "Sure," he said, "and the little beach cottage, too. But then I figure well, this is what life looks like now."

"Pragmatist. You were brilliant in parsing this whole sordid mess about Lindy Fuller. You really dug out the details, the schedule and…whew…how you finally dug out the background on your father's involvement. Tell me you didn't badger your mother into dementia."

He sat back on his elbows, digging trenches in the sand. "Not really. That's happened on its own. I seem to have managed to keep her in the present for a while—long enough to tell me the story." Raymond sat back and took a long drink from the water bottle he and Meredith were sharing. "I hated to press her, but they had shielded me, and everyone else, from the story and the truth. I only fell into it by happenstance of a hurriedly written note rotting in a purse. Lindy's death brought it all together. I know telling it must have been hurtful for my mother, but I have to confess—couldn't help but feel anger and disrespect for my father. I hope I can let it pass. I guess they felt they had put up a wall of silence in order to keep the life for me and mother special as it had always been. I actually felt envious of Tad when I felt the simple family love in Ed's house in Wichita."

"Why you feel so engaged with Tad as family now?"

"That, and he is, after all, my brother…and," he sighed, "I feel on behalf of my dad and family, I owe him."

"Raymond, that debt needs to be retired. You didn't kill his mother or exile him to Wichita. Any more than he was responsible for your parents giving up their Balboa house, exiled to a condo. You were both an effect of the mistakes your parents made."

"Well, we can make the best of it now. I've got more than twenty years on him and have a lot of resources and living I can share. Maybe make up for some of it."

"And he's got a brilliant mind, a nice personality and a wonderful future that you can also share and learn from. We all can. Think about it—an uncle for Riley! It's called family."

"And you're always the optimist," he countered. Both were silent, breathing in the air, the sunshine and the sounds of the surf for a while. Riley and her friends' laughter and squeals occasionally punctuated the calm. A flock of seagulls flew over. Finally, Raymond took Meredith's hand and spoke up, "Last Saturday's unexpected moment of…life's timeout and well, uninterrupted sex, was a great break, an invigorating four hours! Freeing. Brought back the beach cottage and the condo and…I don't suppose there's a way today…?"

"Look around you, Raymond," Meredith giggled gently, squeezing his hand and leaning against him. "With all that energy and curiosity and childhood liveliness with us today," she pointed at Riley and her friends. "There's not a snowball's chance in hell—today—but tomorrow…."

ACKNOWLEDGMENTS

Every one of our readers professes their affection for Raymond, constantly asking for more light shed on the wily celebrity detective. And like us all, Detective T.K. Raymond has his own family stories—skeletons and all. So, the detective, now Captain, takes the lead in Meredith Ogden's world in *Detective in the Crosshairs*. And wends his way through the early Hollywood days of his youth, finding surprises and threats as he makes his way to a previously undiscovered home that is now fulsome with activity, stories and love. But as always, it took a team to walk in his shoes. Thanks go to Deborah Baker—Meredith's wing-woman, plus amazing tour guides: Beverly Lenihan, Barbara Wilson, Butch Wilson, Jim Vincler and Nancy Vincler, Susan Wagner, and the creative interpretations of Cynthia Gunn and Elizabeth Beeton. Appreciation and kudos to Meredith's web-tech maestra Suchi Psarakos for making us all look virtually good. And always Dixon who knows just when to find an "m" space, offer a story suggestion as well as a cool libation when the going gets tough.

ABOUT THE AUTHOR

Penny Pence Smith was "legwoman" (assistant) to a famous Hollywood gossip columnist, a role that grew into a field correspond and Los Angeles Bureau Manager covering the entertainment industry for the *New York Time Special Features Syndicate,* and later correspondent for the *Hollywood Reporter.* Her journalism career began at age 14 as a reporter for her local Southern California daily newspaper. With a Ph.D. in Communication Research she has consulted to high tech, health care, public health and finance companies and taught journalism and communication at UNC Chapel Hill and Hawaii Pacific University. Her *Under a Maui Sun* and *Reflections of Kauai* were best-selling tourism books in Hawaii where she lives with her husband.

Check her Author Page on BookBub and Goodreads for news about future Meredith Ogden adventures and other books: pennystories.wix site.com/penny-smith-books.